THE *WHITE CHRISTMAS* INN

THE WHITE CHRISTMAS INN

Colleen Wright

HOWARD BOOKS

New York   London   Toronto   Sydney   New Delhi

Howard Books
An Imprint of Simon & Schuster, Inc.
1230 Avenue of the Americas
New York, NY 10020

First Howard Books trade paperback edition October 2018

HOWARD and colophon are trademarks of Simon & Schuster, Inc.

For information about special discounts for bulk purchases, please contact Simon & Schuster Special Sales at 1-866-506-1949 or business@simonandschuster.com.

The Simon & Schuster Speakers Bureau can bring authors to your live event. For more information or to book an event, contact the Simon & Schuster Speakers Bureau at 1-866-248-3049 or visit our website at www.simonspeakers.com.

Interior design by Davina Mock-Maniscalco

Manufactured in the United States of America

10   9   8   7   6   5   4   3   2   1

Library of Congress Cataloging-in-Publication Data

Names: Wright, Colleen.
Title: The white Christmas inn / by Colleen Wright.
Description: First Howard Books trade paperback edition. | New York : Howard
   Books, 2018.
Identifiers: LCCN 2018010211 (print) | LCCN 2018012730 (ebook) |
   ISBN 9781501180590 (eBook) | ISBN 9781501180606 (trade pbk. original)
Subjects: LCSH: Young women—Fiction. | Man–woman relationships—Fiction. |
   GSAFD: Christmas stories
Classification: LCC PS3623.R5325 (Ebook) | LCC PS3623.R5325 W55 2018
   (print) | DDC 813/.6—dc23

LC record available at https://lccn.loc.gov/2018010211

ISBN 978-1-5011-8060-6
ISBN 978-1-5011-8059-0 (ebook)

THE *WHITE* CHRISTMAS INN

One

AS THE INN APPEARED on the crest at the end of the snowy drive, nestled in the folds of the gently rolling Vermont foothills, Molly Winslow actually laughed aloud.

Her anticipation had been building ever since she'd turned off the main road. She'd soon spotted the hand-painted wooden sign, almost as big as her car, which featured a Victorian-style painting of the inn itself, done up in holiday glory. The gables were festooned with swags of pine, the windows blazing with warm light, and the drive crowded with guests around a lit fir twice as tall as the inn. There was even a horse and carriage, for good measure.

Molly had picked the inn, out of all the charming establishments vying for holiday traffic on the various travel sites, because of details like this. The reviews for Evergreen Inn had been excellent, but what she had really fallen in love with were the pictures: a single magenta button rose laid beside pats of butter hand-pressed into the shape of chickens or daisies, the incredible hand-pieced velvet crazy quilts featured in every single room, the collection of antique blue glassware that sparkled like sapphire in the pictures of the airy kitchen.

Molly even knew from her deep Internet dive of Evergreen Inn that the sign that led guests from the main road changed seasonally: in fall, a different painting featured Vermont's spectacular show of autumn color, and in spring, the sign was suffused with pink and white apple blossoms.

Whoever had appointed the details of Evergreen Inn, Molly had decided, was an artist. As a kind of artist herself, Molly was drawn to it all. Her whole job was building brand-new worlds out of nothing but a handful of images and words.

But as an artist, she was also aware of the distance that sometimes lay between an artist's grand visions and what they were really able to create, between what they promised and what they could actually deliver.

And this wasn't just a hypothetical piece of wisdom for her these days. The deadline she was under for her next book had been keeping her up at night now for weeks. And during all of those long nights, not a single hint of inspiration had sparked in her mind amidst the giant crowd of worries.

That was part of how she had managed to convince herself that the Christmas trip to Vermont wasn't a frivolous luxury, but a legitimate business expense. It was a chance to leave the worries back home in Brooklyn and get a much-needed change of scenery to coax some inspiration out of hiding before the anxieties caught up with her.

But although some part of her longed to be swept away into another world, she still had enough hard-nosed Brooklynite in her to hold a certain air of skepticism as she wound her way up the long drive. Not very many things, she'd found, actually lived up to her imagination. And even when they didn't—well, a lot of times, it was still a good story.

Which was why, after several bumpy minutes on the winding private lane, when the inn finally became visible beyond a stand of snow-dusted trees, she burst into laughter.

The place wasn't just as lovely as she'd imagined it.

It was better.

She'd thought that the giant fir in the drive was probably just an artist's invention, but there it was, twinkling with lights. Not only was the green roof of the inn trimmed with pine, but the evergreen swags were dotted with red velvet ribbons and trimmed with what looked to be silvered grapevine. A rocking horse stood guard on the wide porch, lacquered bright red, with a buffalo plaid blanket under his kid-sized saddle.

As soon as Molly pulled up into the circle drive around the base of the fir and opened her car door, she picked up an incredible blend of aromas: the clean spice of pine, a faint hint of smoke from the giant fireplace she knew was waiting inside, and a strong scent of cinnamon, which no doubt was wafting out of one of the ramshackle complex's several chimneys.

Not only that, but the light snow that had been falling during the early part of her drive had really started to stick once she reached the country roads of Vermont, coming down in big, fluffy flakes. They dusted the green roof, the bare branches of the oaks, and the pine needles, and fell silently around Molly as she pulled her bag out of the back and crunched through the snow to the front door, feeling as if she'd just awoken in a snow globe.

In fact, she thought dreamily, *maybe that could be a story: a little girl who suddenly finds herself in a snow globe world . . .*

But as Molly stepped through the front door, her thoughts were once again interrupted by the beauty of the real world.

She stood in a roomy, welcoming entryway, set off from the main building by a garland of juniper, whose waxy blue and pink berries were in turn set off by sprays of wild roses. A hurricane lantern with a real flame glowed on a small table just inside the door, beside a small pewter dish filled with tempting golden candies labeled *Rosemary Caramel* in elegant script.

Straight ahead, she could see fire leaping in the fireplace that dominated the large lounge, filled with overstuffed furniture and velvet and faux-fur pillows. It was decorated to the hilt for Christmas, with a tall Christmas tree covered with vintage-style tinsel in one corner, and a large nativity that appeared to have been hand-carved in the other. All around the ceiling, Christmas lights twinkled among the branches of the same pine, juniper, and red-rose swags that graced the entryway.

To her right, she recognized the collection of tables in the inn's stylish dining room. Each of the tables was set with a pine-and-poinsettia floral arrangement, and a vintage light-up Santa stood in one window, his nose and cheeks bright red, as if he'd come in from the cold just before her.

But somehow she didn't notice the woman behind the front desk, to her left, until she heard a small, lively voice call out from behind her.

"You must be Molly."

Molly spun around to find a petite, cheery older woman smiling back at her. Maybe, Molly reflected, she hadn't noticed her because she looked exactly like Mrs. Santa Claus, or at least the perfect grandmother from an old-time Christmas card: just another perfect detail in a place that seemed to be full of them, with her white hair pulled back in a bun, her cat's-eye glasses, and her neat blue-and-green plaid shirt.

"That's right," Molly said, walking up to the front desk, which was a rich reddish cedar counter, varnished to a high shine.

It wasn't until she set her bag down that she thought to wonder how the woman had known her name.

"I'm Iris," the woman said.

"Molly," Molly said instinctively, then grimaced.

But Iris was already on to other things. As she clicked

through the computer screen in front of her, she narrated her actions with a flourish. "Molly Winslow . . . checking in December twenty-third . . ."

She laid a substantial brass key on the counter between them.

"You're in the Robin's Nest," Iris said, nodding at the staircase that disappeared beyond a half wall to her left. "So you'll have the whole top floor. Just keep going up until you run out of stairs."

"Okay."

"Oh, and it's the Christmas holiday, so all your meals are included in the cost of the room," said Iris. "So make sure to eat your money's worth. And that's it!"

"Okay," Molly said again, hardly able to believe check-in could be so easy. Did they just pass out keys to anyone who walked in the door in Vermont? They didn't even check her ID. "I'm all set, then?"

"All set," Iris said with a satisfied air. Then she looked up. "I'll just need to know the name of whoever will be meeting you here so I know where to send them."

"Oh," Molly said, trying to keep her voice light. "It's just me."

Iris didn't actually say, *Alone? At Christmas?* But the incredulity on her face got the point across.

"I'm actually looking forward to the peace and quiet," Molly said. "I'm going to be finishing a book while I'm here."

"A book?" Iris said. The interest in her eyes was quickly chased by confusion. "But your reservation's only for . . ."

"A few days," Molly finished for her. "I know it's not long enough to write a whole novel. I write children's books."

"Oh!" Iris said, delighted. "I've written a children's book!"

Molly tried to keep her shoulders from visibly slumping. At least seventy-five percent of people gave this same response. And then they looked at her as if they couldn't tell why she should make a living doing something that had only taken them an afternoon, or at most a weekend.

And maybe they are right, she thought. Right now, she was having fewer ideas than any of them.

"It's about my grandson, Luke," Iris went on. "When he was a baby, he thought that apple pies grew on apple pie trees. So the story happens in an apple pie orchard, but then—"

"Sounds great!" Molly scooped up the key from the counter and mustered what she hoped was her most brilliant smile. "Thanks so much for your help," she said, backing toward the stairs. "I can't wait to see the room."

"Luke's around here somewhere," Iris said. "If you want, I can send him up with the luggage."

But Molly was already thunking her roller bag up the stairs. "I'm good," she called down. "I've got it. I'm fine. Thank you!"

Two flights later, a third half flight led from a small landing to a door. A felted wreath with woolen leaves and the carefully formed figures of tiny birds announced *Robin's Nest*.

Inside, the room was just as described: a wide, airy attic suite, its ceiling punctuated by a series of skylights, with a high four-poster bed covered in the jewel tones of a velvet crazy quilt, several cozy couches, and a separate room with a large, grandfatherly desk, complete with captain's chair and a pair of daybeds. Like the rooms below, this one was full of Christmassy touches. A candle beside the bed, wrapped with red velvet ribbon, gave off a buttery cinnamon scent that blended with the fresh pine of the juniper and rose swag that hung over the headboard of the bed. And on one of the tables sat a beautiful set of hand-hammered tin figurines: Santa with all his reindeer, who were connected one to another by strings of delicate red thread.

Immediately, Molly hoisted her bag onto the luggage stand at the foot of the bed and began to unpack, hanging clothes in the large wooden wardrobe, which had been hand-painted with a pair of peacocks, and setting a stack of books and her computer on the desk.

The last thing she pulled out of the bag was her mother's giant sky-blue cashmere scarf. Molly had seen it on her mother at least a thousand times, especially in the last days of her life, when no matter what they did, they couldn't seem to make the room warm enough for her. Her heart leapt at the sight of it now, even as it tugged over the fact that this would be her first Christmas without her mother.

The two of them had created all sorts of their own traditions after her father died, when Molly was a child. She'd just never considered what she'd do after her mother was gone.

Probably because she'd always figured she would have a family of her own by that time.

Her thoughts were interrupted by footsteps on the stairs, followed by what sounded like a scuffling at her door.

"Hello?" she called.

"Hey!" a friendly voice responded. "It's Jeanne from downstairs! I just brought you up a few things."

But when Molly opened the door, what bounded through was a gigantic Bernese mountain dog, with his cream and caramel markings, and silky black coat.

It did a quick survey of the room, sniffing the air like a true hound, but then shambled up to Molly, bumping its head against her shins in an ecstasy of delighted wiggles.

"Cassandra!" the woman behind her scolded, struggling to tuck the strands of red hair that had escaped from her ponytail behind her ears as she toted a large wicker-and-wood basket over her arm. "Cassie! Down. Sit!"

The giant dog sat obediently, but then seemed to collapse into the hand-braided carpet, rolling over on her back in a further fit of wiggles.

Molly knelt down to rub Cassie's furry belly. "It's okay," she said. "I love dogs."

"We won't keep you long," Jeanne said. She set the covered basket down on a small table beside the door. "These are just a few afternoon treats. There's cinnamon corn bread, a grilled Vermont cheddar sandwich, and a thermos of hot cider," she said with a smile. And then quickly added, "Although if you prefer hot chocolate, I can run some of that right up."

Molly stood, to the chagrin of Cassie, who couldn't seem to imagine any other activity that could be more rewarding to Molly than rubbing her belly.

"Cider sounds amazing," Molly said. "This whole place is amazing. Everything. From the sign when you turn in, to the garland in the hallway . . ."

"Well," Jeanne said, beaming from the praise, "that's for the wedding. Even we don't usually do fresh roses in winter. Although I did get to make that garland myself."

"Wedding?" Molly repeated.

Jeanne nodded. "A Christmas wedding," she said. "The family's wonderful," she added. "They've been coming here for years. Ever since we opened."

Molly noticed a shadow cross Jeanne's face, but she was distracted from it by the twist in her own heart.

Was she really pricked by the fact there was a wedding going on at the inn? she thought.

But perhaps she was. A wedding meant guests and groomsmen and parties, all reminders of the fact she was spending this Christmas alone.

To shake the thought from her head, she popped open the wooden lid of the wicker basket. Inside, faint steam still rose from the cinnamon corn bread, nestled beside a grilled cheese carefully wrapped in wax paper. And to the side, where they wouldn't melt too fast, were two pats of butter in the shape of Christmas trees.

"This is wonderful," Molly said. "Thank you so much."

"You're very welcome," Jeanne said. "Cassie."

With what seemed to be great effort, the giant dog lurched up from the floor, then descended the stairs with surprising agility at a meaningful glance from Jeanne.

"We're just downstairs," Jeanne said. "If you need anything else. Like to be licked to death by a giant fur rug, for instance."

Molly laughed as Jeanne closed the door behind her.

But in the empty room, she felt a lingering twinge of loneliness.

To ward it off, she pulled the cinnamon corn bread from the basket, broke it in two pieces, and placed one of the wafer-thin pats of butter between them.

Then she padded over to the bed, climbed up on it, and wrapped the scarf around herself, gazing down at the beautiful patterns of the crazy quilt as she waited a few moments for the butter to melt.

Her mother, Molly thought, would be delighted to see her now. She'd love the inn, and everything about the room, and the fact that somebody was still getting some use out of her favorite scarf. She was following her family tradition, Molly thought, of making new traditions.

The first bite of the corn bread was perfect: buttery and warm and rich, with just the right hint of spice.

What, Molly asked herself, *could be better than this?*

Two

"AH-AH-AH!" JEANNE SAID IN a warning tone as her husband, Tim, reached across the large kitchen island, his big, work-cracked hand looming dangerously close to one of the rose cookies she'd just frosted: mouthwatering shortbread, topped with her grandmother's old family recipe for icing, which she'd painstakingly piped into rose after perfect frosting rose. "I swear, you're worse than Cassie."

On the hand-loomed scrap rug by the kitchen fireplace, Cassie raised her head hopefully, then laid her head down with a wounded look when it became apparent that somebody had mentioned her name without having the decency to provide her with at least a scrap of something to eat.

"Come on," Tim said. "Are they really going to miss one little cookie?"

He grinned, but Jeanne gave her head a decisive shake. "Mothers of the bride," she said. "They notice everything."

"I'll tell her the dog ate it," Tim said, going in for the cookie again.

"Tim," Jeanne said, her voice sharp. "I mean it."

Behind her, she could hear Cassie's tags rattle as the dog sat up on alert at the change in her tone.

Tim raised his hands, his grin gone, glancing away from her as if afraid any other little thing he said might set her off.

Jeanne felt frustration rise in her. She'd tried making a joke out of it, and he hadn't listened. Now he was acting like she was the one who was hard to get along with.

But she also felt a pang. The sight of his tall frame, his curly salt-and-pepper hair, and his substantial salt-and-pepper beard still did something to her heart.

"I'm sorry," she said. "I just looked at the books this morning, and these cookies aren't cheap. They're basically nothing but butter."

"Nothing but the best," Tim said.

Jeanne glanced at him, not sure whether this was a harmless comment or a dig. That had been their motto when they'd moved up to Vermont together to start this place, leaving their lives in the corporate rat race behind. At first, they'd traded the line back and forth whenever they made decisions as they converted the old complex of farm buildings into a first-class inn.

Should they get the petroleum-based shingles or the real shake?

Should they order the thousand-thread-count sheets, or the fifteen hundred?

Nothing but the best.

They were smart about it, of course. Tim had found a couple of teenagers from the local farms to hand-cut shake for a few weeks from wood on their property, which was significantly cheaper than buying it from a commercial supplier. And Jeanne had managed to bond with an Egyptian grandmother in the fabric district in New York, who helped her find wholesale prices that meant their high-grade sheets cost them less than the ones found on sale in most department stores.

But five years after they'd opened, just when they'd started to earn a meager profit, the Starlight Lodge had opened practically in their backyard: two hundred luxury hotel rooms just fifteen miles away, with ski in–ski out access to the lodge's private mountain, a ballroom, two swimming pools, and a water park for the kids.

Neither of them had worried about it much at the time, other than to make jokes about the idea of anyone having a "private mountain." They'd been delighted when they opened the inn to be so close to skiing nearby. And they'd been sure that the lovingly crafted, bespoke experience they offered at Evergreen Inn was so different from the behemoth up the road that they wouldn't even compete for the same guests.

But over the next few years, as they'd watched their stream of guests dwindle to a trickle, Tim had started to question the choices Jeanne made about the inn, again and again.

"Does everything we serve really have to be farm-raised?" he'd ask. "What if we just got those little LED candles, instead of burning so many real ones?"

Every little detail around the place, every beautiful little detail, now seemed like an occasion for a fight. Some days Jeanne really believed their troubles must all be her fault, because of her spendthrift habits, despite the fact that she made budget after budget, and stayed up nights trying to find even more ways to squeeze a little more change from them. Some days she only saw red, feeling abandoned and alone, as if Tim had come all the way up here with her only to give up on their dream the second things turned tough.

But however either of them felt, nothing seemed to stop the slow bleed of their meager savings. Two years ago, they'd taken out a loan, in hopes that a few upgrades and some savvy advertising could turn the tide. But despite their best efforts, their bookings had only shrunk. Everyone was too busy driving down the road to the Starlight Lodge.

This year they'd struggled all season to pay off their current bills, and only barely managed to stay current with their loan. And the last time they'd looked at the books together, they'd come to an excruciating decision: they simply couldn't afford to keep the place open after this Christmas. They couldn't live on hope any longer. At the end of this season, they'd shutter the place, then try to sell it for enough to cover their debts, and go back to the city to beg for the jobs they'd hoped to leave behind forever.

She wouldn't have looked at the books at all this morning if she hadn't wanted to get the last set of the month's bills sent off before the end of the year. Writing the checks, and entering debit after debit in their ledger, had left Jeanne with a hollow feeling in her heart, as if each draft she wrote against their account somehow came from inside her.

Tim knew exactly what she was talking about when she'd told him she'd just been dealing with the books. So why would he choose a time like this to make a crack like that?

Jeanne stared at him, frosting bag in her hand, trying to read his face, but he just circled around the counter to give Cassie a good scratch.

"Hey," he said over his shoulder, as the dog squirmed with happiness, "I got that broken door on the garden shed fixed this morning."

"The garden shed?" Jeanne repeated.

Tim nodded. "I thought it was just hanging up on the lip of the threshold," he said, "so I planed that down, but then I realized the whole thing was hung crooked on the hinges. Lucky I did, because I was about to try planing the door to make it fit, and if I'd done that, I'd have had a gap about an inch wide once I fixed the hinges."

He glanced up at her briefly, then scratched Cassie's big white-and-caramel mane.

As usual, Jeanne thought, Tim was all about the task, and not much else. "I told you about the garden shed this summer," Jeanne said. It had driven her nuts the entire season. When she wanted to get the door open, it wouldn't open, and when she wanted to get it shut, it wouldn't shut.

"I know," Tim said, annoyance creeping into his voice. "I didn't forget."

Jeanne felt her own annoyance build in response. Tim's skills as a builder and handyman were one of the things that had let them open the place to begin with—and stay open this long. But these days it seemed like every time she needed him, he was out in the barn or the yard, feeding some farm animal or working on some project. Making repairs to a place that they weren't able to keep.

"But why do it today?" Jeanne asked. "Two days before Christmas?"

"I was trying to get some other things done this summer," Tim said, the irritation in his voice unmistakable now. "Like build that grapevine arbor you thought none of our guests could live without."

"That was a special request," Jeanne said. "For a wedding."

"Would you rather I hadn't done it at all?" Tim asked, standing.

"It just seems like a waste of time," Jeanne said. "To fix the garden shed when we won't even be here by the summer."

Tears sprang to her eyes as she said it. She could remember a time when Tim couldn't stand the sight of tears in her eyes, but now his face just turned dark.

He stalked toward the door that led from the kitchen to the yard, where he stopped and whistled for Cassie. The big dog got to her feet, gave Jeanne a questioning look, but then trotted after him.

Jeanne wiped at the tears in her eyes, realized she'd accidentally swiped stray frosting on her face, then grabbed a paper towel to rub the frosting away.

Maybe it doesn't even matter if we can't save this place, she thought. Her dream had never been about high thread counts or farm-raised beef. It had been about her and Tim. But even though they supposedly ran this place together, she felt lonelier than she'd ever been.

For a long time, she'd blamed their troubles on the financial stress. But even if Tim discovered a million dollars hidden away in some forgotten corner of the barn, would that really solve everything?

It had been so long since she'd felt connected with him that she wasn't sure.

And she didn't even want to think about what it might be like if they didn't have this place to work on together, and wound up back in the city, doing work neither of them wanted to be doing.

Jeanne tossed the paper towel in the trash, took a deep breath, and picked up her bag of frosting to begin the next cookie.

But as she did, a small set of wind chimes on the opposite side of the kitchen began to jingle: a clever warning system that Tim had rigged up years ago to alert her that guests had just come in the front door, without them ringing a buzzer that would disturb the other guests.

There was a good chance it was the wedding party, Jeanne calculated, who were supposed to begin arriving around now.

And if it was, she needed to go give Iris a hand. It was Iris who they'd bought the farm from, years ago. She loved still being a part of the place, and Jeanne and Tim loved having her around. But she wasn't really great with details under the best of circumstances, and the more guests she had to deal with at a time, the more likely things were to go awry.

Jeanne and Tim usually found her occasional mix-ups amusing, like the time she'd handed over an entire wedding party's worth of welcome treats to the first family who arrived, whose thrilled elementary-age children had immediately decimated the bonbons that had been individually wrapped for each guest. Jeanne had managed to bake up several batches of brownies in time to provide treats for the remaining guests, who wound up oohing and aahing over the fact that their baked treats were still warm when they arrived.

Still, Jeanne wanted to avoid any similar surprises with this wedding party. They weren't just special because they might be the last wedding Evergreen Inn was able to host. They were special because they'd been with Evergreen since the beginning.

Jeanne drew a deep breath, untied her apron, and hung it on a nearby hook.

Then she walked through the door that led from the kitchen to the reception area in the front hall, and gave her brightest smile to the two women standing at the desk.

"Welcome to Evergreen Inn," she said.

THREE

THE INSTANT HANNAH SAW Jeanne, the hard knot of nerves that had been building in her stomach all the way up from Boston began to ease.

She darted around the counter and Jeanne stopped beside it as they embraced in a warm hug.

"Oh my gosh," Hannah said. "I'm so glad to see you."

Then she stepped back and looked around. "I didn't think this place could be any more beautiful than it is in the summer," she said. "But look at what you do for Christmas! It's amazing."

Her attention was drawn by a small nativity set up on one side of the check-in desk: the shepherds and wise men, along with the baby and his parents, all done in beautifully cut crystal.

"I've never seen anything like this," she said.

"Oh, I can't take credit for that," Jeanne said.

"It's my grandmother's," Iris piped up. "She brought it all the way up to Vermont with her, when the family first came here from New York. Wrapped it up in flour sacks, and then sat on it the whole way so that nobody would actually mistake it for flour and toss it somewhere."

"It's beautiful," Hannah said. Then she looked around, taking in all the Christmas details: the twinkle lights that dangled near the ceiling level, the swags of fresh juniper, the velvet ribbons affixed to the stairs leading up to the guest rooms.

"It's not just for Christmas," Jeanne said, giving Hannah a squeeze around the waist. "I don't know if you've heard, but we have an important wedding happening here this weekend. For one of our very favorite guests."

Hannah wrapped Jeanne in another hug. "I don't know how to thank you," she said.

From behind the counter, Iris looked up at Jeanne. "More than half this place is reserved in the name of the Green family," Iris said. "Did you have any particular plan about who goes where?"

"Yep, yep," Jeanne said, slipping behind the counter to look at the reservations book.

As Hannah peered over the counter, she felt the companionable bump of her best friend stepping up beside her.

"I'm Audrey," Audrey told Iris and Jeanne, with one of her irresistible grins. "Nice to meet you."

"My maid of honor," Hannah explained, as both women took turns shaking Audrey's hand.

Then she looked at Audrey. "Sorry," she said. "I should have introduced you."

Audrey grinned. "You've had one or two other things on your mind," she said.

"You all ready for the big day, dear?" Iris asked.

Hannah took a deep breath.

"Absolutely," Audrey answered for her. "This is going to be the best wedding of this holiday season. We're running the show with military precision."

Iris raised one eyebrow. "I've never heard of a wedding that went quite . . . that way," she commented.

But Hannah looked at Audrey gratefully. "I thought such a small wedding would keep things simple," she said.

"No wedding is simple," Audrey said. "That's the first rule of weddings."

At this, Iris gave a vigorous nod.

"What's the second rule?" Jeanne asked, raising her eyebrows in amusement.

Before Audrey could enlighten them, her chin lifted and her eyes narrowed as if she'd just picked up some signal only she could hear.

In the silence that followed, the rest of them caught the sound of it, too—the faint, insistent ring of a cell phone, coming from somewhere in Audrey's vicinity.

Audrey began to dig in her pocket as she backed toward the front door they'd just come through. "Excuse me," she said. "I need to take this."

"Her husband's in the marines," Hannah explained, as the door thunked shut behind Audrey. "He's got a few days' leave for the holidays."

"And she's here without him?" Iris said, obviously shocked.

"He's on his way here," Hannah said. "I never thought he was going to be able to make our wedding. We were going to try to live-stream him in from Afghanistan. Audrey had made him promise that he'd FaceTime every dance with her."

"But now he'll actually be here," Iris said, beaming with so much joy you might have thought it was her own husband.

Hannah beamed back. In the midst of all the details and anxiety of planning a wedding, it was good to see other people's joy at her good news. It was a huge blessing that the timing had worked out for Jared to join them, all the way from the other side of the world. Maybe she should spend more time thinking about that than whether the flowers were blue or white, or whatever else she'd been worrying about. Even in those rare moments when she thought everything was finally in order, she was still a bundle of nerves.

"The garland over the door is so beautiful," Hannah told Jeanne. "I've never seen you make one so pretty."

"And you've seen a lot of them," Jeanne said, with a slight smile.

"I guess I have," Hannah said. She and her family had been some of Jeanne and Tim's first guests, the summer they opened, when Hannah was just twelve. And in the years since then, Evergreen Inn had been at the heart of the Green family traditions: summer vacations and a handful of the winter holidays and ski trips. So when it had come time to plan her wedding, Hannah had known exactly where she wanted to hold it.

"I'm just so glad you were able to take us on such short notice," she told Jeanne.

It had come as a total surprise when her boyfriend Trevor had proposed to her that summer, and an even bigger one when he'd insisted, with his usual irresistible energy, that they should get married before the New Year.

She'd been with Trevor since nursing school, when she'd met him as a patient on one of her very first rotations. He showed a special interest in her life, always chatting with her as she made her rounds. At first, she'd thought it was just because they were so much closer in age than the other people on the ward. Most of the other nurses were older. And most of the other patients struggling with diabetes like Trevor was were older, too. So she was surprised when Trevor asked for her number as he was leaving, and even more surprised when he called a day later.

But that was six years ago now. She hadn't exactly been waiting for him to propose that whole time—they'd been too busy becoming adults, getting jobs, and having adventures. And if there was one thing Trevor loved, it was being spontaneous and having adventures. She could understand that. He'd been struggling with health issues related to his diabetes since he was a kid. Some of them were potentially deadly. It only made sense that he would want to live every minute to the hilt. And because he came from a family with a lot more money than Hannah's, he could afford to. It drove Hannah crazy sometimes, but it also kept life full of surprises. She loved that companionship, and the excitement of never quite knowing what would come next.

In fact, that's pretty much how he'd proposed, a few months ago, on a trip to Portland, Maine, for a friend's wedding. He'd spotted a ring he liked in a jewelry store on the boardwalk, and proposed over lobster rolls the very same day. The whole experience was a complete romantic whirlwind.

"I was sure you'd be booked by the time I called," Hannah said. "But I couldn't imagine getting married anywhere else."

"I'm glad we could take you," Jeanne said, but something in her smile looked strange to Hannah.

Just as Hannah was wondering if she'd said something wrong, the front door behind her opened.

She glanced back, expecting to see Audrey stomping her feet against the cold outside, but instead a tall man, around her age, stood in the entryway, shaking the snow out of his blond curls onto the shoulders of his black-and-red-check coat. He looked like an ad for a high-end outerwear company. But he also looked oddly familiar.

"Luke!" Iris exclaimed. "I told you to take a scarf!"

Luke shook his head. "I think I'll live, Grandma," he said.

"Luke?" Hannah said. A host of jumbled memories of the

skinny, smart-mouthed kid who she'd spent hours with during her adolescent years, wandering through the sunlit woods around the inn, or tramping through the snow, hunting for firewood or holly branches, suddenly collided with the full-grown man in front of her.

"You remember Luke," Iris said, in the tone of a grandmother who couldn't quite believe that not everyone in the world found her grandson as unforgettable as she did.

Hannah took a closer look at the young man in front of her. Even over a decade later, the resemblance was so strong that she could still catch glimpses of the boy she'd known in the features and gestures of this stranger.

Especially when he smiled, as he did now, with a quizzical raise of an eyebrow.

"Have we met?" he asked, his tone amused and unmistakably flirtatious.

"You remember Hannah, Luke," Iris said. "It's little Hannah."

Now it was Luke's turn to double take. His get-to-know-you grin was quickly replaced by a dawning recognition.

"Wait," he said. "Hannah . . . Green?"

Hannah nodded.

Suddenly, she found herself in the grip of an enormous bear hug that lifted her off her feet and replanted her, after a brief twirl, about a yard from where she'd originally stood.

"Hannah Green!" he said. "What in the world? I thought I was just going to get to see Grandma on this visit. You look— I didn't know you'd be here, too."

"You're here for Christmas?" Hannah asked.

Luke shook his head. "I'm on my way to Burlington," he said. "To have Christmas with my folks. I just stopped in this morning to see Grandma along the way."

"He likes my apple pie better than his mother's," Iris said. "She doesn't use cinnamon sugar on the crust."

"But we'd never tell her that, right, Grandma?" Luke said. He turned back to Hannah. "So what have you been up to?" he asked. "What are you doing here?"

"She's getting married," Iris announced.

"Oh, no kidding," Luke said, his expression changing. His posture changed, too, his back straightening, arms crossed. "Sometime soon?"

"This weekend," Hannah said.

"Wow," Luke said.

"You met him, Luke," Iris said. "When you came to see me that summer. A few years ago."

"I did?" Luke said.

"He did?" Hannah added, almost in unison. "I don't remember seeing him."

"You were out on a hike with your parents," Iris said. "Trevor came in a little later, and he had some trouble with his car, as I remember."

Luke's eyes widened at the jog to his memory. "Oh," he said. "That guy?"

Hannah nodded and smiled. "That guy," she said.

"Well," Luke said, clapping his hands. "Congratulations."

Before Hannah could thank him, the front door swung open again.

This time it was Audrey, but her face was all wrong: her eyes bright with what looked like tears, and her mouth set in a determined line.

"Audrey?" Hannah asked. "Is everything all right?"

"It's Jared," Audrey said.

Hannah's heart sank. Every time Jared was deployed, she

felt a constant low-grade anxiety about his safety. It wasn't anything like what Audrey must feel as his wife, but the fact that Jared might be in danger was never far from Hannah's mind. Was this the call they had all been trying not to dread for so long? The day before her wedding? "Is he all right?" Hannah asked.

Audrey nodded, but as she did, tears slid down her face. "Yes," she said. She wiped fiercely at the tears, stopping them midway in their tracks. "He's fine. I guess I should just be grateful for that."

Hannah went over and wrapped Audrey in a hug. "What happened?" she asked.

"He's not going to make the wedding," Audrey said. "It's this storm. I guess it's a lot worse than they thought it was going to be. He tried to get into Boston, and then New York, or even Philly, but they're delaying and canceling flights left and right. He's still trying to get whatever he can, but he's stuck in San Diego and right now the closest he can get to the East Coast is Tulsa." Her voice broke as she said it.

Hannah gave Audrey a tight squeeze. "I'm so sorry," she said.

"Me too," Audrey said, squeezing back.

"Luke," Iris commanded from behind the front desk. "You take these girls' luggage upstairs for them, so they can get some rest."

As Hannah released Audrey, Jeanne slid a pair of keys across the varnished wood. "You'll be in communicating rooms," she said. "The Blue Jay and the Gold Finch."

"That's perfect," Hannah said. "Those two rooms with the beautiful footed tub in the bathroom between them?"

"That's right," Jeanne said with a smile.

"And you still have those incredible bath salts?" Hannah asked.

Jeanne nodded. "Made them myself," she said. "Eucalyptus and bergamot."

"How does an amazing hot bath sound?" Hannah asked Audrey.

"I'm supposed to be taking care of you," Audrey said.

"There's plenty of time for that," Hannah said, scooping up the keys to follow Luke, who had already somehow managed to pick up both their suitcases and the giant poufy garment bag that held her dress, and was bounding up the stairs with them.

"I'll be up in a minute with some afternoon treats," Jeanne said.

"Almond brittle?" Hannah asked. It was one of Jeanne's signature delicacies, and Hannah had consumed it in epic portions ever since she was in middle school.

Jeanne smiled. "I might be able to find some of that around here," she said.

At the top of the stairs, Luke stopped at the first door, letting the suitcases thud to the floor. "Okay," he said. "Which is which?"

"This is Audrey's room," Hannah told him. "I'm down the hall."

"That's mine," Audrey said, pointing to her bag.

With a flourish, Luke opened the door and carried the bag in, setting it up on the luggage stand as if it didn't weigh anything more than a box of feathers.

Audrey sank down on the high queen bed, which was covered with a beautiful crazy quilt in shades of midnight and sky blue.

"Can I get you anything, honey?" Hannah asked.

"I just need a minute," Audrey said. "I'll be fine."

"I know you will," Hannah said.

"That's rough," Luke said as Hannah pulled the door shut behind them. "Being split up on the holidays."

"She was so excited he was coming," Hannah said.

"It's a good problem, though," Luke said. "That they want to be together. So many couples seem like they're not even sure they like each other anymore."

Hannah opened the door to her room and he carried her bag in, placing it at the foot of her bed.

"Thanks," Hannah said.

"Anytime," Luke said.

At the door, he turned back. "How are you doing?" he asked.

"Me?" Hannah said, taken aback. "I'm okay. A little nervous, I guess."

"But not too nervous," Luke said with a grin.

Hannah laughed, trying to ignore the hard knot in her stomach that had become her constant companion in the weeks leading up to the wedding. "No," she said. "Not too nervous."

"That's good," Luke said. He looked at her for just a moment longer, as if he was deciding whether to say something else. Then he ducked his head.

"Well," he said. "I wish you both all the very best."

"Thanks," Hannah said. "You, too. Merry Christmas."

"Merry Christmas," Luke said, and pulled the door shut behind him.

Hannah dropped her coat on the chair by the door, hopped up on the bed, and let herself fall back into its velvet folds.

Just as she felt the stress begin to slide off her shoulders, and sink into the loft of the mattress, her phone began to ring in her coat pocket.

With effort, she managed to get herself upright and scramble over to the door to retrieve it before it stopped ringing, the selfie she'd taken of her and Trevor that summer—just after he'd proposed—displayed on the screen.

"Your timing is perfect," she said. "Audrey just got into her room. How are you doing?"

"Good, good," Trevor said.

Hannah breathed a sigh of relief. "I was afraid you were going to have trouble," she said. "Audrey just heard from Jared, and he's not going to make it in time for the wedding. This storm has all the airports in the Northeast shut down, so he's stuck. Where are you?"

"Boston," Trevor said.

"Boston?" Hannah repeated, her mind doing a quick calculation. "Weren't you going to leave this morning? Is the traffic that bad?"

"I haven't left yet," Trevor said.

Hannah felt a deep annoyance rising in her. Trevor was always changing plans at the last minute. It drove her nuts, and he knew it. And now he was changing them on the weekend of their wedding.

"Why not?" she said. "When will you get here?"

"Hannah . . ." Trevor said.

Something in the tone of his voice turned her annoyance to cold fear.

"What?" she said.

At the other end of the line, she heard nothing but silence.

"Trevor?" she asked. "Are you there?"

"I'm not coming," Trevor said.

"You're not coming?" Hannah said, disbelief struggling with exasperation in her voice.

"It's just too much," Trevor said. "It's just too soon."

"Too soon?" Hannah repeated. Every time she parroted his

words, her voice seemed to rise another notch. "Trevor, we've been dating for six years."

"Getting married is a lot different than dating," Trevor said, with the patronizing gravitas of a relationship expert on a daytime television show. "It's just all happening so fast."

"Trevor, you were the one who wanted to get married this year," Hannah reminded him.

"I know that," Trevor said. "I thought that maybe once we got married, I wouldn't feel so . . ."

"So what, Trevor?" Hannah asked.

"Scared," Trevor said quietly.

Hannah said nothing for a long moment, taking it all in. "What exactly are you saying?"

"I'm just not sure you're the woman I'm supposed to marry," Trevor said.

"If that's how you feel about me, then why did you ask me to *marry* you? Why did you take six years of my life?"

"That's not the only thing I feel," Trevor said.

Hannah shook her head in disbelief. "What else do you feel?" she demanded.

As usual, once she got heated, Trevor started to turn into a rock, encased in an iceberg.

"Never mind—"

"I deserve an explanation. You don't get to run away and hide without—" Her voice cracked.

"Look," he said, "clearly you're upset."

"You're very observant," Hannah said.

"I don't think talking is a good idea with you in this mood," he said.

"Mood?" Hannah said, rage bubbling up in her. "Trevor, you just broke our engagement. Two days before our wedding. I never pushed you into any of this. You wanted to get married. If you were having second thoughts, you should've told me weeks ago, before the caterers and flowers and plans. This is just—" Her voice gave in as the tears started stinging down her cheeks. "The most selfish thing, the most *cowardly* thing, you've ever done."

"Well," Trevor said, his tone weary and removed, "was there anything else you wanted to say?"

Hannah looked down at the picture of Trevor's beaming face on her phone, but so many thoughts and feelings crowded her mind that she couldn't put any of them to words.

"No," she said.

"Okay," Trevor said, with just enough mild smugness to let her know he thought he'd won this argument. "Well, I guess I should let you go, then."

"I guess you should," Hannah said.

But she hung on the line until he disconnected the call.

Then she threw the phone down on the bed and walked to the window.

She pressed both her palms to the cool glass to steady herself, and she tried to look down at the yard outside, to get some kind of different perspective, but it was snowing so hard now that she couldn't see anything at all.

FOUR

BOB WAS RIDING SHOTGUN, but as the mild storm the weatherman predicted had grown in force to something that seemed much more akin to a full blizzard, Stacy could tell he'd gotten more and more anxious.

"Why don't you pull over and let me drive," he had suggested, as Stacy made the executive decision to leave the freeway. It was always a tricky calculation in bad conditions. Was it better to stay on the main roads, which were more likely to be cleared, but also more full of traffic? Or would it be safer on a less-traveled road, where they could move at their own pace, with fewer tractor trailers to deal with?

For the first hour of the blizzard, Bob had made a strong case for sticking to the main roads. But even as the traffic slowed to a crawl, wrecks kept piling up. And when they passed a jack-knifed truck, Stacy had had enough. The country roads might not be as clear, but they knew them, from all the time they'd spent at the little inn that had become their family's home away from home. She was pretty sure that they'd be virtually deserted, under the conditions. And she wasn't about to let a careless driver on the interstate keep them from getting to their only daughter's wedding.

So she'd taken the next exit, which let them out onto a winding Vermont country road that she could only see a few yards down, even with her lights on, in what should have been broad daylight.

"I don't know where it'd be safe to stop, honey," she said, in answer to Bob's offer to drive. "I'm not even sure where the side of the road is now. If we stop, I don't know if anyone else will be able to see us. And we're almost there."

Bob put his hand on her leg and gave it a squeeze. "I just wish there were something I could do," he said.

"You do plenty," Stacy said, touched by the note of longing in his voice, because she knew he wasn't just talking about the drive through the snow. "For everyone."

Her own hands ached to reach over and comfort him in return, but it was impossible to take either one of them off the wheel under the conditions.

Out of the corner of her eye, though, she could see Bob shaking his head.

"You wouldn't have to be making this drive," he said, "if I'd been able to afford to fly us all to Aruba."

By nature, Bob was a jokester, but this joke was too serious to make Stacy smile. Instead, she felt a little flare of anger in her heart, which she quickly tried to squash out. She didn't want to walk into her daughter's wedding weekend with any negative emotions, but Bob wasn't the only one who wished that things were different.

Hannah, their daughter, had been dating her boyfriend Trevor for so long that Stacy and Bob had started to wonder privately if he would ever get around to popping the question. But when he finally did, for some reason, he was in a tremendous hurry to tie the knot. He and Hannah had only gotten engaged a few months ago, but he'd insisted on having the wedding before the end of the year.

That meant that almost any venue Hannah or Stacy had ever dreamed of was already booked up. But that was a secondary concern to the major problem, which was that Bob's business as a contractor had been struggling for several years, after a big company had pulled its headquarters out of the small town where he built homes, leaving a huge glut in the housing market. He was both well loved and well respected in town, so he'd managed to hang on while other contractors folded or packed up to seek brighter prospects. And it looked like the market was finally turning. But in the meantime, he didn't have anything like the kind of cash he would have liked to have on hand to throw his daughter a wedding. In fact, he was struggling to climb out of debts he'd had to take on to save the business, and the jobs of the twenty people who worked for him.

After a few weeks of false starts, Stacy and Hannah had come up with what seemed like the perfect solution: holding the wedding at the inn in Vermont where the family had spent summers and a handful of holidays ever since Hannah was a little girl. Miraculously, it wasn't booked up yet over the Christmas holiday. And it was just big enough to host a tiny wedding with a handful of guests from each family, which was all that Bob and Stacy could afford.

Over the course of the planning, both Stacy and Hannah had gotten excited about holding the intimate event at the beloved inn—and grateful that they didn't have a giant guest list that required Excel spreadsheets to keep track of, or hand-making favors for hundreds of guests.

But part of Stacy still had to fight to keep from resenting Trevor's big rush. She couldn't disagree with his choice of bride, and she guessed that it was good that he was so eager to start life with Hannah. But she wished they'd had more time, so they could have the opportunity to give their only daughter the best.

"It's going to be wonderful," Stacy said, trying to ease the sting of it for him now. "In those big weddings, nobody really gets to talk to the bride and groom, and if they do, the bride and groom are so overwhelmed they don't even remember it. This way we'll all get to know each other. It'll be personal. No professional photographer, just Audrey snapping pictures."

"Except she's a way better photographer than any of our other friends," Bob said.

Stacy was grateful to hear the smile in his voice.

"Yep," she said. "We're lucky in a lot of ways. And it's never the wedding that's important. It's marrying the right person."

"I know I'm lucky I married the right girl," Bob said.

This time, when he squeezed her knee, she laid her own hand over his, just for a moment.

Then, at the sound of a roar behind them, she snatched her hand back, gripping the wheel tightly. She couldn't see anything but white in the rearview mirror as the roar grew louder and louder. But from the sound of it, she could tell it was approaching at a far higher speed than their little car was moving.

"What in the world?" Bob asked, twisting to look back.

As he did, the glare of two bright lights appeared in the whiteout of the rearview, high up: a tractor trailer.

It gained on them at a sickening speed, while Stacy did her best to hold her own. She still couldn't see far enough ahead to jam on the gas herself, and even if she did, it would only delay the moment of collision for an instant, at the rate this truck was gaining on them. The only hope was that the driver would see them in time—which wasn't at all a given in these conditions.

As Stacy's fingers clenched around the wheel, the grille of

the truck broke out of the snow, bearing down on them until she couldn't even see the lights on either side anymore.

Then, in a rush, the roar passed to the left of them, crossing over into the oncoming lane of the little two-lane road. A huge clod of dirty ice hit their window, completely blotting out even the limited view Stacy had had of the road. She drove blind for three or four swipes of the windshield wipers, until they managed to fling off enough of the slush and mud to clear the window again. Which did nothing to improve the visibility on the road itself. Now she couldn't even see a few yards ahead. It was more like a few feet. And most of that was full of thick snow.

"What is this clown doing on the side roads?" Bob asked. "Did they close the freeway?"

When Stacy didn't answer, he looked at her. "How are you doing?" he asked.

"We're almost there," she said, more to herself than him.

She squinted into the whiteout.

Then her headlights caught the first smear of color she'd seen for hours: what seemed like a fine painting someone had accidentally left hanging on the side of the road, swaying gently in the swirling snow. The top of the sign had already been effaced by snow, but she still recognized the familiar lettering at the bottom: "Inn."

And just after it, she could see the tiniest hint of a lane leading off the main road, so small she wasn't sure it was even a road until she made the turn onto it and began to follow it up the hill to safety and warmth, and the start of their daughter's new life.

FIVE

"JEANNE!"

Jeanne knew Bob Green's big, booming voice before she saw him. As the door slammed shut behind him, a gust of wind and a handful of glittery snow spilled through the front door into the warm room along with him and his wife, Stacy, the mother of the bride. "Are those for us?"

Jeanne, who had been headed for the stairs with the welcome baskets for Hannah and Audrey, one on each arm, turned around.

As she did, Stacy, a pretty fifty-something blonde, embraced her in a hug, the sparkles of snow on her shearling hood chill, but the light in her eyes warm.

"We're so glad to see you," she said. "And so glad to be here. Can you believe it?"

For what felt like the first time in a while, Jeanne didn't have to force her smile. She'd always liked Stacy, from the first time she'd ushered her family into Evergreen Inn's doors over ten years ago. And over all the years the Green family had returned since, that instant connection had grown into a deep affection.

She squeezed Stacy back, as Bob enveloped both of them in a clumsy bear hug of his own.

"Congratulations," Jeanne said, as all Stacy's laugh lines lit up in a giant smile.

Then Iris bustled out from behind the desk. "You haven't used up all the hugs yet, have you?" she joked, clasping first Bob, then Stacy, in a warm embrace. She stopped when she came to Jeanne, then gave her a big hug, too.

"What was that for?" Jeanne asked.

"You look like you needed it," Iris said tartly, before retreating behind the desk.

In the meantime, Bob had stepped over to inspect the contents of the basket nearest him, pawing through its carefully arranged goodies still very much like a curious and hungry bear. "Warm brownies," Bob said, helping himself to one as he rooted through the rest of the basket with his free hand. "And grilled cheese! Honey, I told you we shouldn't stop for anything before we got here."

"We didn't stop because we didn't want to spend our daughter's wedding marooned on the interstate in Vermont," Stacy said bluntly, helping herself to a brownie.

At her first bite, her eyes closed in bliss and she took a long, deep breath. "I remember the first time I ever tasted these brownies," she said. "And I've made that recipe you gave me over and over. But I still think you must have a secret ingredient. Mine never turn out like yours."

"Vermont moonshine," Bob suggested, taking full possession of one of the baskets from Jeanne's arm, as Stacy slid her own arm through it companionably.

"This is perfect," she said with a sigh. "I always tried to imagine where Hannah would get married, and I never could. But as soon as she said it, I couldn't imagine anywhere else."

The sight of Stacy's face, and her radiant happiness, brought Jeanne's memories of the early days at the inn sweeping back: all the hope and energy they had had when they'd first opened the doors, without a shadow, just for that moment, of the troubles of the present.

"I can't wait to see what you've whipped up for us this time," Stacy said. "I know it's going to be perfect."

"I hope so," Jeanne said.

"I know it will," Stacy said. "It always is."

Bob was the first to hear the sound of Audrey's footsteps, coming down the stairs. But Stacy was the first one to pounce the maid of honor with a hug. "Honey!" she said. "Thank you so much for being here! How are you doing? How is Hannah-belle? How are Trevor and his folks? Did they get here all right? This snow is a mess, but we made it!"

Jeanne could see the struggle on Audrey's face, the attempt to smile through her own pain, and Jeanne's heart went out to her.

But when Audrey came to the foot of the stairs, still without having given an answer, Stacy's face crinkled in concern.

"Honey?" Iris said from behind the front desk. "What's wrong?"

As Audrey took a deep, shaky breath, Jeanne watched her closely. This wasn't how Audrey had looked after she heard her husband wouldn't be able to make the wedding after all. This was something worse.

Audrey opened her mouth to speak, then shook her head and looked down at the swirls and vines of the thick antique carpet at the foot of the stairs.

"Is something wrong with Hannah?" Stacy asked. "Is she all right?"

At this, Audrey raised her chin. Jeanne had seen her take the news of her husband's absence. She had faced it head-on. And Jeanne had a feeling that whatever came next was going to be direct, too, even if it was unpleasant.

"Trevor's not coming," she said.

"Not coming?" Stacy repeated. "Did he get stuck in this storm? When it settles down, I'm sure—"

"He hasn't even left Boston," Audrey said quickly. "He's not coming at all. The wedding's off."

"Why, that . . ." Stacy began, her brow darkening. "That little . . ."

"Nincompoop," Iris finished for her, decisively. She folded her arms, radiating disapproval.

Dazed, Bob handed the welcome basket back to Jeanne without really seeming to see her. "Where's Hannah?" he asked.

Stacy looked at Jeanne, her eyes wide. "Oh, Jeanne," she said. "After all the work you must have done."

"That is the last thing you should think about right now," Iris said.

"You don't worry about that," Jeanne said firmly, as her heart sank and her mind began to race. "You don't worry about that at all."

"Where's Hannah-belle?" Bob demanded, his voice growing louder.

"She's up here," Audrey said, starting back up the stairs.

Stacy gave Jeanne one more stricken look, then followed her husband.

Jeanne sighed and did a bewildered half turn in the entry hall.

Behind the desk, Iris shook her head.

"I guess that means we won't be full this Christmas after all," she said, pulling out the reservation book and flopping it open on the desk before her. "So no room for Trevor Armstrong. And no room for the Armstrong parents. Should I go ahead and run the cards for their deposits?"

Jeanne could hear from the quaver in Iris's voice that she was just as upset for Hannah as Jeanne was, and only trying to find a way to be useful in the emergency. But trying to deal with the details in the midst of such bad news started an ache in the back of Jeanne's head. And when her mind cleared enough to really think about what Iris was saying, the headache only got worse.

"I didn't take their deposits," Jeanne said.

"You didn't?" Iris said.

"They were just part of the Green wedding. I've known the Greens for so long. I thought I'd run the Armstrongs' cards when they got here," Jeanne said.

"The only card I've got on file here is Bob's," Iris said, rifling through the papers on the desk.

Jeanne shook her head. "We can't run that. I'm not going to charge him for the room of a groom who didn't show up."

"No," Iris said. She sat back down, nodding with a certain stubborn approval of Jeanne. "I guess not."

But as Jeanne carried the welcome baskets back into the kitchen, the reality of what had just happened began to crash in on her.

The reservations for the Armstrong family hadn't been a lot, but they had been just enough, along with the Green guests and their meager cash reserves, to pay the mortgage bill that was still due before the new year.

How, she wondered as she set the welcome baskets neatly on the counter, lost in a daze, would they ever pay it now?

In her younger days, she might have burst into tears of frustration. But today, she was too tired to do anything more than lay her head down on the smooth steel of her kitchen counter as tears welled in her eyes without slipping down her face.

"Jeanne?"

At the sound of Tim's voice, Jeanne buried her head in her

arms. On top of everything else, she couldn't face the idea of telling him.

A minute later, though, she could feel the gentle touch of his arm on her shoulder. Blindly, she lifted her head and buried it in his work jacket, which was still cold to the touch and dusted with snow.

He had come in from outside and crossed the kitchen to reach her without even stopping to take it off.

"Jeanne," he said. "What's wrong?"

"Hannah's wedding," Jeanne said. "It's not happening. Trevor broke it off."

Tim's face turned grim. "That guy—" he began, then stopped himself.

Jeanne met his eyes. "I didn't get a deposit for the Armstrong family rooms," she said. "So we're losing all that income."

Tim wrapped her in a hug. "We'll get through it."

She'd heard him say this a million times. And once, it had worked on her like magic. But now it just made her feel like he hadn't been listening.

"How?" she asked, pulling back. "How is it going to be all right?"

"Jeanne," Tim said. "It's just a drop in the bucket."

"It's not a drop in the bucket, though," Jeanne said. "It's cash. Cash we needed to pay the mortgage. And if we don't pay the mortgage, we risk going into default before we're able to make a sale that could make us whole again."

"We can break into my retirement if we have to," Tim said.

Jeanne shook her head impatiently. "That's not how we're supposed to spend that money!" she said. "What are we going to retire on?"

Tim shrugged.

"I just wanted some time," Jeanne said. "I thought I could at least buy us some time. I thought we could maybe land this plane, instead of crashing. Take our time closing up. Give some warning to the people who have helped us all these years. Like Iris. I *still* don't know what we're going to tell Iris."

It had really been a gift when Iris sold them the place. There had been other, higher bidders, but Iris had agreed to sell to them because she believed in their vision, and because they were thrilled to let her still have a part of it, living nearby on her own small parcel of land and working at the inn, for as long as she wanted. And for Jeanne, one of the most painful parts of the inn's troubles wasn't just watching her own dreams die—it was the fact that she wouldn't be able to keep the promises they'd made to Iris. And at Iris's age, how many more reinventions did she really have in her?

"I thought I had this all worked out," Jeanne said. "I thought I could at least get us through to the end of the year. Do this wedding. End with something beautiful. Now I can't even make a single payment."

As she said this, Tim stepped back, his face changed.

"We," he said.

"What?" said Jeanne.

"*We* can't make a single payment," Tim said. "Not *you*. Us."

"I know that," Jeanne began. "It's just—"

"Do you, Jeanne?" Tim asked. "Really? 'Cause I have to tell you, it doesn't feel that way."

"I—" Jeanne began, but Tim was already stalking away from her, across the room. Before she could think of anything else to say, he disappeared again, out the door into the storm.

And before she could do anything else, the chime he'd rigged to the front door began to jangle.

Six

MOLLY PLACED THE LAST colored pencil on the large antique desk, set the beautiful tin box that had held the pencil down beside it, stepped back, and sighed.

It couldn't be a more perfect setting to write.

The slightly oversized sheets of white paper that she liked to draw and dream on were placed neatly in the center of the desk. Colored pencils lay to the left of it in a comfortable jumble, with a fountain pen, graphite pencils, and a handful of stray ballpoint pens to the right.

Above the blank paper she'd laid out all the ideas she'd collected for the book over the past weeks and months: sketches on one side, handwritten notes on the other. It was a trick she'd learned to make the blank page not seem so blank. The notes were a visual sign that she wasn't starting from scratch: all she had to do was glance up from the page to see how many ideas she already had.

And with so many ideas spread across the desk, it was almost impossible that one of them wouldn't spark a new stream of inspiration.

The thick snow falling beyond the window over the desk was ideal as well. There was nothing to annoy her, none of the invading sounds or sights of the city, like car horns or people shouting on the street. But the steady, beautiful motion of the snow was a pleasant distraction, a place to rest her mind between thoughts, or a way to open the door to let new ideas come in.

She retrieved her mug of hot cider from the table beside the bed, took a sip, and sat down.

At the first sight of her sketches and notes, she smiled as if she'd just run into old friends. There was the zebra on the bicycle, the swan wearing a crown, the octopus who wore four different pairs of shoes, the notes about *singing policeman!* and *popsicle chase* and *Christmas wish*.

As she always did, she just sat and let it all wash over her as the heat from the cider seeped comfortably into her palms. She didn't write by thinking, but by listening, setting the stage, and letting the story arrive.

Except that this time, it didn't.

For several minutes, she sat in patient expectation, waiting for all the details she'd collected to begin to come play with each other and create a story: the zebra on the bicycle gets flagged down by the singing policeman, the octopus tears off down the street in a Popsicle chase.

But although the sketches and fragments jostled companionably in her mind, none of them struck a spark big enough to light a whole story.

She watched the falling snow, to clear her mind.

She drank half the mug of cider.

She set the cider aside.

She picked up a colored pencil and doodled for a bit, to give the ideas a chance to come through her hands, instead of her head.

Then she put the pencil down again.

Nothing.

A little knot of fear began to grow in her stomach, as unwanted thoughts crowded in. This was just what had been happening to her back in Brooklyn, and nothing was different here. Nothing could be more perfect about this spot. So why could she still not write?

Suddenly all the memories of the grief and uncertainty and loneliness she'd been wrestling with at home in her tiny Brooklyn apartment came rushing back: the days when she'd cried for her mom, all by herself, the days when she'd worked and worked, and had nothing to show for it at the end of the day—and no one to show it to.

But the memories came back so clear that they didn't feel like memories anymore. The worry and the loneliness felt just as present here as they had there.

Maybe the problem wasn't the place. Maybe the problem was her.

Molly shook her head, downed the remaining cider in a single gulp, and stood up.

I'm just tired, she told herself. *It was a long trip up here. I just need a little break before I get to work.*

And before she could think anything else, she set the mug down on the desk, and walked out of the room.

As soon as the door shut behind her, she felt better.

An incredible blend of delicious smells wafted up the stairs from the kitchen below: cinnamon, and chocolate, and something savory—maybe roasted vegetables and rosemary. And a pleasant babble of voices murmured from the floors below, as well.

Gratefully, she padded down the stairs.

As she reached the main floor and the front desk, she was surprised by a blast of cold air. The front door wasn't actually standing open when she got there, but the reason for the chill was obvious: an older couple stood at the desk, negotiating with Iris.

"Anything you've got," the man said. "If your coal cellar has heat, we'd take that, at this point."

"Actually," Iris said with a smile, "I think we can do better than that."

As she found them a room, Jeanne came through the door, carrying a large basket of brownies.

"Hello!" the man said heartily. "I'm Frank. This is my wife, Eileen."

Jeanne did her best to muster a smile.

"They're looking for a room," Iris said. "I told them they were in luck. A wedding has just been canceled."

"Canceled?" Eileen said, her smile fading.

"Just a second," Jeanne said, depositing the brownies on a serving table in the corner of the entryway.

"Salted fudge brownies," she said to Molly. "Please help yourself."

Molly, who had been doing her best to stay out of the way, quickly realized that directly adjacent to the brownies was the most comfortable chair in the place, wine-colored velvet, with big overstuffed wings.

She took a seat, and helped herself to a brownie.

"Should I give them the groom's room?" Iris asked Jeanne. "Or the parents of the groom?"

Molly watched as Eileen gave Frank a quizzical look, but he just laid his credit card down on the counter. "It doesn't matter to us," he said. "As long as it's a room."

"Groom's room it is," Iris said, with a bright smile.

A blast of snow and wind roared through the front door, seeming to sweep a figure in along with it. When the door slammed shut again, that figure proved to be a white-haired old man with a face so red from the cold that he looked for all the world like Santa's grouchier, skinnier, older brother.

"Dear God," he said, in a clipped British accent. "I signed up for a trip to Vermont, not the Arctic Circle."

"Well, this can't be as bad as the Arctic Circle," Iris said, with a laugh.

The old man fixed his penetrating gaze on her. "You're quite sure of that, are you?" he asked.

Iris raised her eyebrows, unfazed by his British reserve. "Since neither of us has been there," she said, "I'm not sure either of us can be sure."

"What makes you think I haven't been?" the old man said, with a twist of his lip that could have either been a hint of contempt or a grin. On his grizzled features, it was almost impossible to tell.

"I'm sorry," Jeanne said to the man. "I don't believe we have a reservation for you tonight."

"I'm painfully aware of that," the man said. "It would be hard to confuse this establishment with the Starlight Lodge, where I do in fact have a reservation for this evening. But since the Vermont police have now officially closed the roads for the duration of the night, I find myself at your mercy. I realize every hovel in the area is likely fully booked at this point, but I am forced to inquire: Do you perhaps have a room for the night?"

Jeanne's eyes narrowed slightly at the patronizing tone in his voice, but Iris broke out into a wide, welcoming smile.

"Absolutely!" she said. "You came at just the right time. You'll have the last room in the place. Which is also my favorite," she added confidingly as she flipped open their reservation book.

"Your favorite?" the man said. "And why is that?"

"It's the room I grew up in," Iris told him. "Your name?"

"Godwin," the man said, laying his own credit card down on the counter beside Bob's. "Geoffrey Godwin. Are you the owner of this establishment?"

Iris shook her head. "I sold this farm over a decade ago to Jeanne and Tim. But they kept me on to help out around the place. It was my one stipulation."

For the first time since Godwin had arrived, his face thawed into something approximating a smile. "It sounds like you drive a hard bargain," he said.

As Iris collected the cards to run them, Jeanne turned to the rack of keys on the wall behind her, selected two pairs, and laid one on the counter before Bob and Eileen, and one before Godwin.

"You'll both be on the second floor," she said. "Just take the stairs up. You can't miss it."

Godwin collected his key, but as Bob and Eileen gave their effusive thanks and started up the stairs, he made a beeline for the brownies.

"And what are these?" he asked Molly with an arch air.

Molly was slightly insulted, both that he had apparently mistaken her for a waitress, and that he thought that, if she was a waitress, she would ever curl up in an armchair, munching on a brownie while on duty.

But something about his air was so commanding and regal that she didn't quite dare to talk back to him.

"Salted brownies," she said in a servicey tone, then felt a wave of annoyance at herself.

She'd never seen anyone pick up a brownie the way Godwin did. He gazed down at it for a long second, as if it were a creature he wanted to make sure was no longer breathing. Then he narrowed his eyes, reached for the fudgy square, sniffed it, and raised it to his thin lips with the precision of a lab technician.

But after his first bite, his expression relaxed. "Not bad," he said, and took another.

As he did, the front door banged open again. This time, two girls came barreling into the room, one about eight, one about five, both with dark hair and identical puffy jackets, one blue and one orange. They were also both screeching at the tops of their lungs.

"It's cold!" the older one said, hopping about sixty times a minute. "Cold! Cold! Cold!"

The little one's emissions weren't even that cogent. She just let out what seemed like an unending, high-pitched whine, as if she were a tower that gave off a warning signal when the temperature dropped below a certain threshold.

At the sound of the voices, Cassie came bursting through the kitchen door, her tail wagging a mile a minute.

"A puppy!" the littlest girl cried, in an ecstasy of excitement.

"That's not a puppy," the older girl said, trying to defend herself from Cassie's exuberant licking while also petting the soft hair on the top of her big head. "It's a *dog*."

"Just another quiet day here in the country," Iris said. "Cassie, come here."

With enormous reluctance, Cassie broke free from the two girls and bounded over to Iris, who grabbed her collar, holding the big dog firmly behind the desk.

The eyes of everyone in the lobby of the inn turned toward the door, waiting for the girls' parents to materialize.

After what seemed like several minutes, during which both

girls began to vigorously plead for Cassie's freedom, a man emerged from the storm, wrangling a large black backpack, a pair of turquoise suitcases adorned with unicorns, and a large stuffed tiger.

As he struggled with the door, which was being blown on its hinges by the wind, Molly jumped up to catch it.

"Thanks," he said gratefully.

Molly held the door against the wind, but didn't close it, waiting for the girls' mother to join them. After a moment, the man looked back.

"Oh," he said, a slight wince crossing his face. "No. It's just us."

"Daddy!" the older girl called, as Godwin hastily retreated up the stairs. In Molly's absence, the older girl had apparently discovered the brownies and helped herself. "Do you want a brownie?"

"Addison," the man said, his voice exasperated but firm. "Come here. Bailey. Addison."

Obediently, the two girls gathered at his side, composing themselves with angelic expressions that gave no hint of the chaos they had unleashed on the inn just moments before.

"And who might you be?" Iris asked, eyebrows raised.

"I'm Marcus Andrews," the man said, glancing from Jeanne to Iris with a warm if frazzled smile. "I'm afraid you've already met Bailey and Addison."

"Hello," the girls chorused.

Their father sighed. "We were on our way to the Starlight," he said. "But the roads have been closed. Is there any chance you have room for us? We have no place else to go."

Iris looked at Jeanne. Jeanne bit her lip. "I just gave away my last room," she said. "I'm so sorry."

Marcus glanced back at the storm beyond the windows. "You

don't have anything at all?" he asked. "It's actually illegal now for us to be out on these roads."

Jeanne shook her head. "If it were just you," she said, "I'd be glad to have you sleep on the couch in the lounge. But with the girls, I just don't think—"

"Daddy," Bailey said, pulling on his sleeve. "Did you bring Dodo from the car?"

"I brought Prince," Marcus said, pointing to the stuffed tiger. "Why don't you hold on to him?"

"Is it cold in the car?" Bailey asked.

"It wasn't cold when we were in the car, was it?" Marcus said reasonably.

"It gets cold when you turn the car off," Addison said, with an older sister's imperious wisdom.

"Is Dodo cold?" Addison said, her voice rising in childish agony as she drew out the last word.

"Honey," Marcus said, "Daddy's working on something else now." He looked back at Jeanne. "We would take literally anything at this point," he said. "Please."

Molly looked at the swirling snow beyond the uneven glass of the windows, thinking of the journey Marcus would have simply to get out to the car and back now, let alone find another place to stay. Then her mind flashed on the antique daybeds in her room.

"You know what?" she said, stepping forward. "I have room. The girls could stay with me."

SEVEN

"I KNEW IT," HANNAH'S father said, his hands gripping both sides of one of the antique wooden chairs in her room so hard that Hannah was afraid he'd snap the delicate wood to matchsticks. "I always knew he wasn't good enough for you."

Hannah took a deep breath, trying to steady herself.

"You know when I knew?" her father said, warming to his theme. "Do you remember that barbecue we had, Stacy? Where he made such a big deal of how he wanted to stay after to help out? After you girls went inside, he didn't lift another finger. He just stood there and let me scrape down that whole grill myself."

"Honey," Hannah's mother said sensibly. "Maybe he didn't know how to scrape down a grill."

"What kind of man doesn't know how to clean a grill?" Hannah's father asked. "Hannah knows how to clean a grill."

"That's true," Hannah's mother allowed.

"And she knows how to change a tire. Does Trevor know how to change a tire?" Hannah's father demanded, looking at Hannah.

Hannah just stared back at him. Trevor had no idea how to change a tire, a fact which had become evident after they'd blown one on the way to a friend's house in Cape Cod, and she'd had to figure out how to get the jack to work on the sandy shoulder, where it kept sinking in instead of lifting the car so she could remove the blasted tire. Trevor had tried to encourage her, but he couldn't have been described as "helpful."

That was so much the dynamic of their relationship, she realized. She had never really grown out of the role of nurse she had when they'd first met. Of course, as they'd dated, she'd watched his health and been there with him through the times when his condition landed him back in the hospital again. But it was more than that. No matter how long they were together, she was always the one taking care of things. Taking care of him. Now her mind ran back over the dozens of times in their relationship that she'd had to swoop in to save the day: not just changing the car's tire, but hunting down medicine in the middle of the night when Trevor had let his run out, or sweet-talking a local cop into letting them off without a ticket when Trevor decided to do a tightrope walk along the railing of a bridge.

Should I have known then? she wondered now. Because she hadn't. She had to admit that she had liked the feeling of being needed. But maybe there had been all kinds of signs she'd missed.

"Not knowing how to change a tire hardly disqualifies a young man from matrimony," Hannah's mother said.

Hannah looked at her mother gratefully. Her father had gone into full battle mode as soon as she had told them the news that Trevor had called the wedding off, but her mother still seemed reasonably calm.

"You know how I knew?" Hannah's mother said. Hannah's heart sank. "It was when you called him and told him you'd just been rejected by the nursing school at Duke, when you'd worked so hard to get in there, and he asked you if you *wanted* him to come over. I never could believe he asked you that. He should have been on his way the instant he heard the news."

"You know what else he did?" Hannah's father began.

"Yes," Hannah burst out. "I know a thousand other things that Trevor did, and a thousand other things that Trevor didn't do. But do you want to know when I knew?"

Both her parents looked at her, wide-eyed and waiting.

"I knew when Trevor told me this afternoon," Hannah said. "Before that, I had no idea. Not a clue. So if this was all so obvious to both of you, I'm not sure why you didn't bother to tell me."

She sat down on the bed and crossed her arms, doing her best to stay mad, because that at least felt better than crying, which is what she had been doing before her parents arrived.

But it was no use. Even with her arms crossed and her chin lifted, the tears still rolled down her cheeks.

"Oh, honey," her mother said. She sank down beside Hannah on the bed, and let Hannah's head drop onto her shoulder, just as she had done when Hannah was a child. "I'm so sorry. We shouldn't even be mentioning Trevor's name. Nothing matters but you right now."

"That's right," Hannah's father said, visibly relieved at the excuse to flip into a mode of accomplishing things instead of having to feel them. "We should be thinking about what to do. You talked with Jeanne downstairs? We'll have to see what we can get back on the deposit we made."

"You can't get the deposit back, honey," Hannah's mother said. "That's the point of the deposit. It protects businesses from things like . . . this," she said.

"Oh," Hannah's father said. "Jeanne's an old friend. I can't imagine her keeping our money when she hasn't—"

"She's not the one who didn't keep her end of the deal," Hannah said, her voice cracking. "They must have spent everything already, making sure they had all they needed for this weekend. And with this storm, it's not even like there's a chance she could sell it to anyone else."

"We'll talk about all those details later, Bob," Stacy said, with a warning glance to her husband, who sat down with a dissatisfied sigh in a nearby rocker.

"But what about you, honey?" her mother asked Hannah. "What can we do for you?"

At the kindness in her mother's voice, the tears began to flow freely down Hannah's face. Part of her just wanted to go back to being a child, whose problems could all be solved by her mother's kiss, even as she knew she could never be a child again. Another part of her still did feel like a child, in a way that made her ashamed, as if she was just a kid who still didn't understand anything, even though she was old enough now to get married.

"Are you hungry, pumpkin?" her father asked. "I can go get you something to eat or drink. I bet Jeanne's got something amazing down there in the kitchen."

Hannah knew exactly what Jeanne had in the kitchen. She'd spent hours on the phone with Jeanne in the past few months, planning every aspect of the menu down to the contents of the treat baskets that were supposed to be given to each guest on arrival, and the sweets that would be waiting for them on the entryway buffet as they came to check in.

Now the thought of salted brownies and Vermont grilled cheese on fresh sourdough bread just made her stomach twist.

Was this how it was going to be from now on? she wondered. Had Trevor ruined not just her wedding, but all her favorite things?

Until now, the pain of Trevor's call, and the press of the immediate details and embarrassments of the canceled wedding had been the only thing on her mind. But suddenly she got a glimpse of her whole life stretching out ahead of her. With none of the plans she and Trevor had made, it was a wide, blank canvas. And with the pain she felt in her heart right now, that was terrifying.

But both her parents were still looking at her, waiting for her to tell them whether she thought having a sandwich might help.

"You know what?" she said. "I think I just need to be alone."

Her mother and her father exchanged glances.

"Honey," her mother said. "I don't really think that's a good idea right now."

But the thought of spending any more time with her parents, with the wedding dress still hanging up on the mirror over the back of her closet door, was unbearable.

Unsteadily, Hannah stood up.

"I just need to get a breath of fresh air," she said. "I'll be right back."

And before either of them could say anything, she walked out of the room, ran down the stairs, and darted past the front desk, through the front door.

EIGHT

LUKE, WALKING INTO THE lobby from the kitchen, where he'd just dropped off a stack of firewood for the giant old cooking fireplace, caught sight of Hannah just as the door closed behind her.

"Hannah?" he called, although with the sound of the wind and the door closed between them, there was no reason to believe she could hear him.

He turned to his grandmother, behind the desk, with a quizzical expression.

"Where was she going?" he asked. "Did the groom just get here?"

Iris's eyes widened. "You didn't hear?" she asked.

"Hear what?" Luke said.

Iris dropped her voice, and glanced from side to side, as if the sleepy Vermont farmhouse were actually a breeding ground for international spies.

"He's not coming," she said.

"Because of the storm?" Luke said, with a hint of disgust. "I mean, I know it's bad, but all he needs to do is get some chains on his tires and . . ."

"It's not the storm," Iris said. "It's the whole wedding. He called it off."

Luke gazed at her for a long moment, as if the program that had been playing had just frozen for a minute, and he was waiting for it to come back on and make sense again.

When nothing changed, his expression darkened.

"Hannah's wedding," he said. "That moron called off Hannah's wedding?"

"He's actually a very bright young man," Iris said. "He graduated college at the top of his class."

"How do you know that?" Luke demanded.

"He told me," Iris said.

"Of course he did," Luke said. He shook his head. "I never liked that guy."

"You know him?" Iris asked, surprised.

"I met him," Luke said. "A few years ago, remember?"

"Ah!" Iris nodded. "When you came up to pick up that beautiful old sideboard that Jeanne didn't want anymore, and take it down to your mother."

"That's right," Luke said darkly. "I'll never forget it. I was just about to take off, when his car breaks down in front of my truck. And the lawn is too wet to drive something that big through, especially loaded down like that.

"And then when I asked him to move his car so I could get out of there," Luke went on, "it wouldn't budge. So I spent all afternoon trying to figure out what was wrong with it. Turns out, he hadn't added oil in thirty thousand miles."

Iris winced. "It's amazing that car lasted that long," she said.

"I know," Luke said. "They should probably advertise it. But that took my whole afternoon. I had to unload that thing at my mom's place in the dark, around midnight. And the worst part was that when he finally did call a tow truck, he stood there

looking at me like he'd just done me a huge favor, and was waiting for me to congratulate him."

He shook his head, until something else occurred to him. "I
didn't see Hannah on that trip, though," he said. "I don't think
I've seen her since we were both twelve, thirteen years old. What
was he doing up here without her?"

"Oh, she was here," Iris said. "She went out for a hike that
day, and he told her he wasn't interested."

"In going on a hike?" Luke said, his voice rising.

"Well, honey," Iris said. "I know that's what you do for a
living, taking those boys and girls out into the wilderness. But not
everybody does that. That's why there's a job for you."

Luke was shaking his head as if he might never stop. "I don't
care," he said. "Even if he wasn't interested in the great outdoors—which is where all mankind lived for eons before we invented these dirty, overgrown villages we like to call cities—he
should have been interested in going with *her.* For Pete's sake. I
once went with a girl to learn how to groom her dog. Not because I wanted to know how to groom a Pomeranian. Because I
wanted to be with her."

"How do they make their little manes stand out like that?"
Iris asked. "It never seemed quite natural to me."

"They help nature along," Luke said. "With a little bit of
doggy hair spray."

Iris giggled, and Luke grinned. "See?" he said. "It might not
have been what I thought I was interested in. But it made me a
little more interesting, right?"

"I thought you were the most interesting thing in the world,"
Iris told him. "Even before you could talk."

Luke leaned his lanky frame over the counter to plant a kiss on her forehead. "Thanks, Grandma," he said. "I wish all the girls felt like that."

"Well, that might start to seem more like a problem than a blessing, too," Iris said.

Luke shrugged. "That's a problem I'd like to try to solve," he said, with a mischievous smile.

Iris smiled back, but concern crossed her face when she glanced past Luke at the blowing snow outside.

"You better get going," she said, "if you're going to make it to Burlington still tonight. They're already shutting down some of the roads."

"But not the secret back trails of my youth," Luke said with a wink. "If I get out of here before sunset, I don't think I'll have too much trouble."

"Did you pack your arctic parka?" Iris asked.

"I've got a trick or two up my sleeve," Luke told her, then opened his arms. "But I'm not leaving without a hug from Grandma."

Grinning, Iris stepped out from behind the desk to embrace her grandson.

"Thanks for coming all this way to see me," she said.

"Thanks for everything, Grandma," Luke said, giving her a squeeze.

Then he strode into the kitchen, where Jeanne sat, her head bowed over what looked to be a cookbook.

He picked up his bag from the corner by the door and swiped a piece of corn bread from the checked lining of a nearby basket.

"Great to see you, Jeanne," he said. "Thanks for taking such good care of Grandma."

Jeanne looked up, surprised. "Oh," she said. "You're going?"

"Have to get on the road before too much longer," Luke said. "Or you're going to have another guest snowed in here."

Jeanne shook her head. "Only if you want to sleep in the barn," she said with a slight smile.

"Have you ever slept in that barn?" Luke said. "It's better than you'd think."

"In December?" Jeanne asked, her look wry.

"Ah," Luke said, swinging his bag over his shoulder. "Maybe wait till spring."

Immediately, Jeanne's eyes dropped back to the book on the counter before her, as if he'd just said something that embarrassed her—or hurt.

Luke paused for a minute, wondering what in the world could have been wrong with what he'd just said. But when he couldn't think of anything, he put his hand on the doorknob.

"Merry Christmas," he said, opening the door.

"Merry Christmas," Jeanne mumbled in return, without looking up.

From inside the house, it had looked like a complete whiteout outdoors. But when he got outside, he was glad to find that the wind had died down for the moment, so that the snow fell silently in steady flakes. With the snow clouds so low, it felt like the whole world had turned into one big room, with the clouds as a fluffy ceiling.

From his training as an outdoorsman, Luke knew that, however charming it was, prolonged exposure to the elements, especially during a big snowfall, could quickly turn deadly.

For the moment, though, as he tramped through the snow to his truck, he felt as if he was walking through a Christmas card, complete with the real sparkle of the actual snow, which was more dazzling in the dying afternoon light than any drugstore glitter.

His truck was parked a little ways off the main circle drive that led to the entrance of the inn, so he wouldn't be in the way of actual paying customers, which meant that he got a good view of the woods he'd spent so many years in as a kid as he pulled the door of the cab open and tossed his pack on the passenger seat inside.

But as he swung up into the driver's seat and glanced down the hill into the woods, he saw a flash of bright blue among the snow-heavy pines.

Suddenly, he realized he hadn't seen Hannah on his way out the door. He scanned the yard, looking for her in the shelter of the front porch, where he had been sure she must have stopped, since she hadn't been wearing a coat when she darted out the door.

The porch was deserted. So was the rest of the yard.

But a recent image rose up in his memory: the jeans Hannah had been wearing when she darted out past the front desk.

Through the window of his truck, he looked down into the shadows that were starting to gather in the forest. The flash of blue was gone.

He hopped out of the cab.

"Hannah?" he called into the trees. "Hannah!"

She'd obviously wanted to be alone when she ran out, so maybe she just wasn't answering now because she didn't feel like having company.

But as Luke scanned the woods, trying to place just where he'd seen the flash of blue last, he found himself hoping that was all there was to it.

The woods were beautiful in any season, and easy enough for

him to navigate, since he'd known them all his life. Hannah had given him a run for his money back in the day, when they'd played hide-and-seek and tag in the pines. But if she wasn't familiar with them now, she could find herself in real trouble even quite close to the house—especially in this kind of weather.

Luke checked his watch.

On the other hand, she was probably fine. And if he didn't leave now, he might not make it at all.

He scanned the pines, hoping to see another flash of blue, or hear her voice calling back, just to make sure she was okay.

"Hannah?" he called again.

When there was no answer, he slammed the door of his cab behind him and started off into the woods.

NINE

"WHAT DO YOU THINK?" Molly asked, opening the door to her room.

Immediately, both girls spilled into the big attic space. Bailey described a large, clumsy circle on the floor, distracted by just about everything she saw: the antique hobby horse in the corner, the basket of food by the door, the miniature Ferris wheel perched on one of the many end tables in the big room. Addison made a beeline for Molly's bed, touching the velvet quilt with an expression of wonder. "Daddy," she said. "This is so soft."

"That's Molly's bed, honey," Marcus said.

"Where's *my* bed?" Bailey asked, turning around.

"That's right through here," Molly said, leading them into her workroom, with the daybeds and the desk.

She stood aside to let the girls and Marcus enter. Immediately, Bailey hopped up on one of the daybeds, stuffed with quilted velvet cushions that looked like they'd been lovingly hand-dyed.

"This one's mine!" she said.

"You know," Molly said, "there might actually be room for all of you, if the girls doubled up. Or you three could even take my room . . ."

"Under no circumstances," Marcus said. He tousled Addison's hair. "I think you'll find these two are more than enough."

"Well, I'm glad to have them," Molly said, looking at her desk with a flicker of a question: How was she ever going to get her writing done with these two girls in her workroom? "If you're sure you're comfortable with them staying with me."

"I'll be right downstairs," Marcus said. "And these two have recently proven that they can bolt down two flights of stairs in under twenty seconds if ice cream is on the menu."

"Did someone say 'ice cream'?" Addison asked with a mischievous grin.

"I think you'll find the real question," Marcus said with a smile, picking up Bailey, "is how comfortable you are staying with them."

"Daddy," Bailey whispered with all the gravitas of a grand dame of the international stage. "I have a question."

"What's that, honey?" Marcus asked.

As his eyes crinkled with pleasure at the sight of his daughter's face, Molly recognized for the first time how strong he was, swooping up Bailey as if she weighed nothing more than a sack of feathers. And now that the worry of where to shelter his daughters for the night had left his face, she could also see how handsome it was: blue eyes and dark curls, lit by a genuine, warm smile.

"I need another brownie," Bailey stage-whispered.

"I'm sure you'll have another brownie," Marcus said, a teasing note in his voice.

At this, Bailey's expression turned suspicious. "*When?*" she asked meaningfully, as if this was a game she'd played, and lost, before.

"At some point in your long and pleasant life," Marcus told her, his forehead against hers, "I'm sure you will have another brownie."

Bailey swatted at his shoulder, delight at his joke mixing with frustration at not getting her way. "But I want a brownie now!" she said.

"What are these?" Addison asked.

While Bailey had been negotiating for brownies, Addison had wandered over to Molly's desk, which was still spread with blank paper, surrounded by her notes and sketches.

"That's my . . ." Molly stopped before she said "book." It didn't look like much of a book yet, even to her. And she didn't relish the prospect of explaining to Addison why it didn't look more like a book yet—or when exactly it would be finished.

Marcus glanced at her.

"You're working on a project?" he asked.

"I'm a writer," Molly said, trying to keep her voice low. "I'm working on a manuscript."

Marcus's eyes widened in interest, but over at the desk, Addison had been doing her own investigation. "Did you draw this?" she asked, holding up one of Molly's sketches: a panda reading a book. She wore an expression of consternation, and her tone was slightly accusatory. Almost exactly like Molly imagined her editor to look when she called to check on the progress of Molly's most recent manuscript.

Molly knelt down. Kids were full of surprises, and every one of them was different, so in all her years of working with them, she'd never been able to come up with a list of foolproof rules for dealing with them. But if she knew one thing, it was that it always helped to get on their level.

"I did," she said. "What do you think of it?"

In Marcus's arms, Bailey began to squirm. "Daddy!" she said. "I want to see!"

Addison waited for Bailey to scamper over, then showed her the sketch.

"What does this look like to you?" she asked Bailey.

Bailey looked from her sister to the picture, as if she wasn't sure whether this was a trick question or not. Then she decided to take a high tone, to make sure everyone there understood how obvious the answer was.

"It's Peter Panda," she said.

Instantly, Addison's eyes were on Molly, with all the intensity of a TV lawyer in the last moments of a courtroom drama after the big reveal.

Molly raised her eyebrows. Bailey was right. Peter Panda was one of her oldest characters, and one of her personal favorites. But he'd never had a starring role in any of her books, so she was surprised that Bailey had identified him so unerringly.

Addison waved the sketch in front of Molly as if it was a critical piece of damning evidence in Molly's case.

"Molly Winslow draws Peter Panda," she said, her eyes narrowed. "Did you copy this from her?"

"No, I did not," Molly said seriously.

"But it looks *just like* Peter Panda," Addison insisted.

"That's right," Molly said. "It is."

Addison stared at her, stumped.

"Now, Addison," Marcus broke in. "It's just a drawing of a bear. You hardly need to accuse Miss . . ." He looked at Molly and grinned. "I'm sorry. You did tell me your name earlier, but I—"

"It's Molly," Molly said, and raised her eyebrows at Addison with a friendly smile.

For some reason, perhaps because she was still too young to have stopped believing in miracles, Bailey caught on faster than Addison.

"Molly Winslow!" she shouted. "You're Molly Winslow!" She threw her arms around Molly's neck and held on with such vigor that Molly had to struggle not to fall on the ground herself.

"Bailey," Marcus said, "I'm sure she's not . . ." He looked at Molly for help. "I mean, you're not . . . are you?"

Molly smiled and nodded.

"No way!" Marcus said, suddenly almost as excited as his kids. "Are you kidding? You're kidding, right?"

Molly managed struggle to her feet with Bailey still in her arms, as Addison dashed back to the desk to see what else she'd missed.

"I'm sorry," Marcus said. "I can't believe it. You're one of our very favorites."

"You're *my* favorite," Addison said, still perusing the sketches scattered around Molly's blank page. "I've read everything you ever wrote."

"A thousand times," Marcus stage-whispered to Molly.

"This is your new book?" Addison said, turning around.

Molly hesitated. For some reason, discovering that she was standing in a room full of passionate fans just made her realize how far she had to go to actually call the next book a book.

"It's a . . . start," she said, offering a bright smile that she hoped might distract from the total lack of anything on the blank page in the center of the desk.

But Addison was not about to be put off by a simple smile.

"How does it start?" she asked.

Even Marcus turned to Molly now, obviously as eager as the two girls were to hear the first scoop on the new story.

"Ah," Molly said. "I'm still working that out."

"That's probably one of the biggest decisions you have to make in a story, right?" Marcus said. "How it starts? I guess once you decide that, everything pretty much goes from there. It's a big deal."

Marcus was just trying to relate to what her life must be like as a writer. And actually, his guesses were surprisingly accurate. But they still made the weight of the unfinished book, which had been pressing down invisibly on Molly's shoulders, and her heart, feel heavier and heavier.

"Yeah," Molly said as Bailey began to squirm in her arms.

"What's it about?" she asked.

"Um . . ." Molly said.

Bailey stared into her eyes, waiting for an answer, as Molly looked back, wishing that she could read the answer in Bailey's wide brown eyes.

When Molly didn't answer, Bailey's brow furrowed. "Is Peter Panda in it?" she asked.

Then she began to squirm again.

Molly set her down, and she ran over to join her sister, who was still staring at the sketches on Molly's desk.

"Are all these characters going to be in the book?" Addison asked.

With both girls' backs turned to her, Molly couldn't hold her game smile on her face any longer. She shook her head, wishing she had better answers for all of them.

But before she could compose herself, Marcus apparently noticed the change in her face.

"Okay, girls," he said. "I think that's enough questions for now."

Addison turned around, an impish grin on her face. "Why?" she asked.

Her dad's face broke out into a big smile. "Is that *another question*?" he asked.

Bailey began to bounce up and down on the balls of her toes. "Are we playing the question game?" she said.

Molly smiled. She'd loved the game herself as a kid, with its simple rules: everyone had to speak only in questions, and the first one who didn't, lost.

"Can I play?" she asked.

Addison's eyes widened. "Do you know the question game?" she asked.

"Doesn't everyone?" Molly said.

"Daddy!" Bailey cried. "Molly Winslow knows the question game!"

"You lost!" Addison crowed. "That wasn't a question!"

Bailey's face crumpled in disappointment.

"Well, technically," Marcus said, "neither was that, Addison."

"But Bailey did it first," Addison insisted. "The game was already over."

"I think maybe it was a tie," Marcus said, kneeling down to embrace them both.

But now it was Addison's turn to squirm free. "I didn't lose," she said indignantly. "Bailey did."

Molly's heart went out to her. Justice was clearly on Addison's side, and she remembered the frustration when she was a kid of listening to adults tell half-truths to smooth things over, as if kids were too dumb to notice, when in fact she had noticed almost everything. But Molly's heart also went out to Bailey, who was so much younger than everyone, and had only lost the game in a burst of childish enthusiasm.

"Come on, Addison," Marcus said gently, trying unsuccessfully to circle her waist in another hug. "It's just a game. It doesn't matter."

"It does!" Addison said. "There are rules! You have to follow them!"

Tears began to run down her cheeks.

"Why are you crying?" Bailey asked, her voice full of concern.

Then a smile flashed across her face. "That was a question!" she announced gleefully to her dad.

"Okay," Marcus said. "Okay, ladies. It's been a long day. I think it's maybe time for us to start thinking about getting ready for bed. Who wants to help me bring our things from downstairs?"

Bailey's glance turned crafty. "And brownies?" she asked.

The mention of brownies even distracted Addison momentarily from the various injustices of the world. "Bailey and I should share one," she said. "Since we tied."

Marcus looked up at Molly, barely able to suppress his laughter. "She's training to be a lawyer," he said.

"I can see that," Molly answered.

Addison was already marching toward the door, quickly trailed by Bailey. "I'll split the brownie in two," Addison told her seriously. "And then you can choose."

"Why can't I split it?" Bailey demanded.

"Your pieces are never the same size," Addison said reasonably as they slipped out of the room. "If you split it, I'll just take the bigger one."

Marcus sighed, following them. "I don't think I'm ever going to be able to thank you enough for this," he said.

Molly raised her hand to wave away his concern. "It's nothing," she said.

"You can let me know if you still feel that way tomorrow morning," Marcus said, disappearing through the door with a grin.

As he did, she checked the ring finger of his left hand for the first time. No ring there, or on any of his other fingers.

What happened with their mother, she wondered as she heard the voices of the girls chattering down the stairs, *to leave this sweet family alone at Christmas?*

Ten

"MADDIE," JEANNE SAID, SINKING down on the stool beside their landline kitchen phone, as she held the receiver to her ear. "It's great to hear your voice. It's been a crazy day."

"For you, too?" Maddie Perkins said.

At the sound of Maddie's voice, some of the frustration and worry Jeanne had been feeling began to seep away. Maddie had served as their supplier and caterer for big events at Evergreen Inn from the day they had opened.

In fact, Maddie's business had opened around the same time the inn did: supplying local goods to local restaurants and event spaces. Maddie wasn't a transplant like Jeanne and Tim. She'd grown up in Vermont, a farm girl herself, raised with several hundred head of dairy cattle on her mother's farm, which had been in the family for generations, and even boasted its own rare but delicious brand of Vermont cheddar.

And Maddie brought all the same attention to detail and passion for perfection to her work that Jeanne brought to hers. Jeanne always knew that whatever she ordered from Maddie would be exactly what she'd asked for, or better—whether it was dozens of pink- and brown-tinted farm-raised eggs, or perfectly turned crescent rolls, one of Maddie's personal specialties. It was largely their partnership with Maddie that had allowed them to expand into hosting bigger events, while still keeping the quality their guests had come to expect from the inn.

But unlike Evergreen Inn, Maddie's business was flourishing, because Maddie wasn't in competition with the Starlight Lodge. In fact, they were now her biggest customer, placing such big orders for locally sourced produce that Maddie had had to comb the entire state looking for small farmers who could help her meet them.

Still, over the past decade, Maddie and Jeanne had become fast friends. And hearing her voice made Jeanne feel less alone in the swirl of all the storms, both outside the windows of the inn, and inside herself.

"I think it may be the craziest day we've seen here at the inn," Jeanne said.

"Worse than those Brits with their antique convertibles?" Maddie asked.

Jeanne smiled at the memory. Evergreen Inn had been a featured stop for a group of British tourists who spent a few weeks each summer driving vintage American cars through the countryside. But when they'd tried to leave the morning after the feast Maddie and Jeanne had prepared for them, not one but three of their convertibles failed to turn on, which had spurred a three-state hunt for vintage car parts.

"Well, first of all, the wedding's off," Jeanne told Maddie.

"This storm?" Maddie said, taking in a quick breath.

"The groom," Jeanne said. "Cold feet. Last minute."

"That poor girl," Maddie said. "And your receipts. Did you get a deposit?"

"Not on the rooms," Jeanne said. "But we've had a whole fleet of surprise guests show up. I guess they've closed the interstate down now."

"Well, I hate to say it," Maddie said, "but that's a relief."

Jeanne's brows knit.

"What do you mean?" she asked.

"It's been a crazy day here," Maddie said. "I was calling to tell you that we aren't going to be able to make the delivery for the wedding. I'm so sorry, Jeanne. When I realized the storm was setting in, I actually loaded up everything early, thinking I could beat it and still get home. I didn't think our refrigerated delivery truck would make it with the wind and such, but I got everything into our four-wheel drive and got about half a mile down the road before the engine seized up from the cold. Carl came to rescue me on his snowmobile, but we couldn't get anyone to come tow the car, and now everything in it is frozen. I was holding out hope till the last minute that someone would be able to come and tow us, but there's no way the lettuces survived this long. Or the fruits."

"Or the canapés . . ." Jeanne added, still in shock.

Maddie sighed. "I was terrified that meant we'd be ruining someone's big day, but I guess if the wedding's off . . ."

Jeanne's mind raced to catch up with what was happening. If Maddie didn't come, Jeanne thought, what did she have left in the kitchen? Not much, she knew without even opening a cupboard or the fridge. She had deliberately let her stocks run down so there would be room for the huge amount of food required to serve a wedding, even one as intimate as Hannah's had been planned to be.

I should have known, she thought, the guilt overwhelming her. If total strangers were pulling off the road into her driveway looking for shelter, why would she expect that Maddie would be able to make it here with a truck full of hand-harvested canapés? But Maddie had always been so consistent—wondering whether she would be there or not felt like wondering if the sun would come up. It wasn't even worth a thought, because there was simply no question about it.

"But I've still got guests," Jeanne said. "The place just filled up with stranded travelers. I don't even know if I've got enough to serve them dinner, let alone get through the next few days. If there's anything you could get to me, anything at all . . ."

"I'm sorry, Jeanne. I really am," Maddie said. "I really hate to leave you in the lurch like this."

"I know, Maddie," Jeanne said.

"And they just started announcing that they don't want anyone on the roads. Not just the interstate. Any of them," Maddie went on. "I'd love to help you, but we need to be safe."

"Of course you do," Jeanne said, feeling a little pang of shame that she had even pressed Maddie, who was obviously trying to do her best.

"I'm sorry," Maddie said again. "You know if there was anything I could do—"

"I know," Jeanne told her. "You've never let us down before. And this isn't your fault. I'll figure something out."

"Thanks, Jeanne," Maddie said. "Stay warm."

"You, too," Jeanne said.

She put the phone back in its cradle and went directly to the refrigerator, half hoping that while she was on the phone some genie had filled it with succulent sausages and piles of fresh fruit, fairy-tale-style.

But the door swung open on a chilly, brightly lit void.

Aside from a few dishes for the rehearsal meal she'd already prepped, there was almost nothing fresh left in the fridge, only staples like milk and butter, and not enough of those to reliably hold out for days with a full house of guests. Everything else was supposed to come in from Maddie.

She shuffled through the cupboards, confirming what she already knew. Aside from healthy quantities of baking supplies, there was nothing: no meat, no cheese, no vegetables, no fruit.

In the potato drawer, she found a ten-pound bag of workmanlike Idaho reds, half-gone.

Were there at least enough for hash browns tomorrow morning?

She started to count them out on the counter, two at a time.

By the time she got to fourteen, tears were sliding down her face.

When she got to twenty, Tim came in, shaking snow off his blue watch cap as he stomped the snow off his boots.

"I checked on all the animals. Everyone's cozy in the barn, and I gave them extra hay. Made sure the piglet's pen was dry so she doesn't freeze to death in this . . ." As soon as Tim saw her face, he was silent. "What's wrong?" he asked.

Jeanne shook her head, unable to get the words out at first.

Tim started to put his arm around her shoulders, then hesitated, as if waiting to make sure she didn't shake it off.

But when she just kept crying, he drew her closer to him. "Hey, Jeannie," he said. "What's wrong?"

"It's Maddie," she said.

His eyes widened. "Something happened to her?" he asked.

Suddenly, Jeanne realized how much more terrible the news could have been—which only made her feel like a baby for being so upset. And none of this, of course, helped her be any less upset.

Jeanne shook her head. "No, no," she said. "It's the catering and supplies. They can't get here tonight."

"Oh," Tim said, stepping back and crossing his arms.

She could practically see him biting his tongue to keep from adding, *Is that all?*

"I don't have anything else here," she said. "I've got finger sandwiches and some brisket for the rehearsal dinner, but that's not enough for even a single meal tomorrow. And the place is full now. We had three more groups arrive while you were out."

"That'll cover some of the shortfall from the wedding," Tim calculated.

"But now we have to feed them," she said. He wasn't listening.

"They don't expect five-star service in the middle of a blizzard," Tim said. "You always think of something."

Jeanne felt herself getting flushed with anger, because he was exactly right. She did feel like she was always the one who had to think of something—because he never seemed to be thinking about what she was worried about at all.

"People expect all kinds of things," she said. "And anyway, I'm a cook, not a magician. I can't make something out of nothing."

"Nothing? Really?" Tim said, and pulled the refrigerator open. But at the sight of the empty shelves, he froze.

"Wow," he said, and turned back to Jeanne. "How many people did you say we have here tonight?"

"All the rooms are full," Jeanne said. "And some of them are kids, Tim. We can't let them go hungry."

Tim took a deep breath. "Okay," he said. "Hold on. Maddie's pretty far away, like twenty, thirty miles, right?"

Jeanne nodded.

Tim's brow furrowed, thinking. "What if we went over to Hiram Fletcher's?" he said. "I know he's got sausages and cheese, and he's only a mile down the road."

Jeanne's mind began to search through their neighbors. "And Daphne Hines has got incredible produce growing in her winter greenhouse. It's not just lettuce and vegetables. I saw nasturtiums over there the last time I stopped by."

But just as quickly as the light of hope had lit in her eyes, it died out. "But how would we get there?" she asked. "I just talked with Maddie, and she said all the roads are closed now."

Tim frowned along with her, but a second later, he broke out in a grin. "Well," he said, "they're closed if all you've got is a car or a truck."

"What were you planning on taking besides a car or truck?" Jeanne asked. "Your motorcycle?"

"This is why you should have let me get that old used snow-mobile that showed up in the paper this summer," Tim said with a look of mischief.

Jeanne just shook her head.

"Remember that old sleigh that Iris's father had stashed in the back of the barn?" Tim asked.

Jeanne shook her head. Maybe he was trying to cheer her up, but she just wasn't in the mood for jokes. "That thing is a wreck," she said. "One of the blades is broken in half, and even if it weren't, the mice ate all the leather off the seats. They're nothing but springs and stuffing now."

"Not anymore," Tim said.

"What do you mean?" Jeanne asked.

"I fixed it up," Tim said.

"Why?" Jeanne yelped.

Tim shrugged. "I like to fix stuff."

Jeanne shook her head slowly. "If you had asked me, in a million years, would we ever need a *sleigh* . . ." she began.

"But now we've got one," Tim said, going over to the door to pull on his boots. "Get your coat. Or get two of them."

"Why?" Jeanne asked again.

"You've got to come with me," Tim said. "I can barely find the turnoff to Daphne's in broad daylight. Plus, you're going to need to tell them what you want to order."

Boots and coat on, he pulled a wool overshirt from the rack and held it out.

Somewhat dazed, Jeanne put it on. "I guess Iris can take care of the place while we're gone," she said.

"We're going for a sleigh ride, Iris," Tim told the older woman in the front hall, as Jeanne yanked her oldest work coat out of the hall closet and managed to yank it on over the work shirt. "So that means you're in charge now."

"What makes you think I wasn't to begin with?" Iris said, raising one eyebrow with a merry smile as the two of them tramped out the front door, heading for the barn.

ELEVEN

FOR THE FIRST FEW minutes after Hannah ran out through the front door, she hadn't even felt the cold.

It had just been a relief to step out into the white, silent world, where there were no other voices speaking and every sound was muffled by the snow, both in the air and on the ground.

She'd headed for the woods without even thinking, because it was the woods that had always been her sanctuary while they were staying at the inn, whether she'd had a spat with her parents or was frustrated with Trevor or worried about a friend.

At first, they were just as familiar as they always had been. She'd always been a bit of a tomboy, climbing every one of the trees that presented any kind of tempting foothold. So she knew many of the trees by heart, and even how they'd changed over the decade since her family had been visiting the inn, their trunks growing thicker, their twigs turning to branches.

And even when the cold did begin to set in, it came as a relief. She was grateful to feel anything other than the sickening drop of her heart, which felt like it had gotten on a roller-coaster ride that might never stop falling.

Plus, she was wearing the thick, white, cashmere, cable-knit sweater her mother had bought her as a special part of her wedding "trousseau." It was incredibly soft, but it was also incredibly warm. And Hannah knew she was so close to the house that she could make it back in just a few minutes if she started to get really chilly.

Lost in her thoughts, she didn't know how long she wandered among the familiar pines before she tucked her fingers up into the cuffs of her cozy sweater, or how long after that the cold began to seep through the sweater itself in earnest.

Still, she resisted going back into the house, back to all the practical questions that had pressed on her within its walls, back to her parents' pain, and her own, until the bite of the cold was so sharp it was impossible to ignore anymore.

When she finally began to look at her surroundings, searching for a familiar sign to lead her home, she realized why the cold had intensified. While she'd been out in the woods, the sun, which had been dropping toward the horizon when she left the house, had fallen beyond it. Light was quickly fleeing the woods as night came on.

At first she thought that should actually make it easier to find her way back: just look for the lights of the inn, in the gathering darkness.

But as her glance darted from tree to tree, she didn't see anything that looked like the welcoming light of home: just the fading glow of the sun beyond the snow clouds that were pouring the blizzard down. The snow turned bluer and bluer as even that light faded.

Around her, on all sides, a slight slope led up into the trees.

From this, Hannah recognized she was in the low valley in the trees that had been a favorite hiding spot of hers in younger days.

The problem was that part of what made the valley special was its uniformity. From the bottom of it, all the slopes looked the same. She knew she was close to the inn, but she had no idea in which direction the buildings lay.

As she tried to think what direction to choose, she drew the sweater closer around her—a mistake. The snow that had fallen on her had been sitting on the wool, a hairsbreadth away from her warm skin, for long enough now to start melting, so when she tried to snuggle into the sweater to warm herself, she only got painful hits of ice-cold water on the gooseflesh of her arms.

The sting of them sent her charging up the low rise of the valley's natural bowl, hoping that if she got some more elevation, she'd be able to catch sight of something.

But when she stumbled up to flat ground again, all she saw was more snow, and more trees—and none she recognized.

By now, whether it was from cold or from nerves, or some of both, she was having trouble catching her breath.

Panic building in her chest, she dove back down into the bowl of the valley, trying to follow her footsteps before they were erased by the storm, so that she could at least keep track of which direction she had already gone. Even knowing where she'd failed was at least some information that might help her get back home.

By the time she struggled down the slope to the bottom of the valley's bowl, the cold had set her whole body on high alert. She didn't have a single thought of her parents, or the wedding, or even Trevor. Everything in her just wanted to survive.

And to do that, as the grip of the cold tightened on her, something told her to keep moving.

So when she got to the bottom of the bowl, she just kept going, right up the slope in front of her.

She crested it, half hoping she'd immediately see the lights of home, which should only be steps away, if she could just figure out the direction to go.

But instead, she found herself in more snowy forest—snowy forest that looked to her for all the world exactly like the one she'd found on the opposite side of the bowl.

Tears sprang to her eyes, and she was immediately surprised by the way they began to sting where they slid down her face in the cold.

Should she go to the left or the right? Or back down into the valley?

As she wondered, a gust of wind blew her a few steps to the right, and she just continued to follow it, putting one foot in front of the other into the blinding snow. As the night had come on, the woods around her had darkened so that all she could see clearly were the hundreds of individual flakes that flew directly around her face, and the black hulks of trees when she got close enough to them.

But most of the time, from what she could make out now, she was in a blizzard that could have just erased the whole forest, for all she knew.

Maybe because of the drop in temperature, the wind had picked up as well, so that the snow no longer fell in peaceful quiet, but whipped into her eyes. The wind slapped her hair, now damp with snow, against her cheeks, and let out intermittent loud shrieks as it blasted through the trees.

But when she started to imagine that it was calling her name, she felt her stomach drop with despair. Was this what she'd read about, when people were freezing to death, the hallucinations they started to have as their dreams took them under?

"Hannah!" the wind called again.

It sounded as if it was getting closer.

Then something caught her by the elbow, and she screamed.

"Hannah," the voice said again, more gently. "Hey. You okay?"

An arm descended around her shoulders.

Hannah had to push her damp hair away from her eyes to see Luke's face, but somehow she had already placed his voice.

He gave her an encouraging grin, and her face crumpled with tears.

"Luke," she said.

"What are you doing out here?" Luke asked as he steered her through the woods.

Hannah shook her head. "I don't know," she said. "I just needed a minute to myself. I thought I could find my way back to the house, but I couldn't. I was completely lost out here," she said, getting herself together enough to wipe at the tears on her face.

"No, you weren't," Luke said, as they stepped out of the woods, into the familiar curve of the driveway, with the lights of the inn twinkling just beyond. "Look how close you got."

Hannah shook her head. "I don't think I'd have ever found it if you didn't come after me," she said.

"Sure you would have," Luke said lightly, as they came up the stairs to the inn. "You were headed in the right direction. You just didn't know it."

"Thank you," Hannah said, when the door finally closed behind them, shutting out the dark and the wind.

Hannah's teeth chattered involuntarily as a shiver threatened to spread through her entire body.

Luke grinned. "No problem," he said. "I'm a trained professional. You want to get that damp sweater off?"

"A trained professional?" Hannah said, peeling off the soaked cashmere. She tugged down the tank top she wore underneath. Luke hung the sweater on a hook, taking a big red-and-black plaid blanket out of a basket by the door.

"I'm an outdoor guide," he said. "I spend most of my time leading people around in the woods."

"Rich businessmen?" Hannah asked, as he wrapped her in the blanket. "Out to risk their lives because they don't get any other excitement?"

Luke looked at her, bemused. "I see your little run-in with the Vermont winter didn't take the edge off your smart mouth," he said. "I remember that from when we were kids."

"All of me is smart," Hannah said, surprised to feel herself smiling. "I can't help it."

"Not smart enough to put a coat on when you go outside, I notice," Luke said, raising his eyebrows.

Even under the blanket, Hannah was still shivering as she stepped out of the entryway into the lobby.

Iris looked up at her. "Oh, honey," she said. "What happened to you? Didn't anyone ever tell you not to go out in the cold without a hat on?"

"I think you probably told her that yourself at least a dozen times," Luke said with a grin as he hustled Hannah past her.

"Apparently, I didn't tell her often enough," Iris retorted as they slipped into the lounge.

"Okay," Luke said. "Let's get you over by the fireplace."

"This is your professional opinion?" Hannah said, following him through the lobby to the giant stone fireplace in the lounge, where a glowing fire danced in the massive iron grate.

She sank down beside it gratefully, feeling the radiant heat seeping into the chill that had set into her bones.

"Thank you," she said. "I shouldn't hassle you about your job. I can tell you're good at it. And obviously, I needed a guide tonight."

"It's mostly with kids, actually," Luke said, turning his back to her to pour a cup of hot chocolate from the gleaming copper thermos that Jeanne had left on a nearby end table, along with an assortment of homemade crackers and cheese. "Although maybe I *should* try to round up some rich businessmen. It might be easier to pay the bills."

"Kids?" Hannah said.

"Yeah," Luke said, putting the mug of chocolate in her hands. "They're all different, but they're all struggling somehow. Taking them out in the woods takes their minds off their problems, lets them know there's more to life than their cell phones and high schools. And learning outdoor skills builds confidence."

"To actually solve their problems," Hannah said.

"Some of them, I hope," Luke said.

"I remember you always liked to show kids around," Hannah said. "As soon as a new kid checked in, you were always like, Hey, come out to the woods with us!"

"Do you remember the first time we played in the woods as kids?" Luke asked.

"I do," Hannah said. "I thought I'd found the entrance to Aladdin's cave, and you told me you'd been all over the land, and there were no caves for miles."

"We were both right," Luke said.

"It's more like an overhang than a cave," Hannah said.

"But I never noticed it before you pointed it out," Luke said.

"And I would never have found that spot if you hadn't taken me," Hannah said. "Although apparently my time in the woods didn't manage to cure my smart mouth."

"Yeah, but I never thought that was a problem that needed solving," Luke said. "I always kind of liked it."

Hannah smiled again and raised her mug of hot chocolate.

"Sit down," she said. "You're not going to make me drink alone, are you?"

Luke glanced out the windows, into what was now definitively night. "Ah," he said. "I'm sorry, but I've got to get going. I'm still trying to get to my mom's tonight. I would have started out earlier, but . . ."

"Someone got lost in the woods," Hannah said with a rueful look. "And you had to go fish her out."

Luke grinned. "It was my pleasure, really," he said. He watched her for just a moment longer, then clapped his hands like a camp leader winding up for a new activity.

"Okay," he said. "Got to get going."

"What do you mean?" Hannah asked. "Aren't the roads closed?"

"You forget, I'm a trained professional," Luke said.

"Are you sure you should be doing that, even as a professional?"

He shrugged. "It's that or not make it home for Christmas. It's an epic storm. No telling when the roads will open again, when we're this far out of town."

"Okay . . ." she said. She drew her blanket more tightly around her shoulders.

"Be safe."

"Always," Luke said. "Merry Christmas."

"Merry Christmas," Hannah called after him as he walked out of the lounge, turned the corner into the lobby, and disappeared.

Twelve

GEOFFREY GODWIN TRAMPED DOWN the flight of stairs that led to the lobby, stopped at the foot of them, and frowned.

Iris resisted the urge to frown back, and then the sudden urge to laugh. The atmosphere of the lobby, with the warmth of the antique furniture, the sparkle from Jeanne's decorations, and the smells of chocolate and cinnamon that pervaded the whole first floor was so wonderful, and Godwin's expression was so suspicious, that it was actually comical.

How could anyone, Iris wondered, *be dissatisfied in a place like this?*

With a sharp glance that seemed to take in every detail, Godwin surveyed the room, showing no expression of delight at any of the touches that usually elicited smiles, or even gasps, from other guests: the bowls full of hand-painted Victorian glass bulbs, the grapevine swags Iris had helped Jeanne dip in pale blue glitter, with sprays of juniper and dried roses peeking out from between the curls of the vines, the rolled beeswax candles on the mantel, the cinnamon wreath hanging on the mirror over the mantel of the entryway's fireplace.

It wasn't until his gaze came to Iris that his expression changed. Iris wouldn't have called it a softening. It looked more like surprise, as if he was startled to discover he hadn't been alone in the space all that time.

"Hey. Is this fireplace original to the inn? What's the construction date for this place?"

Iris's brows knit.

"My name is Iris," she said, with a satisfying arch of her brow.

At this, a slight twinkle came to Godwin's eye, as if some of the Claus family spirit had managed to survive within the chill of his Grinchy exterior.

Iris girded herself, ready to fire back some comment of her own if it turned out that his amusement was at her expense.

But apparently, he was capable of laughing at himself.

"I'm sorry," he said. "Iris. I do forget my manners from time to time."

If he hadn't been so curious about the big old house, Iris might have made him stew for just a bit longer in his apology. But whatever the limits of his manners, Iris seldom met anybody who asked such intelligent questions about the place. And there was no topic of conversation she liked better herself.

"This house was built in 1868," she said. "By a Union soldier who had recently returned from the Civil War."

The skepticism flared in Godwin's eyes again as he raised his bushy white eyebrows. "This is a pretty nice spread for a simple soldier," he said.

"Well, it didn't start out like this," Iris shot back, coming from behind the desk. "You can see the whole footprint of the original home here," she went on, pointing to the lounge, with its giant fireplace. It was spacious enough as a single room, but quite modest as a family home.

"So how did all this come to be?" Godwin asked, gesturing at the sprawling floor plan that now surrounded the lounge, and up at the multiple floors that rose overhead.

"Piece by piece," Iris said. "As he and his descendants had

more funds and opportunity. This beauty," she said, nodding at the merry flames that danced in the fireplace in the lobby, directly across from her own desk, "was also built by the original owner, after an especially good harvest—and after he and his wife had had enough children that they were eager to have a room of their own. His wife actually created the faces on both of them. You can tell because she had a fondness for pink stone. When they were clearing the nearby fields, she'd have the kids bring her any stone that had a hint of color in it. And in this one . . ." she said, bending over to hunt for exactly the stone she wanted in the lobby fireplace.

When she found it, she straightened, grinning and pointing. "There's a fossil!"

"You don't say?" Godwin said, leaning forward and squinting so that he could see for himself: a beautiful, perfectly formed spiral shell, encased forever in stone. "That's quite a specimen," he said. "And you seem to know quite a bit about this place. You said you lived here at one point?"

"All my life," Iris said simply.

"You mentioned the original owner and his descendants," Godwin asked. "Are you by chance one of them?"

Iris nodded, smiling with pride.

"So the same family has been on this land for over a hundred years," Godwin calculated.

"Almost a hundred and fifty," Iris said.

"That's getting rarer and rarer," Godwin mused. "Especially here in the States. It must be a special family."

"Be careful," Iris said. "If you give me any more compliments on my family tree, I'm liable to pull out pictures of my grandchildren. And there's no telling where that ends."

"Heaven forbid," Godwin said, with a theatrical shudder that

Iris couldn't be sure was a joke, or not. "And how long has it served as an inn?" Godwin asked.

"I sold the place to Jeanne and Tim a little over ten years ago," Iris said.

"Sold?" Godwin said, his eyebrows leaping in surprise.

"The expenses had gone up so much that I wasn't sure I could keep up with them," Iris said. "And none of the kids or grandkids wanted to come back and live out here in the sticks. I didn't want to get in a place where I couldn't control whose hands it fell into. I'd never want to see this land broken up, or the house torn down. And Jeanne and Tim loved it as much as I did. *Almost* as much," she amended, with a smile.

"And your only stipulation, as I remember, was that you be allowed to stay here to work," Godwin said.

"That's right," Iris said. "I don't know what else I'd do with myself otherwise."

Godwin gave her a long look. "I suspect you'd think of something," he said finally.

"And what about you?" Iris asked. "What brings you to Vermont?"

At her question, all the friendliness went out of Godwin's expression. His eyes began to dart around the room, not as if he was absorbing details, but as if he was looking for a way to escape.

"That's a long story," he said. "And not a very interesting one, I'm afraid."

"I think all stories are interesting," Iris said.

But instead of picking up on the thread of her conversation, Godwin glanced into the lounge. "You'll excuse me to continue my explorations?" he asked.

"Of course," Iris said. "Let me know if you have any more questions."

"You may regret having said that." Godwin stepped into the next room, peering around it with the same sharp, calculating glance with which he'd regarded the lobby.

His demeanor was so precise, and his gaze so intense, that Iris wondered for a minute if he was a man with a military history, or even a spy.

She smiled at herself. That explanation, however outlandish, would explain his capacity for observation, and perhaps his brusque demeanor, but it raised a whole host of other questions, like what a dangerous spy might be doing in the wilds of Vermont on the day before Christmas.

Still, as Iris returned to her desk, she couldn't help but wonder what, exactly, he had refrained from telling her about himself—and why.

Thirteen

"NO, DADDY, NO, DADDY, no, Daddy, no!" Bailey protested.

Marcus, who was still standing in the doorway of Molly's suite, which the two girls had just barreled into, shot a glance of mild exasperation and commiseration at Molly, then looked down at Bailey.

Bailey wasn't in full meltdown mode; there were no red-faced tears or hiccups. But she clearly had deep feelings about the topic under discussion, which was what book they were going to read before the girls went to sleep.

And after she had made her point clear, she folded her arms and stuck out one hip, like a miniature general laying claim to all the territory he could see around him.

Addison, who had been heading obediently to bed before Bailey's outburst, looked at her sister with mild surprise, then adopted a waiting air, not sure yet whether to take the role of responsible big sister or to join her in a righteous protest.

"But I thought *The Christmas Pony* was your favorite book," Marcus said, crouching down to negotiate eye to eye.

"It is," Bailey said, as if that only made the current predicament worse.

"Well," Marcus said, with a puzzled air, "is there something else you'd rather read?"

Bailey shook her head decisively. "No!" she repeated.

"Okay, Bailey," Marcus said. "Then I have to admit I don't understand. What exactly is the problem with me reading this book to you?"

He had carried the book into the room with him, and now he held it out, trying to entice Bailey with what had apparently until recently been her favorite book in the world.

But Bailey, implacable, simply turned her nose up at it.

"I don't want you to read it," she said, then turned and pointed at Molly with a sweeping gesture, as if she were a character revealing the identity of some long-lost family member in a daytime drama. "I want *her* to."

"Oh," Marcus said, and glanced back at Molly to check her reaction.

Addison, in the meantime, seemed to have decided this was a demand she could get on board with. She'd been hanging back, a bit to the side, but now she took up a spot beside her sister and crossed her arms as Bailey nodded to her in solidarity and satisfaction.

"She writes books," Addison argued. "So she must be good at reading them."

"And she is prettier than you," Bailey added.

At this, Marcus, who had locked eyes with Molly, ducked his head in embarrassment. "Well, I won't argue with that," he said. "But Molly is already doing us a pretty big favor, letting you stay in her room tonight. And I'm not sure she wants to read you the book."

Bailey was willing to consider this parry. She took a measuring glance at Molly, who gave her a smile in return, then turned back to her dad.

"We should ask her," Bailey said.

"Well," Marcus said, rising to his feet. "Why don't you go ahead?"

"Would you read the book to us?" Bailey said.

"I would be glad to read it to you," Molly said. "It's a favorite of mine, too." The book wasn't one of her own, but it was a Christmas classic, and something she often pulled out around this time of year herself.

"And tuck us in," Addison added, not to be outdone. And probably, Molly reflected to herself wryly, knowing a sucker when she saw one.

"Now, wait a minute," Marcus said. "Just because she said she'd read you a book doesn't mean she's signed up for nanny duty."

"Tuck us in!" Bailey sang, her eyes suddenly as wide and irresistible as a puppy's. "Will you tuck us in? Please tuck us in!"

Molly laughed. "I think that could be arranged," she said.

"You two are amazing," Marcus said, shaking his head. "I'm going to have you come to my next salary negotiation."

"Daddy," Bailey said in her high piping voice. "What's a salary negotiation?"

"Something that I hope you don't have to worry about for a good long time," Marcus said, beginning to shoo them toward their room.

He glanced back over his shoulder as they began to trundle along in basically the right direction. *Thank you*, he mouthed as they went.

Molly nodded and shook her head. "It's no problem," she said.

"I'll just get them changed, and then . . ."

She nodded as he disappeared into the room that had so recently been her office.

Seemingly almost instantly, Bailey reappeared, shoving her arms clumsily but with determination through the sleeves of a ruffled pink flannel nightgown.

"Okay!" she announced, hopping around with an amount of energy that seemed to portend that the odds of her surrendering to sleep any time soon were slim. "We are ready for our *stoorrry*!"

But the way she sang the word "story" melted Molly's writer's heart. Bailey drew out the syllables with expectation.

"Yes, ma'am," Molly said, giving a little salute as she walked into the girls' room. "One story, coming right up."

By now, Addison had changed into white footed pajamas.

She helped Marcus smooth a blanket out on one of the daybeds, then sat down on it while he picked up a sheet to begin to make up the second one.

Bailey took Molly's hand, led her over, and waited for her to sit down, before clambering up onto the daybed and settling in comfortably at Molly's side.

"All right," Molly said, running her hand over the beautiful cover image of a silver fairy peeking out between the branches of a snowy pine. "Are you girls ready for a story?"

"Yes!" the girls chorused.

Molly glanced at Marcus, who gave her a friendly nod. Suddenly, she felt slightly shy. She was used to reading to big groups of kids, in classrooms and bookstores. And years ago, when they were little, she had read to her brother's boys. But reading in such an intimate setting, with an adult who was a virtual stranger in the room, was a weird feeling for her.

As she started to read, however, the wonder and momentum of the story took over, as a father went through all kinds of travails to bring home the present his daughter wanted most: a Christmas pony.

"Read it again!" Bailey demanded, when Molly closed the book after reading the last page.

"Again?" Molly teased her. "Did you already forget everything that happened?"

"Maybe he'll do something different this time," Bailey said.

"He never does anything different," Addison said sleepily.

"How do you know?" Bailey said. "We haven't read it again yet."

"Okay, girls," Marcus said. "Molly only signed up for one story. And these girls know that one story is the family standard," he said, with a wink at Molly. "They're just trying to see if they can pull one over on you."

"I can't believe that," Molly said, looking from Addison to Bailey in pretended shock. "You girls would never try anything like that, would you?"

Addison got up with a sigh and padded over to the second daybed, which her father had just finished making up, complete with the stuffed tiger, which Molly was surprised to see was actually the older girl's toy, not Bailey's.

But Bailey wasn't yet ready to admit defeat.

"Daddy," she said, borrowing her sister's tone of command, which she was likely all too familiar with. "You have to leave."

"I do?" Marcus said with a laugh. "And why is that?"

"Because Molly is tucking us in," Bailey said.

Molly smiled, seeing the opportunity for some negotiations of her own.

"I can't tuck you in if you're not in bed," she pointed out.

Instantly, Bailey scrambled under her covers, then peered up at her dad. "Okay, Daddy," she said. "Time to go."

"I don't have to go," Marcus told Molly.

"Oh, no," Molly said. "I think I've got this well in hand."

With a smile, Marcus leaned down to kiss first Addison, then Bailey. "All right, girls," he said. "Sleep tight."

"Good night, Daddy," Bailey said, hanging on to his hand for a few more seconds so she could give it one last kiss.

"I'll be right downstairs," Marcus whispered to Molly. "In case you need reinforcements."

Molly nodded as he slipped out the door.

Fourteen

"I CAN'T BELIEVE IT," Jeanne said, her eyes wide. "It's like a miracle."

"Well," Daphne Hines said, "I like to think that every nasturtium blossom and head of lettuce is its own little miracle. But a whole big pile of them, that actually takes a lot of work."

Jeanne grinned at Daphne, and then looked down at the bunches of fresh chives in her own hands.

"Can you spare another two or three of these?" she asked.

"Heck, take them all!" Daphne said. "Lord knows how long it's going to be before anyone else can find their way down my drive. And once these things pass, you know . . ."

"They're past," Jeanne said.

"You're doing me a favor," Daphne said, "taking them off my hands. I hate to see things go past and not get used. And if I had to sit in my house for the next week, just watching all these chives and lettuce and squash go past ripe to rotten . . ."

"I have a whole inn full of guests who are going to be absolutely delighted to help you with that problem," Jeanne said.

Tim, who had been outside, carrying yet another carton of greens and vegetables out to the sleigh, came into the greenhouse at the far end. He started to make his way down to them through the long, narrow paths between table after table of fresh produce. Daphne had somehow coaxed it all into being, safe under the arched glass of her greenhouse, despite the chill of the Vermont winter.

"Is that it?" he asked, his voice almost cheerful.

"No!" Jeanne said, her eyes wide with delight. "Look what else she just showed me!"

She held up the bunches of spiky greens in both hands.

"Fresh chives!" she said. "In December. In Vermont!"

Tim's face crinkled in a smile. "Will wonders never cease?" he said.

"*And* parsnips," she said, pointing to a stash of the white, carrot-shaped roots that she and Daphne had piled on a nearby table.

"*And* red potatoes," she added, rattling a bushel basket on the floor with her foot.

"They're not quite ready yet, but I'm going to let her take them."

"By which she means they are the sweetest fingerlings I think I've ever seen," Jeanne said.

"And you have seen your share of fingerlings," Tim added.

"That's because no grower in their right mind would sell them when they're this young," Daphne said with a grin. "There's no possible profit in it. Not if you want to charge a sane price for a potato. But," she said, raising her hands in a shrug, "it's Christmas."

"I can't believe you have all this," Jeanne said. "And that you're letting us have it. Thank you."

"Oh, you're welcome," Daphne said, raising an eyebrow. "But I'm an old softie. It's easy to get just about anything out of me. What I can't believe is that you were able to shake down Hiram Fletcher for half a sleigh's worth of meat and cheese. That man treats his freezer and smokehouse like they're the Vermont outpost of Fort Knox."

"I helped Hiram out around his place this summer," Tim said. "So we got to know him."

"Well, what in the world did you *do* for him?" Daphne asked. "Build him a magic table that makes sausage on command?"

"He'd been trying to get his old milk filter running, and he was afraid if he couldn't figure it out, he'd have to buy a new one."

Daphne shook her head and clicked her tongue. "Farm machines," she said. "Any one of them will set you back a year's profit."

"I figured it out for him," Tim said mildly.

Jeanne looked at him, remembering how effusive Hiram had been in his praises of Tim's talents as a handyman. And Hiram was not exactly an effusive man by nature. But Tim made it sound as if he hadn't done much at all.

"Well," Daphne said, "all you needed to do was tell me about that poor girl, with her good-for-nothing groom running off at the last minute. If that girl has a broken heart, she needs to *eat*!"

She gave a deep belly laugh, and patted her own substantial girth as she did. "That's not how I got this, though," she said. "My problem is I eat when I'm sad, *and* I eat when I'm happy."

As she spoke, Tim carefully settled the parsnips atop the fingerling redskin potatoes, and covered them with the chives.

"You got a blanket out there for those?" Daphne said, her expression suddenly serious.

"Yes, ma'am," Tim said.

"That's good," Daphne said, nodding. "Those chives are skinny enough, they might just freeze out in the open on your way home. But at least you don't have to worry about refrigeration," she said brightly.

"No," Jeanne agreed, "that shouldn't be a problem."

"Last one?" Tim said, hoisting the basket.

"Last one, but one," Daphne said, patting Jeanne on the shoulder. "Come with me, honey," she said, nudging Jeanne down the greenhouse aisle toward the door that connected the greenhouse with the Hines family home.

"I'm going to send her home with half a dozen jars of my apricot balsamic preserves," she said.

"Oh, Daphne," Jeanne said. "I couldn't."

"That's right," Daphne said, grinning back over her shoulder. "You couldn't refuse!"

A few minutes later, Jeanne and Tim's faithful draft horse, Magnus, bobbed his head in greeting as Jeanne stepped out of the Hineses' house. Daphne waved goodbye to Tim while Jeanne tried her best to keep her balance as she wrangled a six-jar box of jam down the front steps, which were nothing but faint mounds under the huge snowfall.

When she hit what seemed like solid ground, she slogged her way through the knee-high snow, then stretched to pass up the box, while Tim leaned down to collect it from her.

As she climbed into the front seat of the sleigh, he stashed the jam carefully under the blanket, among their other many treasures: a side of high-grade beef, bacon, sausage, three kinds of cheddar, and an experimental Brie, along with piles of lettuce, crisp radishes, squash, several pounds of cranberries, and even half a bushel of apples.

Jeanne smiled happily as Tim straightened up and flicked the reins, spurring gentle old Magnus into a hopeful trot that dragged the sleigh forward with him, almost silently except for the faintest singing whisper on the loose snow.

"This turned out even better than I thought," she said.

Beside her, she could see Tim glance over. His expression was happy, too, but he clearly had a comment he was holding back, despite the relief in his eyes.

"This was a wonderful idea," she said, sliding her arm through his. "Your idea."

At a tug of the reins, Magnus pulled a bit to the left to stay on Daphne's drive, causing the bells at his halter to ring.

Jeanne actually giggled. "It's almost too perfect," she said. "When I first saw this old sleigh, I think I might have had visions of filling it with food and driving to our neighbors' one day. But I don't think I imagined there would be actual jingle bells involved.

"And this sleigh looks incredible," she added. "I mean, sky-blue upholstery. I couldn't have picked anything better myself."

"I know what you like," Tim said, pressing his lips together so he wouldn't look too self-satisfied.

"Thank you," Jeanne said, squeezing his arm.

"Honestly," Tim said, as they slid on through the darkness, "I'm just glad we found a real reason to use this thing. I was afraid it was just going to be one more fix-it project I did that didn't really fix anything."

"I think you could say this one actually saved the day," Jeanne said, squeezing his arm again.

"Well," Tim said, "I guess some stories do actually have happy endings."

As he said it, Magnus balked, then reared back slightly.

In the moonlight, Jeanne could see the shadow of a fox dart across the snow.

Then the sleigh, which hadn't braked when Magnus did, ran straight into the big horse's rump. It wasn't moving fast enough to hurt him, but it gave him such a scare that he charged forward a few yards, dragging the sleigh along with him.

Jeanne felt a sickening drop as the sleigh left the even path of the drive and began to slide down the grade.

"Whoa, Magnus, whoa!" Tim said, pulling the big horse to a stop.

Jeanne surveyed their position, relieved to see that they had only drifted a few feet off the path.

But when Tim turned Magnus's head back toward the road and prodded him into action, the sleigh didn't budge.

Confused, Magnus turned his head toward them again, as if awaiting further instructions.

"Come on, Magnus," Tim said, flicking the reins again. "Just put some heart into it."

This time, the big horse truly did strain, the muscles of his powerful back popping and his hooves sliding in the snow as he scrambled against the weight of the sleigh. He continued pawing the ground and trying to yank the sleigh forward until Tim pulled back on the reins.

"Tim," Jeanne said. "Why'd you stop him?"

"If he could have pulled us out," Tim said, "he already would have. Something else is wrong."

"Maybe if you just give him another chance," Jeanne suggested.

Tim dismissed her thought with a single shake of his head. "Nope," he said. "It's not Magnus's fault. Something else is wrong."

He hopped down into the snow, which went up past his knees in the hollow of the ditch beside Daphne's drive, and began to slog around the sleigh. The runners were totally lost in the deep snow, which came up almost to the lip of the sleigh itself on the side that listed the most into the ditch.

"Is it stuck on something?" Jeanne asked, twisting around so that she could see his progress. "What can we do to get it free?"

"If I knew that," Tim said, annoyance creeping into his voice, "do you think we'd still be here?"

Fifteen

ALONE IN HER ROOM, curled up under a thick cream-colored wool afghan, Audrey hit connect and waited for her Skype to come up with Jared's image on the other end.

As the application hissed, bouncing through the wires to connect with Jared, and letting her know it was still in action with a little singsong tune, she smiled at the leap in her heart.

Over the months of their separation, those sounds had become so connected with seeing him and talking with him that she reacted to them the way she reacted to hearing his knock on the door: a little flush in her cheeks, a little thrill of anticipation, a little jolt of happiness, just to know he was there.

But some part of her was amused at the fact that she now responded to the sound of an Internet connection like a twitter-pated teenager.

And some other deep part of her, one she very rarely let out, ached over the fact that this was what she and Jared had been reduced to: faces on screens, in moments stolen at odd hours. She missed seeing his face in person, kissing his cheek or giving him a squeeze. She missed the deep comfort of companionship, long hours spent together without having to say or do anything in particular. She missed just sharing jokes or thoughts or observations as they came up, instead of having to keep up the constant conversation of a call.

Tonight, from the disappointment of not getting to see him over Christmas, that part was still raw and stinging.

But then Jared's face appeared on the screen, and she forgot everything she had just been thinking.

"There's my favorite girl," Jared said, grinning. "Man, you look beautiful, baby. How are things up there?"

"Where are you?" Audrey asked, squinting at a dazzling array of colored lights in the background.

"Orlando!" Jared announced, as if he were delivering the news that he was standing on the front porch, just waiting for her to open the door.

She could tell that he thought of it as some kind of big victory, but all she could think of was how far away Orlando was from Vermont.

"East Coast, baby!" Jared said. "You won't believe what I had to do to get a seat on this last flight. We may have to have a conversation about it if anyone ever comes claiming that we owe them our firstborn child. Plus," he said, "they've got some pretty great light displays here on the concourse."

He tried to turn his screen around so she could see, but all it did was show her a smear of lights.

"Are you stuck there all night?" she asked. "They're not going to give you a room?"

"No, nah," Jared said. "They're still talking about getting us rooms. I'll believe it when I see it."

"I think it's the least they could do," Audrey said.

"Well, they don't control the weather, baby," Jared said. Then he grinned. "Yet."

Audrey smiled.

"That's what I like to see," Jared said, grinning back. He glanced over his shoulder at the concourse behind him. "Besides, if I do wind up sleeping on the floor here, it won't be the worst place I've ever had to sleep."

"Maybe not," Audrey said. "But usually if you don't get to sleep in your own bed, it's for a matter of national security."

Jared shook his head. "You're willing to put up with that, huh?" he said. "Just not flight delays?"

Audrey grinned back. "I'm never willing to put up with it," she said. "I just do."

"Tell me something good," Jared said. "Tell me about the wedding. How's it going?" His tone turned gossipy as his eyes lit up with a mischievous grin. "What are Trevor's parents like? I could never guess what kind of people turned out a guy like him."

A few days ago, Audrey might have stuck up for Trevor against this dig. But now her face darkened.

"Trevor's not coming," she said.

"Ah, man," Jared said. "He got caught in the storm, too?"

Audrey shook her head. "Nope," she said. "He could have made it. But he never left. He just called the whole thing off."

It took Jared a minute to process this. Then it was his turn to shake his head. "Wait," he said. "It sounded like you said the wedding is off."

"That's right," Audrey said. "Trevor's a no-show."

Audrey rarely got a glimpse of Jared the warrior. Around her, he was never anything but gentle, always trying to make sure she was happy and to make the best of their time together.

But suddenly, he got a look on his face that she suspected was the one the enemy saw when they met him in battle.

"Well, that little . . ." he said.

He didn't continue, at a loss for words.

A moment later, he'd mastered the emotion, his face full of

nothing but concern. "How is Hannah?" he asked. "How's she coping? You know, I never liked that punk. Not from the first time I met him. And it didn't get better after that, let me tell you."

Audrey suppressed a smile. "You didn't exactly make a secret of that," she said.

"I didn't?" Jared said with mock surprise. "What gave it away? Do you remember when he showed up at Jen's wedding and wouldn't eat anything they brought him? He was on some kind of cleanse."

Audrey giggled.

"They brought him a chicken breast," Jared went on, "and he was like, 'Can you take this back and get the skin off it?' I was like, 'Dude! Give me your plate. I will take the skin off it myself.' I never understood what Hannah saw in that guy."

"That isn't really the problem with Trevor," Audrey said.

"It's not the biggest one," Jared agreed. "The biggest problem with Trevor is—"

"The biggest problem with Trevor," Audrey said, "is that he doesn't think anyone else has any problems except for him."

"Yeah," Jared said, raising his eyebrows as he thought this over. "That could be it."

"They went through a lot together," Audrey said. "She was always taking care of him. If she hadn't always had to do that, I wonder if things might have been different. But it's hard to leave someone when they need you so much."

"I guess so," Jared said, sounding skeptical.

"And Trevor was there when her mom was sick," Audrey added. "He came to the hospital with her every day. And nobody's perfect," she said, raising her eyebrows meaningfully at Jared.

"Ha!" he said. "Now that I'm off the market, you mean, right?"

"Of course, baby," Audrey said. "That's exactly what I meant."

As Jared's smile at their jokes faded, he began to shake his head, his expression sober again. "Poor Hannah," he said. "I hope she finds herself a better man one day, but still, this has got to hurt."

"It does," Audrey said.

"And at Christmas," Jared said. "What a jerk, to let it get this far if he wasn't serious. He couldn't even tell her the day before? He let all of you get all the way up to Vermont before he even mentioned anything?"

Audrey nodded. "Yep," she said. "And maybe if—" She couldn't get the thought she wanted to say out, because her voice choked and her eyes filled with tears.

"Honey," Jared said. "Hey. What's wrong?"

Audrey shook her head, trying to fight the tears back down. But they weren't going, and Jared looked more concerned with every second that passed. "It's nothing," she said. "It's just that, if he'd told us earlier, I would have stayed in Boston. And maybe I could have gotten a flight to Orlando and—"

She trailed off again, but Jared, as he so often did, had already caught her meaning.

"Maybe we could have spent Christmas together?" he asked.

Audrey nodded, smearing away the tears that were running down her face. She did her best not to dissolve when she was talking with Jared. He already knew how much she loved and missed him. And his life as a soldier was tough enough without him having to deal with her outbursts.

"You know what?" she said. "I could still try. This storm has to break sometime. I could leave first thing tomorrow morning, and—"

"Look, sweetheart," Jared said. "Even if you'd been there, we'd never have found out about the storm in time to get you a ticket out. Especially not with everyone on the entire East Coast trying to rebook at the same time."

"I guess," Audrey said. "But maybe I could have gotten in the car and—"

"Baby!" Jared said. "Have you taken a look outside? They've got eight inches on the ground already, even in Boston. It's supposed to be two feet by morning. I'm not sure one of our tanks could make it through at this point."

"I just wish you were here," Audrey said.

"Me too, baby," Jared said. "Me too. But you know what?"

Audrey shook her head. "What?"

"That's a good problem," Jared said. "That we want to be together."

Audrey looked at him, skeptical.

"When we've got a real problem," Jared said, "is if we don't care whether we're together or not."

"Maybe," Audrey said, starting to smile.

"I'll take this problem over that one, any day," Jared said.

He glanced back over his shoulder, as something indistinguishable squawked over the public address system in Orlando.

"That's lodging for the night," he said. "They're paging my group about lodging."

"Go, go," Audrey said. "Get yourself a room at the inn."

"It *is* Christmas," Jared said with a grin. Then he kissed his fingers and pressed them to the screen. "We'll be together soon, baby, I promise. I'm going to do everything I can to get there.

And just knowing you love me, that's all I need for Christmas. That's enough for me."

"I love you," Audrey said.

"I love you, too, baby," Jared said. Then the connection beeped and cut out as he shut down the application from his side.

For a long moment, Audrey stared at the screen, sending up a prayer that he'd find a place to lay his head that night.

Then she shut her computer and stood up.

She thought she had heard Hannah come into the room next door while she and Jared were talking.

If she had to be stuck here instead of with Jared, at least she had a mission. And her mission was to take care of Hannah.

She'd better go check on her.

Sixteen

"HELLO, DEAR," IRIS SAID when Molly padded down the stairs, into the lobby of the inn. "Marcus is right in there."

She nodded at the lounge with a merry smile, as Molly wondered just what made Iris so sure she was in search of Marcus.

Then again, Molly realized, Iris wasn't wrong. Molly had come down there looking for him.

"Oh," she said, smiling back. "Thanks."

In the cozy lounge, Marcus scrambled to his feet when Molly finally came padding down the front stairs. The warmth of the dancing fire behind him grew more and more inviting the closer she got to it.

"Is everything okay?" Marcus asked. "You need me to take over?"

Molly shook her head, sinking down in the large stuffed leather sofa opposite the one Marcus had been sitting on.

"They are both dreaming peacefully," she said. "At least, as far as I can tell."

Marcus sighed with relief. "You're some kind of miracle worker," he said. "Half the time, it takes me at least twice this long to get them down."

As Molly laid her head back on the cushions, she felt something incredibly soft beside her cheek. "Oh my goodness," she said, reaching up for it. "What in the world is this?"

"It looks like fur," Marcus said as she pulled it onto her lap: a thick white fluff, backed with substantial red satin. She ran her hands over it, dazzled by the incredible pleasure of the softness.

"It's probably left over from the days when Iris was queen of the north," Molly said.

"You can make a story out of anything, can't you?" Marcus said, his eyes crinkling in a smile.

Apparently not any*thing*, Molly thought to herself, thinking of the blank pages still waiting on her desk, now between the sleeping girls.

But there was something she liked about the friendliness in his eyes. And it was good to be reminded that other people saw her as a storyteller. Maybe it would help her start to see herself that way again.

"The world is full of stories," she said.

"Ah," Marcus said. "But not everybody sees them."

As he said this, he crossed behind the couch to a little table set with a silver thermos and a plate of cookies.

"Are you much of a reader?" Molly asked as Marcus poured a stream of hot chocolate into a beautiful blue mug.

Marcus glanced over his shoulder. "You mean of anything longer than children's books?" he asked with a self-deprecating look.

"Children's books count as books!" Molly exclaimed.

"That's right, that's right," Marcus said. "I forgot my audience. Here," he said, setting down a steaming mug and a plate with a few brownies on it in front of Molly.

"They're delicious," he added, taking up a seat on the couch across from her. "I was tempted to eat them all before you got here, but I managed to restrain myself."

Molly looked down at his offerings.

"Do you like brownies?" he asked. "And hot chocolate?"

Molly shook her head, picking up the mug to give it a taste. "I don't like hot chocolate at all," she joked. "And I especially don't like brownies," she added, popping one in her mouth.

Marcus laughed. "Well, besides children's books and blueprints," he said, picking up the thread of their earlier conversation, "I can't claim to do much reading."

"Blueprints?" Molly asked. "Are you in construction?"

"Maybe I should be," Marcus said. "That seems to be where the money is. But no, I'm an architect."

Molly's eyes widened. "So also an artist," she said.

"I think I used to tell myself that," Marcus said with a wry smile. "Many years ago. Before I'd lived in the real world for as long as I have now."

"I don't know much about actual architecture," Molly said. "But I always feel like I'm . . . building something when I work on a story."

Marcus nodded. "That's interesting. Because I always try to make a place that isn't just the setting for a story. It tells one itself."

"I'd like to see a place like that," Molly said.

"So would I," Marcus said. "But I'm afraid not much of what I try to build actually gets made."

"You must make *some* things," Molly said.

"I make many, many things," Marcus said. "It's just that they don't usually wind up to be what I started out making."

"I understand that," Molly said.

"Oh, no," Marcus said. "You forget I'm familiar with your work. You're an artist. No question."

"Well, thank you," Molly said. "I wonder if you're not more of one than you think."

"Maybe," Marcus said. "But you certainly don't want to be around an artist who thinks he's a great artist. I can tell you that much."

"Amen," Molly said. She popped another brownie in her mouth. She'd encountered several self-appointed geniuses over the course of her own career. She snuck a glance at his face, which was glowing in the warm light of the fire. "Thank you for these," she said. "They're wonderful."

"You're more than welcome," Marcus said. "The truth is I'm never going to be able to thank you for taking us in from the cold. Let alone for playing babysitter to the girls."

"It was hardly babysitting," Molly said. "They're wonderful. It was fun to get to spend some time with them."

"We'll see what you think after you've spent a little *more* time, then," Marcus said, but with a smile that made it clear he adored his girls. "I can't tell you what a great surprise it was for them to get to meet a favorite author. I mean, any author at all would have been a thrill for them. But you're very high on their list of all-time favorites."

"That's a high honor," Molly said. "They're very bright girls."

"I like to think so," Marcus said. "But I'm afraid I might not be an impartial judge."

"Dads aren't supposed to be impartial judges," Molly said with a smile.

"I guess not," Marcus said. "In any case, you turned this whole day around for us. Until we met you, everything had been going wrong."

"What happened?"

"First of all, we left Mr. Wimple at home, and didn't realize it until we were two hours on the road."

"Mr. Wimple?" Molly said.

"A stuffed bear," Marcus said. "And a *very* old friend of the family. So old that Bailey doesn't remember life without him."

"I can see why that might have caused some upset in the travels," Molly said.

"Although around that time, we did have the distraction of driving directly into one of the biggest storms on the Eastern Seaboard in the past ten years," Marcus said.

"That would be a major distraction," Molly agreed.

"But not as major as one might hope," Marcus said. "When you have happened to leave poor Mr. Wimple at home. On Christmas, no less."

"What will poor Mr. Wimple do at home all by himself?" Molly asked.

"Exactly," Marcus said. "And furthermore, what is the point of opening presents on Christmas if Mr. Wimple is not there to enjoy them with you?"

"Well, it's never the gifts that make Christmas, Christmas," Molly said. "It's who you're with."

"My girls have certainly learned that lesson," Marcus said.

But the smile he gave at that joke dissolved even as he said it, as if some other, much more serious thought had chased it away. He shook his head and raised his eyebrows, staring into the middle distance.

Instantly, Molly knew that he was referring to whatever had happened with their mother. But instead of asking him about it, she stayed quiet, letting him take his own time, and choose his own words.

After a moment, he looked back at Molly. "It's been three years since we lost their mom," he said. "Cancer."

The way he said the single word carried a whole world of hurt with it: fear, sorrow, anger, loss.

He took a breath. "People told me it would get better," he said. "At first I didn't believe them. Turns out, it's true. It does get better. But it never goes away."

Molly nodded. She knew the feeling, from losing her own mom and dad: how the spike of pain finally faded, but there was an ache that never did.

"She must have been special," Molly said.

"Well," Marcus said, a smile breaking through his more somber thoughts, "since you've met the girls, you know a lot about her. They both got her smarts, and her spirit, and her smile."

"They're great girls," Molly said, smiling back.

As she said it, the front door slammed. Both of them turned their heads as a snow-dusted figure emerged into the entrance area, stomping his feet and brushing snow from his hair.

"Another stranded traveler," Marcus said.

Molly shook her head. "That's Luke," she said. "I met him before. He's related to Iris at the front desk."

As they watched, Luke had a quick conversation with Iris, then strode into the lounge, straight up to the fireplace.

He nodded at the two of them as he held his hands out to the flames, obviously trying to coax some feeling into them after a blast of cold.

"What's it like out there?" Marcus asked.

"Well," Luke said, "I didn't get too far before a Vermont state trooper turned me back. But from what I could see—it's snowy." He grinned.

"Yeah," Marcus said. "That's how we wound up here."

"I thought I might be able to use my country wiles to get to Burlington tonight," Luke said. "But I guess I'll be spending it here. I've just got to see if they can find me a space, now that all the rooms are booked up. Maybe in the kitchen, by the fire," he joked. "Gram said I could sleep on her floor, but she snores so loud I wouldn't get any sleep."

"Well," Marcus said, gesturing to the lounge. "This is my room for the night. You're welcome to crash on the other couch. And I think you might be able to find a blanket or two," he added, nodding at the huge stacks of fuzzy wraps that were piled on the various chairs and couches around the room.

"That would be great," Luke said. "Thanks, man."

Molly took this as her cue. "I'm going to get out of your bunkhouse," she said, "and get back to my own."

Marcus stood up with her. "Thanks again," he said, looking into her eyes with a grateful smile. "You let me know if you need anything at all."

"Good night," Molly said, a shy smile of her own forming in return.

Luke nodded at her, and she suddenly felt awkward that he was there, watching the exchange.

She padded toward the stairs, then looked back. Marcus was silhouetted against the fire as he bent over to make his bed for the night. The shadows of the nativity scene danced in the corner, mirroring the play of the fire in the fireplace.

We made some more room at the inn, Molly thought as she went up the stairs.

Seventeen

"I'M SORRY, HONEY," HANNAH'S mother said, blotting at Hannah's damp hair with a towel that had been warming in a basket by the fire in her parents' room. "We didn't mean to upset you."

Hannah nodded. "I know, Mom."

When Luke had first brought her back to the house, her whole body had just been in survival mode. All thoughts had been driven from her head except the bite of pain as the cold seeped into her extremities, the rising panic as it became harder to breathe in the frigid air. She thought at first that she had managed some genius trick, chasing out any thoughts of Trevor in the face of much more elemental concerns.

But as she began to warm up, the mug of hot chocolate and the heat of the welcoming flames on her skin, a dull, low-grade dread began to build in her, despite the cozy surroundings and the sweetness of the chocolate.

It didn't come with any thoughts yet, but she knew they wouldn't be far behind. Which is why she had climbed the stairs back to the second floor. And why she had walked past the door of her own room, and gone instead to her parents'.

That helped, but it didn't drive the heaviness in her heart away. If anything, it seemed to be getting heavier, just barely perceptibly, moment by moment.

"You know we love you, Hannah-belle," her father said from

the easy chair he'd sunk into across the room. "We just didn't know the right thing to say."

"I'm not sure there is a right thing to say," Hannah's mother said. She gave Hannah a squeeze. "But we'll get through it. We always have."

Usually, Hannah loved her mother's hopefulness. And usually it gave her hope of her own. But tonight, nothing seemed to be making a dent in the pain that throbbed a little more with each beat of her heart, like an injury waking up as the anesthetic wore off.

At the door of her parents' room, there was a gentle knock.

Hannah's parents exchanged a glance. "You expecting someone?" Hannah's father asked.

Her mother shook her head.

For a minute, Hannah's heart leapt with the crazy hope that it was Trevor, having changed his mind, come through the storm to beg for another chance. They could still make it work, she calculated quickly. There was no reason the wedding couldn't go on like they'd planned, just as long as he was here now.

But when her father went to the door, it was Audrey's head that peeped through. "Have you two seen Hannah?" she half whispered. "I just went to check on her, but she's not in her—"

Before she could finish, she caught sight of Hannah.

"Hey, honey," Audrey said, "where have you been?"

To Hannah's relief, Audrey's voice wasn't full of the sympathy that laced her parents' voices. As much as Hannah appreciated their concern, it was hard to deal with them, even when they weren't busy shouting insults about Trevor. She felt like she needed to feel better, so that they could feel better. And the fact was, she didn't know right now if she would *ever* feel better.

But Audrey just gave Hannah the same matter-of-fact treatment she always did, even when Hannah didn't answer her question.

"I just went downstairs looking for you," she said. "And someone put a fresh plate of warm sugar cookies out by the front desk. I think it's a sign that we're supposed to drown our sorrows in Christmas cookies."

"Well," Hannah's mother said, a serious expression on her face. "I don't know if now is exactly . . ."

But Hannah was already hopping down off her bed, shedding the towel her mother had placed around her neck, and the blanket Luke had wrapped her in when they'd come inside.

With a grin, Audrey swung the door open. Gratefully, Hannah escaped through it, into the dim hall.

"Don't worry," she heard Audrey promise over her shoulder. "I'll take good care of her."

"Thanks, sweetie," Hannah's mother said.

"You heard from Jared?" she asked Audrey as they headed for the stairs. Her mother's comment reminded Hannah that she wasn't the only one having a bad day.

Audrey sighed. "He's in Orlando," she said. "But I don't know when they're going to start letting flights land in the Northeast again. At least they gave him a place to stay in the airport hotel. I wonder if I should have just told him to stay in San Diego. At least he could have gotten some rest there. I'm afraid now he's going to spend his entire leave in airports, and by the time the snow clears it'll just be time for him to turn around and go back."

Hannah gave Audrey a quick squeeze and the two of them started down the stairs, following the buttery scent of fresh-baked sugar cookies.

But when Hannah reached the last step, she looked up to see

the back of a tall man who looked remarkably like Luke, dressed in a sweatshirt and a pair of loud red pajama bottoms printed with large multicolored Christmas bulbs. He was filling a plate with cookies from a tray on the low buffet in the entryway. He had so many cookies piled on the plate that it looked like they might topple over.

"Luke?" Hannah said.

Luke turned around. When he saw Hannah, his eyes darted around the room like he was looking for an escape, and his face flushed a bright red. He looked down at his pajama bottoms, and after a second his face broke out in a wide grin.

"I don't know which I should be more embarrassed about," he said. "The pajamas or the cookies. In my defense," he said, lifting the plate, "the cookies are dinner. My grandma just set them out, and they're amazing."

"What are you doing here?" Hannah asked. "Didn't you just leave?"

"That eager to get rid of me?" Luke asked, putting on an expression of mock hurt.

As he did, Audrey came down the stairs behind Hannah.

"Hello," Audrey said, in a tone of voice that carried the clear implication of, *And who in the world is this?*

At the interest in Audrey's voice, Hannah caught a momentary glimpse of Luke in a new light: a handsome stranger, tall, friendly, and grinning. Years ago, if they'd accidentally run into someone like Luke, it would have been the highlight of their evening.

But they weren't just two young girls anymore, out to explore the world together, Hannah thought. So much had happened since then, for both of them. Hannah's stomach turned. She took a cookie from the tray.

"I'm Audrey," Audrey said when Hannah failed to introduce her. She stuck her hand out, and Luke shook it.

"Pardon my pajamas," Luke said. "I'm crashing on the couch tonight."

"You couldn't make it out?" Hannah asked. She nibbled on the cookie.

"And this is Hannah," Audrey said, in a tone that conveyed her apologies for Hannah's bad manners.

"Oh, I know Hannah," Luke said, grinning. "Hannah and I go *way* back."

"Really?" Audrey said, turning to Hannah with a *we'll discuss this later* look.

"Hannah was my first love," Luke added.

Hannah choked on her cookie. Audrey slapped her back, and Hannah slowly swallowed.

"That's right," he said, eyebrows raised. "You could climb a tree, and you knew all the lyrics to my favorite Guns N' Roses album. I was twelve. I couldn't think of anything else I could want in a girl. Come to think of it, I'm not sure I can now."

"You two *dated*?" Audrey asked.

Hannah began to shake her head vigorously.

"Of course not," Luke said. "I had no idea how to talk to girls back then. And this one," he said, nodding at Hannah, "was too busy climbing trees to notice me."

"I haven't climbed a tree since then," Hannah said. "I don't know if I still can."

"Don't sell yourself short," Luke said. "You've still got it."

He picked up a cookie from his plate and took a bite of it. "You'll excuse me, ladies," he said, heading for the lounge. "You arrived just in time," he called over his shoulder. "If you'd waited any longer, I'd have picked that tray clean."

As Hannah stood there, watching him disappear into the shadows of the lounge, Audrey picked up a pair of plates and filled them with a few of the cookies that had survived Luke's raid.

"You want to sit down here for a while?" Audrey asked.

Hannah shook her head, looking into the lounge, where she could already see one figure stretched out on a couch near the fire, apparently dead to the world. Luke was settling in with his plate.

"Someone's already sleeping in there," she said. "Let's go back upstairs."

Audrey barely let Hannah get one foot inside the door of her room before she turned on her, eyes wide with excitement.

"You know that fine-looking man down there?" she asked. "You two were *childhood sweethearts*?"

"Hardly," Hannah said, biting into one of the warm cookies and feeling a faint twinge of pleasure at the perfectly balanced butter and sugar, with just a hint of vanilla. "Mostly, I remember him wanting to argue about the best brand of truck. I didn't care what kind of truck was best, and that drove him nuts. Also," she added, "throwing pinecones at me in the forest. He thought that was *hilarious*."

"But he is so *handsome* now!" Audrey said. "And so nice!"

Hannah remembered his kind words as he led her into the house, and how gentle he'd been when he'd wrapped the blanket around her.

"He is nice," she agreed. "But I'm not exactly interested in romance at the moment."

Audrey shook her head. "Well," she said, "whenever you are ready . . ." She trailed off with a meaningful look.

Hannah tried to smile, but couldn't manage it.

She set the plate of cookies on the table beside her bed.

"Thanks for coming to check on me," she said. "But I think I just want to be alone for a while."

"You sure, honey?" Audrey asked.

Hannah nodded.

"Okay," Audrey said, heading for the door. "Well, I'm just next door."

"I know," Hannah said. "Thanks."

When the door closed behind Audrey, Hannah's thoughts returned to Luke. Audrey was right. He was handsome, and more than nice—kind.

But her heart was too heavy to even feel a tingle at the thought of him.

As she looked around the room, her gaze fell on her wedding dress, still hanging up on the old antique wardrobe where Audrey had placed it when they first came into the room. It was white and pristine and hopeful, as if nobody had told it yet what had gone on today.

With a sigh, Hannah got up, pulled the dress down, stuffed it into the empty wardrobe, and closed the doors.

Then tears began to slide down her face.

The wash of doubts and anger and sadness returned, without her mother or Audrey or someone else to distract her. Her mind kept replaying the same images and questions over and over. She remembered the good times with Trevor and ached that there would never be any more. She remembered the bad times and couldn't stop asking herself why she hadn't seen the warning signs. And all of the times she had pushed Trevor to take care of himself or be more careful, and he'd pushed back, with a laugh or a sharp comment.

Should she have just let him be?

Should she have tried to be more free and easy herself?

But then what about all the times he'd been so grateful to her, telling her that she was the only one who really knew what he needed, the only one he couldn't live without . . . his little "emergency kit." She used to love when he called her that.

Her stomach turned over at the thought now. That he'd discarded her without a second thought. At the very moment when it mattered most.

Her heart, which had been so open and hopeful in the days leading up to the wedding, hadn't been remotely prepared for any kind of rejection, let alone the end of such a long relationship.

It was bad enough that Trevor had wasted everyone's time, money, and energy. But now she felt broken, like there was something fundamentally wrong with her. She wanted to believe she was worthy of love, but now, perhaps for the first time in her life, she was afraid she would never find it . . . or that she didn't deserve it. But then again, Hannah thought, she was supposed to be his girlfriend, his *wife*, not his nurse. Maybe she'd lost sight of the thing that mattered most.

Looking around at the empty inn room, she became acutely aware of the fact that she had never had a relationship where her partner put her needs above his own. And now she was alone. When she was broken, who would take care of her? As Hannah sobbed into her pillow, she feared that no one would ever want to.

EIGHTEEN

"I KNOW WE'RE STUCK, Jeanne," Tim said through gritted teeth. "If we weren't, I assume we'd be moving."

"I'm sorry," Jeanne said, in a tone of voice that made it pretty clear she really wasn't. "I just thought maybe you hadn't noticed it wasn't working, because you hadn't stopped pushing."

"I noticed."

Jeanne sighed, then shivered. Usually, temperatures stayed pretty close to freezing when snow was falling, but tonight, long after the sun had gone down, the cold was starting to turn bitter. And the snowfall around them showed no sign of coming to an end. "If it's not working," she said, "maybe we should try something else."

"Okay, Jeanne," Tim said, standing back from the side of the sleigh where he had just been straining with all his might, pressing his shoulder into the curve of the sleigh in hopes of knocking it free of whatever obstruction lurked under the snow. "What do you suggest?"

"I don't know," Jeanne said. "What's out of the box?"

This had been a favorite question of theirs for years. It was asking that question that had actually prompted them to dream of starting Evergreen Inn in the first place, instead of just continuing to claw their way up the corporate ladder in New York.

And it was a question they had returned to again and again as they made decisions about the design and hospitality at the inn.

But when she said it, Tim just shook his head.

"I don't know, Jeanne," he said. "What's out of the box?"

Jeanne felt a pang in her heart, hearing the beloved question in such a dismissive tone.

In front of the sleigh, Magnus flicked his tail and whinnied.

Tim stared at him for a minute. Then he turned back to Jeanne, his expression serious.

"You know what?" he asked. "How about this: we leave the sleigh here, and take Magnus back home. That will at least get you home and out of the cold. I don't want you here all night."

"I don't want either of us here all night," Jeanne shot back. "But what about the produce?"

"Well," Tim said, making a clear but failing attempt to sound positive. "We could leave it out here until we figure out a way to bring it back. It's freezing outside, so it'll just be kind of like leaving it in a big fridge."

"Except it's not a fridge, is it?" Jeanne said, in a tone that made it clear how crazy she thought his idea was. "It's a freezer. You're talking about leaving butter lettuce, and chives, and top-of-the-line meats in a freezer."

"You know, Jeanne," Tim said, "it's not the end of the world. An hour ago, we didn't have any of this at all."

"Well, if we only came out here to bring it out in the cold, where it was going to freeze into nothing," Jeanne said, "we might as well not have even come out at all."

"What do you want me to do, Jeanne?" Tim asked.

"I don't want you to give up!" Jeanne exclaimed. But it wasn't until her voice cracked and tears sprang to her eyes that she realized that she was talking about something else. Something much bigger than the sleigh, or the produce.

Tim seemed to realize this the same moment she did. But instead of softening his mood, it just seemed to make him feel worse.

"I never gave up, Jeanne," he said. "But sometimes you have to admit when you're beat."

He sighed and laid a hand on Magnus's back to comfort the old horse.

"It's just facing reality," he said.

At this, a ferocious resistance rose up in Jeanne. Without really knowing what she wanted to do, she leapt down from the seat of the sleigh, where she'd been sitting so that she could guide Magnus forward if Tim was able to get the sleigh free.

Tim caught her arm and steadied her as she wobbled, trying to get her footing.

"Hey," he said. "What are you doing?"

"What is this stuck on, anyway?" Jeanne said, kicking at the snow around the sleigh.

Tim looked at the deep piles of white that surrounded them, rising up past both their knees.

"The snow's three feet deep," he said.

But Jeanne was already digging at the snow with her hands, picking up armfuls and throwing them into the storm. Half of it blew back in her face, but she made headway anyhow, digging down until she could see the glint of the sleigh's runner, and the frozen tendrils of the grass buried deep beneath the snowfall.

"What do you see?" asked Tim, who had tramped over to her, holding his arm over his face to avoid the small storm she was creating herself.

But as she revealed the terrain around that part of the runner, she couldn't find the obstruction. She brushed and pushed snow away for a foot in either direction, but found nothing but clear ground.

"I can't see anything," she said. "It's not stuck on this part."

By now, Tim had started to pitch in. He circled around the sleigh, creating a storm within a storm of his own, as glittery flakes whirled up from where he tossed them away from the sleigh runner.

"You got anything?" she called to him.

"Not yet," he answered, his voice thin beyond the noise of the wind.

Then Jeanne's hand hit something. Where there had been level ground, a chilly, black outcrop of rock appeared, almost even with the grass at first, but quickly building to the size of a boulder.

The sleigh runner, no match for it, had been lifted into the air by its bulk, tilting at an increasingly severe angle. Beyond the rock, the sleigh left the ground completely, jutting toward the night sky through the snow with no traction at all.

No wonder they hadn't been able to move.

"I think I found it," Jeanne said.

When Tim tramped around the side of the sleigh to see, she had already begun to calculate their chances of ever clearing the rock. And they didn't look good.

"It's huge," Jeanne said, brushing the snow away from the rock face as Tim came up behind her. "And if we go any farther, I'm afraid the weight of the sleigh on the fulcrum might split the whole runner. Or the whole sleigh.

"Maybe," she said, twisting back to squint at Tim through the wind, "we could get some of the produce on Magnus. Enough to have something for tomorrow. You could take a load, and I can go back to the house and stay warm with Daphne, until—"

Tim didn't even answer. Instead, in the middle of her sentence, he bolted for the back of the sleigh, kicking up a huge cloud of snow behind it.

"Tim," she called. "What are you doing?"

When he slogged back to her, he was grinning.

"We can do it," he said.

Jeanne looked down at the rock and the runner doubtfully. "I just don't think we should risk . . ." she began.

"We're not going to," Tim said, heading for the front of the sleigh. "We're going to go backward."

He leaned his weight into the front curve of the old sleigh, shoving it backward with all his might. The sleigh inched back perhaps a foot, but even in the midst of the storm, they could hear the screech of the metal runner against the rock.

"Here, come help me," Tim said, waving for her to join him.

Jeanne stomped through the snow to the front of the sleigh, put her shoulder to the opposite site from Tim, and pushed.

The sleigh, which had been stubbornly holding its position, giving up ground only an inch at a time for Tim, suddenly came free and slid back noiselessly into the fresh snow behind it.

Magnus, startled by the sudden pressure from the rig, whinnied and took a few nervous steps back himself.

"Magnus!" Tim said, reaching for his dangling reins. "Okay, boy. You ready for this?"

"Wait!" Jeanne said.

She ran ahead of them, into the snow between them and the road, kicking as much as she could out of the way, to make sure there weren't any more hidden obstructions in the path: a fallen log, another big rock.

A yard or two later, she had made her way to the drive.

"It's clear," she called. "I think it's clear from here."

With a comforting clucking sound, Tim led Magnus forward, into the wind. It took a few steps for the harness to become taut again against the weight of the sleigh.

Jeanne held her breath without realizing it as she watched, waiting to see if the sleigh itself would move on the new path Tim was cutting.

Then she had to scramble into a snowbank to get out of the way, because the big horse and the onrushing sleigh slipped back up onto the driveway so fast.

"It worked!" Tim said, laughing. He ran over to help her out of the ditch on the other side of the drive. "That was amazing, baby," he said.

Then he brushed the snow away from her face and kissed her, full and sincere.

At his kiss, Jeanne felt a wave of emotion roll over her: tenderness and hope that were so familiar that it took her a minute to even recognize them. She gazed up at him and noticed a twinkle in his eye that made him look twenty years younger. The past and present flooded her senses, and in a moment of pure giddiness a giggle escaped her lips.

Then he was grabbing her hand and pulling her up beside him into the sleigh, and flicking the reins to set Magnus trotting home. They rode in companionable silence on the short ride, Tim gently humming "Sleigh Ride."

When they burst through the front door of the inn, each loaded down with bags and boxes of produce, Iris looked up.

"Thank goodness," she said. "I was wondering if I should send the dogs out after you."

"Parsley, Iris!" Jeanne said, waving an evergreen bunch of the herb from the top of the box she cradled in her arms.

"In December!" Iris said. "Will wonders never cease?"

Godwin, their English guest, had been standing at the front desk, apparently talking with Iris.

As Tim dropped a box of meats and cheeses near the coat-rack and went back out into the night for more, Godwin padded over like a guard on duty, assigned to give a full inspection to any suspicious deliveries that might come to the house.

"What's all this?" he asked, looking askance at the snow scattered all over the inn's neat rugs, and the box Jeanne had just set down at her own feet.

But Jeanne was in no mood to be cowed by a grouchy Brit.

"Supplies!" she said. "Our caterer couldn't get through because of the snow, so we took out an old sleigh and picked up a thing or two at some nearby farms."

Telling the story that way made it sound a lot breezier than it had actually been, she realized. But it was all true, still. And she felt proud as she said it.

"A sleigh?" Godwin said. He gave Iris a questioning glance.

She smiled back and waved toward the door. "Take a look," she said. "It's a beauty. It's the sleigh my grandfather bought to bring his bride home after their wedding."

"Winter wedding?" Godwin said, arching his brows as he headed for the door. "Or was it still snowing in Vermont in May?"

"You never know," Iris said.

"It's stacked full," Jeanne added proudly as Godwin came over. "We're not even done unloading. We've got everything from fresh rosemary to Vermont's finest small-batch cheddar."

For the first time, Godwin looked impressed. He peered out the door, then looked back.

"It's an actual sleigh," he said, with an air of wonder. "Straight off a Christmas card."

Almost merrily, Jeanne nodded.

"I've heard of farm to table," Godwin said, admiration in his voice. "But sleigh to table . . . that's something new."

Nineteen

MOLLY TOOK A DEEP breath, her eyes still closed, enjoying the first moments after waking and the last taste of sleep, the warmth of her comforter, and the faint kiss of winter sun pouring through the attic windows onto her face.

She opened her eyes and allowed herself to be dazzled by the crystal icicles hanging from the nearest window, and the deep blue of the morning sky, now completely clear. It was hard to believe this was the same sky that had brought the huge storm the night before.

Maybe the world was always giving us lessons, she mused, in how quickly things could change. Storms came up with no warning, but they also disappeared without a trace.

Maybe, she thought, after this last tough year, losing her mother, the new year could be like this new morning, a clear sky full of possibility.

As these thoughts slid through her mind, she also felt the unmistakable undercurrent of a story swimming just below the surface of her thoughts, leaving ripples on the surface.

But in the dawn light, she was full of confidence that she knew how to catch a story, even a skittish one. If she just got to her desk, with pencil in hand, they could never resist coming out of hiding for long.

Suddenly eager to be up and at it, she threw her covers back, turned over, and found herself looking into a pair of small, delighted faces.

Both girls, Addison and Bailey, were standing beside her bed, watching her.

God only knew how long they'd been there.

And they weren't in their pajamas anymore, but had dressed themselves. Relatively well, it turned out, except perhaps for the red knee socks Bailey had chosen to complement her pink skirt.

"Well, good morning," Molly said.

"You're awake!" Bailey said, climbing right into the bed with her, almost immediately followed by her sister.

"Bailey wanted to play," Addison said, in the tone of one old matron exchanging opinions with another. "But I told her she had to wait till you woke up."

Molly had a quick mental flash of what it might have been like if Bailey had tried to play with her *before* she woke up. "That's good," she said.

"What were you dreaming about?" Bailey asked, running her hands over the soft nap of the velvet coverlet.

"You know," Molly said, "I don't remember."

"Do you have a boyfriend?" Addison asked.

Molly shook her head. "Nope," she said. "Not right now."

"Why not?" Bailey said, with some of the same tone of outrage Molly sometimes felt herself on the topic. "You're so pretty!"

"*And* nice," Addison said in a corrective tone, with a look shot toward Bailey.

Molly glanced at the clock. It was early, but not too early for the girls to go wake Marcus, if he wasn't already up.

She could feel the story still, flitting this way and that in her mind. She couldn't tell just what it was yet, but she knew it was there. That was more than she'd felt for weeks, and she didn't have any intention of letting the moment slip away.

"You know what, girls?" she said. "I usually write in the mornings. So I think I'm going to need to take a bit of time to write."

"Oh! Writing!" Bailey said, her voice rising to a squeal and her hands clapping almost involuntarily, as if someone had mentioned going to a circus, or eating ice cream.

"We never saw a writer write before," Addison said. "Can we watch you?"

"You know, I've never had anyone watch me write before," Molly said, trying to find a gentle way into a refusal.

"That's all right," Addison said. "We don't mind."

"It's just that—" Molly tried again.

"We can be quiet!" Bailey announced. "SO QUIET!" she added, at the top of her lungs.

"Shh!" Addison said. Then she turned to Molly, her eyes wide and serious, to offer her own bargain. "We can help," she said. "If you have trouble."

"Well, that's very nice," Molly said. "But—"

"'Have you ever gone for a walk in the woods?'" Bailey asked.

Molly looked at her, startled by this new turn in the conversation.

"'Eveline hadn't,'" Bailey went on. "'All her life, she'd lived in sight of the forest. But until the day the moon turned blue, she never went in.'"

Now it was Molly's eyes that widened, in astonishment, as she realized that Bailey was reciting Molly's own book to her, from memory.

"'Why did you come to the forest?'" Addison asked, skipping ahead in the story quite a bit.

"'I don't know!'" Bailey answered with glee, still reciting the text Molly had written years ago.

"'Who's the biggest bear in the forest?'" Addison asked in what was clearly a favorite game of theirs.

"'Me! Me! Me!'" Bailey bellowed, hopping up and down on the bed with so much vigor that the old antique vibrated from the force.

"That is . . . amazing," Molly said.

"See?" Addison asked.

She slid down from the bed and surveyed the room, hands on her hips.

"Okay," she said, looking over her shoulder. "Where should we go to write?"

As she said it, a quiet knock sounded at the door.

"It's Daddy," Bailey stage-whispered. "Don't answer."

"Who is it?" Molly called.

Bailey clutched at her arm as if she were about to be fed to the giant bear in her story. "Don't tell him we're here!" she wailed.

"It's Marcus," Marcus called. "Bailey? Are you okay?"

Immediately, Bailey burrowed under the covers.

"Come on in," Molly said, doing a quick check of her flannel pajamas to make sure she was decent.

Marcus stepped into the room, somehow already shaved and dressed, and looking for all the world like a model in an advertisement for the perfect country Christmas: denim shirt, gray wool sweater, neat jeans.

"I've come to collect the inmates," he said with a smile. "I hope they haven't been too much trouble this morning."

"Not at all," Molly said. "We just woke up."

"*Molly* just woke up," Addison amended.

"Where's Bailey?" Marcus asked genuinely, his eyes darting around the room in search of his second daughter.

"I don't know!" Molly said, with a meaningful glance at the wriggling lump under her velvet coverlet.

"Oh no," Marcus said. "Do you think she wandered out in the snow? Should we all go out looking for her?"

The lump under Molly's blankets squirmed with delight and anticipation, but Addison was on a mission and had no intention of being derailed.

"Daddy," she said. "Molly needs to write. We're going to help her. You can go."

"Oh, I can, can I?" Marcus said. He raised his eyebrows and looked at Molly.

"Is there any truth to this tale?" he asked.

"Well," Molly confessed. "I do usually work first thing in the morning."

"But not, I suspect, with a pair of young assistants?" Marcus said.

Molly shook her head.

"Okay, girls," Marcus said, clapping his hands. "Round up! We're interrupting the prime creative moments of one of our country's best writers."

"She needs help!" Bailey piped up from under the blanket.

Molly glanced toward her, thinking wryly that Bailey had no idea how right she was. "It's okay," she said. "Really . . ."

But Marcus was implacable. He flicked the blanket back to reveal Bailey, momentarily frozen in shock at being discovered, and immediately pounced on her, lifting her lightly up onto his shoulder, where she struggled as ferociously as if he were abducting her.

"No!" she cried. "I want to stay!"

"They have waffles downstairs," Marcus said.

At this, Addison came to attention like a trained hound on the trail of prey. Even Bailey stopped squirming, hanging on to her father's neck so she could look seriously into his eyes.

"What kind of waffles?" she said.

"Does it matter?" Marcus said. "Aren't all waffles delicious?"

When Bailey's expression started to turn dark again, he relented.

"They are orange-and-lemon waffles," he said. "With powdered sugar *or* maple syrup."

"And butter?" Addison demanded.

"I believe I saw some butter down there, yes," Marcus said.

The girls weren't the only ones transfixed by the description of the menu. Even Molly could feel her mouth watering.

"We can take Molly," Bailey said peremptorily.

"Yes!" Addison said, bouncing on the balls of her feet.

Molly glanced between them gratefully, touched that the girls would want to spend time with her, and already trying to decide between maple syrup and powdered sugar on her waffles. If the other food she'd had at the inn was anything to measure by, they were probably some of the best waffles known to humankind.

"No," Marcus said, his tone so firm it almost sounded angry.

Involuntarily, Molly raised her eyebrows, startled, and looked at him.

Marcus's expression seemed untroubled, but it was also so flat that all traces of his joking earlier had vanished.

"I mean it, girls," he said, reaching his hand out for Addison's. "Come on."

Both of the girls seemed to get the message that he was serious, and they both fell right into line. Addison marched across the room and claimed the hand he offered, while Bailey slid down from his neck and took up her station on his other side, fitting her tiny hand into his as well.

Marcus shook his head as he looked back to Molly. "Thanks for taking care of them," he said. "We'll be out of your hair now."

Molly felt a pang of disappointment as the door closed behind them, and the sting of something else.

Why hadn't he wanted to have breakfast with her? Did he think that was just a little too much? Was he trying to make it clear that she wasn't welcome to join them in everything, just because she'd opened her room up for the evening?

But he'd seemed so friendly and open the night before. Had she said or done something when they talked that made him uneasy?

And where were all these questions coming from, she finally wondered. It hadn't even been a full day since she'd met them. Why should she care whether they wanted to have breakfast with her or not?

She'd come here to write, and that's what she'd do, she decided.

But when she sat down at her desk, the presence of the story that she'd felt so clearly when she first woke up had vanished.

She tried sitting quietly, to give it a chance to rise up again from the depths of her imagination.

She shuffled the sketches on her desk, then shuffled them again.

But no story emerged from the depths of her imagination.

She tried sketching abstract shapes, and then the open window, with the snowy hills beyond it.

And then she began sketching something in earnest, with a

little thrill of anticipation, curious to see what would be revealed when she was done.

But when she finished, she hadn't created any new character.

It was a sketch of the two girls, staring up at her, the first faces she'd seen that morning.

TWENTY

"GOOD MORNING, BOBCAT," LUKE said, stopping at the table where Hannah and Audrey sat finishing their breakfast, in the light-filled dining room next door to the lounge. One whole side of it was nothing but windows, filled with antique glass that had warped ever so faintly over the years. The panes bent and refracted the sunlight that poured through, making it somehow warmer and more gentle.

"Bobcat?" Audrey said, not even making an attempt to stifle her amusement.

"Sure," Luke said easily. "She's always been Bobcat." He turned to Hannah. "You never told her that, Bobcat?"

Hannah shook her head. She appreciated Luke's attempts to cheer her up, but last night hadn't been an easy one, full of doubts and questions about Trevor, as well as some moments of genuine fury. Everyone else was fresh and rested, but she felt exhausted.

"He came up with that when we were twelve," she told Audrey. "I couldn't get him to stop calling me that."

"And you won't have any more luck now," Luke said. "For one thing, now it's classic. For another, what are you supposed to call a girl who drives a piece of expensive construction equipment around the circle drive at fifty miles an hour?"

"It wasn't fifty miles an hour," Hannah protested. "Those things don't go that fast."

"I was there," Luke said sagely. "I saw what I saw."

Even in her weakened state, Hannah couldn't let this pass. "I thought you called me Bobcat because you could never beat me in a race," she said, with a hint of a wicked grin.

"There she is!" Luke said, grinning back. "That's the Hannah I know."

Hannah felt a little surge of pride as he said it, but it was quickly followed by a twinge. They hadn't seen each other in years. They couldn't really know each other, after all that time. Not the way Trevor had known her.

But he was right, at least, about the girl she used to be. Which one was more true to who she really was? she wondered. The girl he remembered, or the woman she was now? And where had all the fire inside that girl gone?

Luke clapped his hands. "Okay, kids," he began.

"What is this," Audrey interrupted, "summer camp?"

"It's winter camp," Luke said. "And your morning activity, Bobcat, is to help me feed the sheep."

He looked at his wrist, pretending to read an imaginary watch. "Get your boots on," he said. "I'll see you at the door in three minutes."

"I don't know if I feel like . . ." Hannah began.

Under the table, Audrey delivered a quick kick to her shin. "She'll be there," she said.

"I didn't even bring boots," Hannah objected to her.

"We will find you some boots," Audrey said. "Boots are the least of our worries. Think of those poor sheep. Don't you care about their needs?"

"That's the spirit," Luke said, winking as he walked away.

Five minutes later, Hannah stood in the entryway of the inn, bundled in a wool flannel jacket and boots, both procured by Audrey after a conversation with Iris, who had proven to wear her same size shoe.

"Bobcat!" Luke said in greeting. "You ready for this?"

Hannah squinted against the blinding morning light that now bounced off the fields of snow that blanketed the surrounding countryside. "I'm not sure I'll ever be ready for this," she said.

"Come on," Luke said, throwing open the door. "You were born ready."

The air outside was crisp, but so cold it took her breath away. When she first stepped out, the cold felt like it froze her immediately to the spot. But then something in her told her to *move*, *now*, so that she wouldn't freeze where she was.

Luke had already bounded down the front steps, which someone had cleared that morning, and started to cut his own path through the knee-high snow, toward the barn.

The gulps of freezing air made Hannah feel exhilarated. She didn't usually feel every breath, or notice every step she took, but she felt each piercing inhalation now, all the way down to her lungs, and every step was an accomplishment that made her feel a little more alive, and a little more as if she was still making progress.

"Remember this place?" Luke said, undoing the latch to swing the door open.

Hannah slogged her way through the last few steps to the door, then stumbled from the snow into the dry, dusty barn with relief.

"The hayloft," she said, looking up. "You can see for miles from up there."

"You used to climb up there, too?" Luke said. "I thought that was only my spot."

Hannah smiled. "Guess not," she said.

From the left, a set of noses began to poke themselves through the slats of the sheep pens, some white and some black.

"Oh my gosh," Hannah said. "I forgot how cute they were."

"They're pretty cute," Luke agreed. Then he turned to the sheep. "You guys hungry?"

In answer, the sheep shuffled in excitement.

"Here," Luke said, handing Hannah a bag of feed. "Dump this in the trough. I'll grab some hay."

"How much should I give them?" Hannah asked, looking down at the earnest faces gazing back up at her.

"Just so there's a couple inches on the bottom. Think of it as an appetizer. And then we'll give them some hay."

As Hannah poured the feed out, walking backward along the low gate that ran the length of the trough, the sheep dove into their breakfast, jostling against one another and smacking their lips. Watching them, a feeling of satisfaction stole over her, along with something that felt surprisingly like contentment.

When Luke came back, a bale of hay on his shoulder, she looked up and smiled. "This is kind of great," she said. "I think maybe I should have been a shepherd."

"You're not the only one," Luke said with a grin, pulling out fistfuls of hay and tossing them into the trough. "People love taking care of animals. I've seen the most hardened kids, you give them an animal to take care of, and suddenly they become a different person. One kid I worked with, when he first came to us, no one in the program could get him to even say a word to them. So I put him in charge of the rabbits at the ranch. From the first day, I could see him out at the hutch, having whole conversations with them."

"And then he started talking to everyone else?" Hannah asked.

"It's not quite that simple," Luke said. "It took him a long time. For a while, I'd go out there and as soon as I got in range, he'd stop talking. But eventually he kept on, even after I got near. And then, one day, he finally said something to me."

"It sounds like he must have gone through something terrible," Hannah said.

Luke got a faraway look in his eyes. "It was the kind of thing I wouldn't ever want to talk about if it happened to me," he said. "I couldn't blame him for just clamming up the way he did."

The trough full, Luke set the remainder of the bale of hay down beside the pen.

"So what about you?" he asked. "You feel like talking?"

"Oh," Hannah said, surprised. She had been lost in thoughts of what would make a kid decide he never wanted to talk to anyone again. And that made her own pain, fresh as it was, fade in comparison. It was hard to even think of them in the same sentence.

But something about the way Luke looked at her made the emotions of the past day rush up again in her heart, begging to be let out, because there was someone here who seemed strong, and ready to listen.

Maybe, she thought, she was reacting to Luke just like one of the kids he worked with. Still, she couldn't resist the urge to answer his question.

"It's not even a good story," she said. "It's just—everything was hard for me and Trevor for a long time. But I thought that if you love someone, that's what you do. You stay even when it's hard."

Luke nodded but didn't offer any comment.

Hannah shook her head and wrapped her arms around herself. Now that they'd stopped moving, the cold was starting to seep into her again.

"Here," Luke said, moving toward the far end of the barn. "Walk with me."

Hannah fell into step beside him, meandering down the length of the barn. "I guess I thought we had finally gotten over it," she said. "I thought things were going to be all right from now on. But I guess not."

"Well," Luke said. "There's more than one way for things to be all right."

Tears sprang to Hannah's eyes, as anger bubbled inside her. "I know that!" she said. "Of course it's better not to marry Trevor if he doesn't really love me." This was the first time she'd said this out loud, or even thought it, and for a moment she was speechless at the sound of it. "It just . . . hurts," she added, her voice cracking.

"Listen," Luke said. "When we were growing up, you were the toughest girl I knew. And not bad-looking, either," he said, with a self-deprecating wink. "I wasn't kidding when I said you were my big crush back then. And you had some tough competition. Nelly Furtado," he said. "You totally beat her out. I promise you, Trevor is not the only man in the world."

"What did you like best about me back then?" Hannah said wryly. "My braces or my glasses?"

"I liked your spirit," Luke said simply.

At this, the tears began to roll down Hannah's face in earnest.

"I just don't feel like I have much of that left," she said. "I remember feeling that way when I was a kid. Like I could do anything. I loved it. But then you grow up, and you find out—you can't. You can't even get your boss to approve your idea when you know it's better than his. You can't even get the man you want to marry to love you back."

She was afraid Luke might get upset himself, as Trevor sometimes did when she was having a hard time. But Luke just looked at her, waiting to see if she had anything more to add.

She took a deep breath. "I know these aren't the worst problems in the world," she said.

"But they're yours," Luke said. "And they matter."

By now, they had reached the end of the barn, where a dozen fancy chickens were roosting in various wire hutches.

"They're so pretty," Hannah said.

"Look at the green and black on those tail feathers," Luke said, crouching down to get eye to eye with one particularly curious rooster, who strutted back and forth just behind the chicken wire.

But Hannah was looking at something farther back. At first her eye was fooled, because the smooth oval shape was familiar, but the color wasn't: a pale aqua.

"What's that?" she asked, pointing.

Luke followed her gaze, peering pack into the dim depths of the coop.

"Well, look at you," he said. "Not bad for a city girl."

"Is it an egg?" Hannah asked, her excitement rising at the prospect.

By now, Luke was already pulling the door of the coop open, and reaching in. "Yep," he said. "And I bet it's not the only one. Man, is Jeanne going to be glad to see these."

He turned back and grinned up at Hannah. "We thought we were just gonna feed the sheep," he said. "But it looks like now we can feed a whole lot more than that."

Twenty-One

"THAT'S NOT HOW YOU do it," Addison said, frowning as her little sister broke off a piece of her waffle and dipped it in the generous silver cup of maple syrup that had been set to the side of Bailey's fluffy waffle.

Unfazed, Bailey completed her dip, thoroughly dunking the light, cakey confection, flavored with both orange and lemon peel, in the syrup, making sure to douse the whole thing as completely as possible. Somehow, she managed to keep her chubby little fingers pristine.

"It's like ketchup," Bailey said reasonably.

Marcus looked from one of his daughters to the other, bemused, as Addison looked at him for backup, outrage building from mild to serious in her blue eyes. Bailey blithely tore another piece off her waffle and dunked it in the syrup.

He often found himself in this predicament as a single dad. Part of him couldn't help but admire Bailey's inventiveness. When you came right down to it, she was right. Enjoying her waffle this way wasn't much different from getting through a bag of fries. And Bailey was so prim about it that there was nothing that could be construed as impolite in her comportment, even if it didn't exactly match the generally accepted conventions.

But he knew that Addison's ferocity in the matter wasn't *just* the glee of knowing something her little sister didn't. Sometimes

Addison seemed to feel even more responsibility than he did to make sure that her little sister understood the ways of the world around them. It was her way of protecting her sister, and even though she could be imperious about it, Marcus was always touched by the spirit behind it.

"Hey, Bailey," Marcus said. "How about you just pour some of the maple syrup *onto* the waffles? Then you don't have to do all the work to dip every piece."

"I don't mind," Bailey said lightly, thoroughly dunking another piece of waffle.

"Well, honey," Marcus said, "that's not really how people eat waffles."

At this, Bailey immediately got the stubborn look on her face that her mother used to get when she was determined to do something. Marcus's heart both swelled and dropped at the sight of it.

But Bailey, aware she was outnumbered at her own table, was now scanning the small dining area for reinforcements.

At the table next to them, populated by an older couple who had already been seated and were chatting quietly, she found her backup.

The man was executing a modified version of Bailey's strategy, cutting off pieces of his waffle and then using his fork to dunk them into the syrup, rather than dousing the whole mess to begin with.

"He's eating like I do!" Bailey said, loud enough that the couple, diverted from their own conversation, looked over.

The older man, dressed in a chunky blue sweater, grinned at her, dunked a bite of waffle in syrup, and gulped it down.

"See?" Bailey said, bouncing in her chair.

"He's using a fork," Addison pointed out.

"That's true," the older man said, quickly grasping the situation. "But you know how to use a fork, don't you?"

Bailey nodded vigorously.

"I'm Eileen," the woman said, sotto voce, to Marcus, extending her hand. "This is Frank."

Marcus shook her hand as Frank waited for Bailey to pick up her fork.

"Are you ready for this?" Frank asked.

Bailey nodded again.

"Okay, let's go," Frank said.

As if they'd spent all morning working to choreograph the ballet, Bailey and Frank each used their forks to whittle a small piece off their respective waffles, doused them in syrup, then raised them to their mouths.

As they took the bite, they looked at each other and grinned.

"Thanks," Marcus said. "I'm Marcus."

"I'm Addison," Addison announced, and then spoke for her sister, who was still enjoying her bite. "This is Bailey."

"Okay, girls," Marcus said. "Let's let Frank and Eileen finish their breakfast. You probably came on vacation to enjoy being away from kids," he said to Frank and Eileen with an apologetic smile.

"Oh, no," Eileen said. "We just got our last kid out of the house. And now we don't know how we're going to live without them. They've both flown off to Europe this year. Our son is staying with his fiancée's family. And our daughter is on a research boat in the North Sea. It's the first Christmas we've ever spent without either of them."

Beside her, Frank shook his head vigorously. "Honestly," he said, "neither of us could figure out how Christmas was going to feel like Christmas without kids. And your kids," he said, smiling at the girls, "are obviously of the absolute highest caliber."

Addison preened under the praise, sitting up even straighter in her chair, while Bailey, pretending to be too cool to notice the compliment, ate another forkful of her waffle with a performer's flair.

"Have you two been here before?" Marcus asked.

Eileen shook her head. "We didn't even plan to be here *this* time," she said. "We got forced off the road by the snow, and luckily, they had a place open when we floundered up the drive."

"Us, too!" Addison said.

"Daddy was afraid we were going to have to build an igloo in the snow," Bailey added.

"I never said that," Marcus protested with a smile. "I never said anything *like* that."

But as Bailey cocked a skeptical eye at him, he marveled again at how his youngest daughter always seemed to be able to read his thoughts, no matter how well he was trying to hide them. He had wondered how in the world to provide a warm shelter for his family if they weren't able to find a place to stop on the harrowing drive, more than once.

"Well," Frank said. "I don't know how the kitchen managed to turn out a breakfast like this, under the circumstances." He winked at the girls. "I've got to tell you, I'm a bit of a waffle aficionado. And these are some of the best, anywhere on the globe."

"You make it sound like we're seasoned world travelers," Eileen said with a smile. "Which might be *somewhat* misleading."

"What are you talking about?" Frank said. "We've been to Key West. Isn't that another country?"

Eileen shook her head. "It depends who you ask," she said.

"New York," Frank went on. "London. Saint Louis. Southern California. All quite different countries."

Marcus glanced at Addison, whose brow was knitting in concentration.

"And I've had waffles in all of them," Frank said. "You don't deny that, at least, do you?"

"I do not deny that," Eileen said. "I'm not sure I remember ever visiting a place where you didn't have waffles."

"I rest my case," Frank said.

As he and Eileen were talking, Bailey had finished off her waffle, and was now peering covetously at the large, fluffy one on Frank's plate.

"Are you going to finish that one?" she asked.

"Bailey!" Addison protested, making sure the gathered company knew that at least *one* of the children in this family knew their manners. "We just met them!"

"My dear," Frank said, taking another bite, "I'm afraid I am."

As he did, Luke came into the dining room, carrying a loaf of bread and a blue ceramic dish of butter toward the buffet on the side table in the corner, where juice, milk, and water were already set out.

"Fresh bread," he announced as he came through. "Anybody want a piece?"

"I do, I do, I do!" Bailey said, bouncing again as if her chair had been spring-loaded.

"Well, here you go," Luke said, stopping to put a piece on her plate. She pounced on it with delight.

"And how are you young ladies enjoying the snow?" he asked.

"It's very pretty," Addison said politely.

"Pretty?" Luke said. "But what's it like when you *play* in it?"

"We didn't go outside," Bailey informed him. "We stayed in here."

Luke's eyes opened in mock shock. "Stayed in here?" he said. "Why on earth would you do that when there's so much beautiful snow outside?"

At this, both girls glanced at their father, checking to see who this strange guy was. But when they saw that Marcus knew Luke, and even seemed friendly with him, they began to open up.

"Our sled is at home," Bailey told him.

"Well," Luke said seriously, pretending to consider this, "is your sled the only sled in the world?"

Bailey searched his face for a moment before breaking out into a grin. "No," she said, giggling.

"Has it occurred to you," Luke said, "that there might, in fact, be other sleds *right here, at this very inn*?"

"We can go sledding!" Addison said, glancing at her dad for approval. "Dad! Are we going sledding?"

"What do you say, Dad?" Luke asked. "My favorite sledding hill is right past the drive. And I'd be glad to take them. As you may know, I'm a trained professional."

"It's fine with me," Marcus said. "If the girls want to go."

Bailey, who had been making very quick work of her slice of bread, popped the last bite into her mouth, and slid down from her chair.

"I'm going! I'm going!"

"We need snow pants," Addison said, slipping off her chair as well to follow Luke. "We have coats and hats and gloves in the hall."

"Well," Luke said as the girls trailed after him, "let's see what we can do about that."

Smiling at Frank and Eileen, Marcus excused himself to help get the girls into their things.

A few minutes later, fully bundled up in hand-me-down snow pants the inn kept for just such emergencies, the girls roared out the door, squealing with delight at the sight of a pair of sleds that Luke had brought back earlier that morning from a trip to the barn.

As Marcus watched them scamper through the snow toward the crest of the steep but gently sloping hill the inn sat on, he felt the same little cocktail of freedom and loss he felt whenever his girls weren't with him. It felt good to have a minute to himself, but also a bit lonely.

For some reason, as he turned away from the window, wondering what to do with himself, his mind wandered to Molly, writing upstairs.

It was a strange feeling to find himself thinking about anyone but Elyse, the girls' mother. In the days after her loss, there had been times when he wished he could stop thinking about her, and times when she was all he wanted to think about, as a way to keep her alive, at least in his own mind and heart.

That's what this trip had been about, in fact. Elyse had been a serious outdoorswoman, and there was nothing she loved more than skiing. She and Marcus had taken a visit to the Starlight Lodge together shortly before her diagnosis, and it was one of the last purely happy memories he had of her. He'd made the reservation this year as a way to help the girls get to know a place and an activity that their mother had loved, and as a way to try to stay in touch with her memory himself.

But more and more, memories of her had begun to recede from his mind as he dove into the details of daily life. Marcus wasn't sure if that was a good, healthy thing, or if he wanted to fight it with all his might. In those moments, just a look into his daughters' eyes was enough to reassure him she'd never be fully gone.

As he thought back on his last interaction with Molly, he suddenly wondered if he hadn't been too short with her when he was trying to hustle the girls out of the room.

Had he seemed rude to her? He felt a little pang of shame at the thought. That was the last thing he had meant to do, especially since she had been so kind to them.

Then again, he thought, there was no reason to think she had noticed anything about him at all.

He doubted, actually, that she had given it a second thought.

Why would a famous writer spend any of her precious time thinking about him?

Twenty-Two

JEANNE LOOKED AROUND THE kitchen, feeling a warm rush of satisfaction.

The yeasty smell of bread emanated from her beloved old cast-iron stove, which gave it a thick but flaky crust unlike anything else you could produce with even the most modern appliances. The zing of citrus zest, orange and lemon, wafted from her waffle batter with a faint but unmistakable bite. The three dozen eggs that Luke and Hannah had brought in from the barn sat in a wire basket in the center of the kitchen island, and she'd been enjoying endless dreams about what they might become: afternoon omelets, evening meringues, savory crepes, a light, fluffy cake.

She already had the jump on lunch, with quick-pickled onions and goat cheese prepped into gorgeous croquettes for a light salad, and the beginning of a rich beef stew bubbling on the stove.

As she poured a pleasingly frothy ladleful of waffle batter onto her solid, ancient waffle iron and brought the top down with a faint sizzle, she smiled.

As she did, Tim came in from outside, stamping his feet against the cold, bearing a load of firewood for their wood-burning stove.

"Just in time," Jeanne said. "There's still a few logs there on the side, but I was starting to worry what was going to happen when those ran out."

Tim dumped the armload of logs he'd split himself into the fireproof metal box beside the stove, then came around the kitchen island to give his wife a kiss.

"You're so cold!" she said, and shivered.

"Have I ever let you run out of firewood before?" Tim asked with a smile.

Jeanne actually stopped to think about it for a moment. But when she had, she gave him an answering smile. "Nope," she said. "Not in over ten years."

"That's what I thought," Tim said, sneaking one of the delicious crusty tendrils of waffle dough that had spilled out of the waffle iron, down the side, where it had cooked to its own kind of perfection. "I just wanted to check. This," he said as he got a taste of the waffle, "is delicious."

"You want one?" Jeanne asked. "I've got to send this out as soon as it's done, but you can have the next one. You know that crazy old Brit we took in last night? The one who looks like he'd much rather be spending Christmas tormenting people in a medieval dungeon?"

"Did we have more than one crazy Brit check in last night?" Tim asked with a grin.

Jeanne shook her head at his teasing.

"Well," she said, "he's ordered basically the entire breakfast menu, such as it is."

"You managed to produce an entire menu?" Tim said, mouth agape. "Last night, we were just hoping nobody would go hungry."

"Well," Jeanne said, "I had a few ideas, so I just had Iris print them up. It's nothing much. Just the orange-lemon waffles."

"My favorite," Tim said. "If they only let me have one food in heaven, it would be your waffles. In fact, that's how I'll know if I'm there or not. By whether they've got your waffles."

Jeanne grinned under the praise. "I put some of Hiram's bacon on there, in case anybody wanted a side of meat. And then I found some steel-cut oats in the pantry, so I put them on, with walnuts and apples stewed in brown sugar and brandy. And then I made up an apple-cheddar cheese toast, and an old-fashioned cinnamon toast, with butter and cinnamon sugar, just because plain toast is always so dry and boring."

"I smell what you're cooking," Tim said. "It all sounds like a feast."

"Well, he ordered all of it," Jeanne said. "Oatmeal, waffles, both kinds of toast. And bacon. So much bacon. I sent him out a single order, and he sent back a request for more. And when I took that one out, he asked for another. Before I even set it down."

"I guess he worked up an appetite last night," Tim said. "Fighting his way through the storm."

"Well," Jeanne said, "I would have thought some of the edge would have been taken off that by the fact that he ate half a basket of those salted brownies."

"That's a lot of brownies," Tim observed. "For such a skinny guy."

"Another mystery," Jeanne said. "Maybe that could be our next business. Figure out whatever lets him eat that much and still look like a scarecrow, and then sell it." She pulled the waffle free from the iron, and settled it gently on a turquoise ceramic plate, beside the butter, syrup, and orange slice garnish she'd already arranged there.

"But we've got lunch almost prepped already," Jeanne added,

picking up the plate to take it out to the dining area. "Fresh bread, salad with goat cheese croquettes, bacon-beef stew . . ."

"So who did all this already this morning?" Tim said, looking around the kitchen. "Did we hire another three chefs, too?"

Jeanne shook her head. "It's just your wife," she told him. "She's a genius."

But as she turned to go, Tim wrapped her in a hug from behind, sheltering her shoulders with his own. "Tell me something I don't know," he said, kissing her cheek, his own cheek still chilly from bringing the firewood in.

Jeanne sighed. Despite the chill, she let her head drop back on his shoulder and pressed her cheek to his.

"Today feels good," Tim said. "Doesn't it?"

Jeanne felt a twinge as he said it, because beyond it lay all the many days they'd lived through together that hadn't been great. But today, she wasn't going to dwell on those days, either. The kitchen was beautifully stocked and full of activity. The cozy house was full of guests, and a good many of them were enjoying the fruits of her and Tim's labor at this very instant, in the dining area.

"It feels just the way I always hoped it would," she said, setting the waffle plate down so she could thread her fingers through his at her waist.

"Even if this is our last Christmas here," Tim said, "it's a good one."

Jeanne lingered a moment, giving him one last squeeze before she pulled free. "We can't let our crazy Brit's waffle get chilled," she said, picking up a spatula from the counter to give Tim a playful squat. "Back to work, buster. The day's not over yet."

Twenty-Three

UP IN HER ROOM, Molly had already devoured every last crumb of the corn bread she'd saved from the welcome basket Jeanne had brought up the day before.

She'd read every scrap of the notes she'd been taking for herself over again, and then she'd collected them all neatly and tucked them away in a folder off the desk.

That had given her the room to sit and dream over the sketches that surrounded the blank page in the middle of the desk. She'd arranged them from small to large, then rearranged them according to various qualities: the alligator and the minnow, for instance, could both swim, while the robin and the kitten couldn't, or at least didn't want to. She spent a bit of time entertaining the idea of a book about an elephant who was also, improbably, a champion swimmer, before rearranging all her characters again by who she would like to walk her home on a dark and stormy night, from most to least.

She spent some time staring out the east window, because she had heard a creativity guru recently talk about the importance of letting your mind wander. And when her mind didn't seem much inclined to wander over the freezing landscape, she tried the next window, with similar disappointing results.

Finally, she decided that what she must really be in need of was a change of scene—and maybe a replenishment of her welcome basket.

She hadn't made it to breakfast yet, although she'd eaten her fair share of the remains of yesterday's cornucopia. She didn't like to eat breakfast before she'd written a page, and she hadn't actually written a page yet. And some part of her felt a little shy at the prospect of accidentally barging into Marcus and the girls' meal. Marcus had made it clear he didn't want her to be part of it, and the dining area was so small that it would be hard to avoid them if they were seated at the same time, especially if the girls saw her and wanted to talk.

The delicious smells wafting up the stairs—bacon, cinnamon, lemon, orange—had kept the idea of a delicious snack high on her mind. And they only got stronger, and more delicious, as she descended the stairs, telling herself that since it had been a good hour, there wasn't any reason to worry about running into Marcus in the dining room—or anywhere at all.

So of course the first person she saw when she descended the last step was Marcus, standing near the door in a full workman's snowsuit and watch cap. Inexplicably, he had nothing on his feet but socks.

And of course he was the only person in the whole room, which made it impossible for her to get by without doing something to acknowledge him when he looked up and met her eyes.

"Hey," he said.

"Hey," Molly said, instantly averting her eyes so that he didn't think she was trying to entangle him in some long, unwelcome conversation. Staring at the carpet, she started for the dining area, mostly by following her nose.

"How's the writing going?" Marcus asked.

"Oh," Molly said. She was startled to a stop by his question, and then immediately wished she hadn't been, because she didn't have anything like a good answer to give him. "I came down because I think I might need a little break."

"It's important to give your mind a rest on creative projects," Marcus said. "A lot of my best ideas come when I get up from my desk."

Molly nodded, trying to look like that was exactly what she was doing: just wandering around the inn, waiting to be smacked on the nose by one of her best ideas. "Yeah, I know what that's like," Molly said, wishing her best ideas would hit her just a little bit more often.

But part of her was also bemused, and maybe even a little annoyed. This morning, Marcus hadn't been able to get his girls out of her room fast enough. Now he seemed weirdly eager to talk.

"Well," he said. "What about going for a walk?"

From the way Molly looked askance at him, then peered out the window to double-check that, as far as either of them could see, the world was still blanketed in several feet of snow, he quickly realized that he'd need to give further explanation.

He leaned over, practically creaking in the thick overalls, and picked up a snowshoe from the bench by the door. "Ever used one of these?" he asked.

Molly shook her head. "Not once," she said. "But I have to say, I did always kind of want to. When I was a kid, I wanted to be a duck, because of their big webbed feet. I mean, I didn't want that for *too* long," she amended quickly, but when she glanced at Marcus, she could see that he was smiling.

"I wanted to be a pigeon," Marcus said. "Because I thought their feathers looked like gasoline in puddles."

"It's maybe a good thing not all wishes come true," Molly said

wryly. But she was also looking around the entryway, warming to
the idea of getting out of the house.

Marcus was right. Sometimes a walk around the neighbor-
hood was all she needed to get started again when she was in a
story's tricky spot. And maybe that was what ailed her now—
having been cooped up in the house for so long, because of the
storm.

"I just don't have any serious foul-weather gear," she said,
looking at his overalls in mild disbelief. "Do you always travel
with those?"

"These?" Marcus said, looking down at himself. "No, these are
Tim's. He loaned them to me. But I saw a pair of Jeanne's in the
back room. I bet she'd let you borrow them."

"And there are enough snowshoes?" Molly asked.

"There's another pair right here," Marcus said, waving one
triumphantly.

"Ha, okay," Molly said, heading for the kitchen. "Let me see
what Jeanne says."

Five minutes later, Molly marched out the front door of the
inn, bundled into a thick, squeaky pair of blue work overalls, with
slightly-too-large snowshoes sloshing on her feet.

She must look something like a cross between one of the
blow-up floats in the Thanksgiving parade and a genuine Eskimo.
But because she felt absolutely unattractive, some of the shyness
she had felt in the face of Marcus's handsomeness disappeared.
At this point, there was no chance of impressing him, so she
didn't feel any need to try.

And snowshoeing was surprisingly delightful. She knew what
it was like as a kid to try to play in snow that deep, punching
through the icy crust so that your legs got stuck. But the snowshoes seemed to work like magic, distributing the pressure of

each step so that she and Marcus both tramped easily over the pillowy drifts, never sinking in.

Marcus struck out toward the crest of the hill where the inn sat, a thin ridge of bare trees, with not a single human footstep between them and it.

As Molly followed him, the pressure that she'd felt indoors seemed to melt from her heart and shoulders, and she grinned into the sparkling world, feeling like a kid herself again.

Until Marcus turned back and shot a question over his shoulder. "So how's that new book going?" he asked.

"What book?" Molly called, hoping to deflect him, and her own worries, with a joke.

It did get a laugh from Marcus, but it didn't knock him off his conversational track.

"It must be amazing," he said. "To get to build the whole world from scratch. I'm always having to deal with what's already there when I'm working on a building. Building codes. Client demands. The strength of steel." He laughed. "But if you write the book, you can make the strength of steel whatever you want."

Molly tramped beside him for a few steps, thinking this over. "I remember feeling that way when I first started writing," she said. "But sometimes having all that freedom is harder than it might seem."

"What makes it hard?" Marcus asked.

Molly thought for a few more steps. "I guess," she finally said, "when you can go any direction at all, it's hard to choose just one of them."

"The blank page," Marcus said. "We have it in architecture, too."

"It's strange," Molly said. "I used to get such a thrill from it. It never felt scary to me. It felt like pure possibility. And I always figured I'd only get more confident as I published more books. But instead, I'm even less certain. There are all these voices in my head, reviewers, my editor, my agent. I'm having trouble finding my own voice. And if I can't find that, I'm not sure what's the point of even being a writer."

She took a deep breath.

"I thought I was just tired," she said. "After my mother died, it wasn't an easy time."

"I can understand that, too," Marcus said. They were both quiet for a moment, listening to the sounds of nature around them, and the soft crunch of snow beneath their feet.

"But I can feel myself getting stronger now," Molly said. "And I still don't know what I want to write."

"You'll find it," Marcus said.

"I wish I were as sure about that as you are," Molly said. "But I'm not. And it makes me question everything. What have I spent all this time doing, if I can't remember how to be a writer now? And what if I never remember? What will I do then?"

Marcus seemed to know better than to try to give her an answer, maybe because he'd had to face similar questions in his own life.

After a minute, he looked over with a wicked grin. "Okay," he said. "I know what you should write about."

"You do?" Molly said, raising her eyebrows to make her skepticism clear.

Marcus nodded, undeterred. "Yep," he said. "Your next book is about a pair of penguins. They meet in the middle of a big storm, when both of them stumble into the same cave, and then they have to learn how to use snowshoes, because—"

Molly's laugh interrupted him. "I like the opening," she said. "But I'm not sure I can do much with the snowshoe premise."

"Well," Marcus said, looking very pleased with himself. "I'm glad I could help. Now you at least know one direction you don't want to go."

Molly shook her head as they came to the top of the ridge. Below, a whole valley spread out. On the far side of it, so distant that it looked like a toy, was a large complex of buildings, sun glinting from a few of the windows.

"I think that's where the girls and I are supposed to be right now," Marcus said. "Starlight Lodge. It looks different from here."

"Things often look different," Molly said, "when we get some distance from them."

"You know," Marcus said. "When I first visited the Starlight, it felt like everything you could ever wish for." He turned back to Molly. "But this place turned out to be so special I wouldn't wish for anything else."

Molly stared back into his blue eyes, wondering if there was anything more to what he was saying, or if he was just genuinely captured by the charm of the place, and its setting.

"Even sleeping on the couch?" she joked, since she wasn't sure what else to say. "With the girls upstairs in the attic?"

"I think maybe *because* of that," Marcus said.

Discombobulated, Molly glanced away from him, back down into the valley. But this time, she caught sight of something.

"Look at that," she said. "Is that a car? On the road?"

Marcus squinted, then nodded. "I think you're right," he said. "Maybe they're finally getting them cleared. That's good news, isn't it?"

But it didn't feel like good news to Molly. It felt like the world she'd left behind was starting to close in on her again, even though she hadn't managed to begin the manuscript she'd come here to finish. And it felt like some other temporary but precious world was being torn away from her—the world blanketed with this beautiful snowfall, and the girls sleeping in their beds, and him.

She glanced from him to the road far below, not sure what to say.

But before she could think of anything, a snowball whizzed through the air and caught him solidly on the back of his head.

Instantly, both he and Molly whirled around, then tottered as their snowshoes got tangled. Marcus caught Molly by both arms to stabilize them.

By then, the sleigh that Luke had been driving, with Addison and Bailey in back, had drawn up farther down the hill, but was still within striking distance for someone with a good arm.

Addison and Bailey had collapsed in each other's arms, laughing.

"All right," Marcus pretended to fume, bending over to shape his own snowball. "Which one of you two little scamps did this?"

"Daddy!" Bailey announced. "Luke took us on a sleigh ride!"

"It wasn't us!" Addison squealed. "It was Luke!"

By the distance of the sleigh, and the solidness of the hit, this was a believable accusation, and confirmed by the mischievous grin on Luke's lips.

"Girls," he said, pretending to be hurt. "Now, why in the world would I ever do a thing like that?"

In answer, Marcus fired his own shot down the hill, which smacked with a satisfying thud against the side of the old sleigh.

The big horse that was drawing it lurched off, taking the sleigh around the bend, although the sound of the girls' laughter echoed through the morning even after they'd vanished out of sight.

Twenty-Four

"HEY, HONEY," AUDREY SAID gently. "Hannah. Wake up. It's already after noon."

Hannah rolled over and threw an arm over her face.

She'd gone back to her room to shower after breakfast and, alone with her thoughts, decided to crawl back into bed instead. She had woken up several times already, but always managed to convince herself that the memories that resurfaced each time she did were some kind of bad dream that could be resolved with more sleep.

But the look on Audrey's face, and the fact it was so late, woke her up for good.

The broken engagement had come as a shock, and like any other kind of shock, it had left parts of Hannah's heart and mind numb. Even as waves of grief and anger had washed over Hannah in the past day, it still hadn't felt fully real.

But today, the actual day she was supposed to get married, she suddenly felt it all. It didn't feel like she was trying to absorb a shock anymore. It felt like this was just what life was like now: strange and painful, with no hint of when that would change, if ever.

As she came fully awake, she groaned and buried her face in the down pillow, hoping that the feathers might block out the memories of the previous day.

"It doesn't matter," she said. "There's nothing to do."

Gently, Audrey plucked at her arms. "Honey," she said, "it's up to you. But I've done everything I could to distract your mom from coming in here. And if you wait any longer, she's going to be the one waking you up, not me."

This managed to get Hannah at least marginally upright. "I'm up," she said. "I'm up. See?"

"How about you actually get your feet on the floor?" Audrey asked.

She gave Hannah's shoulders an encouraging squeeze as Hannah scooted toward the edge of the bed. But when Hannah began to lose momentum, Audrey lost her patience and threw the covers back.

"Ugh," Hannah said, glaring at her. "You are so mean to me."

"Yes, I am," Audrey said.

Hannah groaned again, but this time she got out of bed, and a moment later, Audrey was marching her downstairs.

"It's not lunch yet," Audrey said. "But I have engaged in high-level negotiations with the kitchen to secure you sustenance."

"I'm not that hungry," Hannah said.

"That," Audrey told her, "is because you haven't tasted this fresh bread yet."

As they came down the stairs, Iris, who was deep in conversation with a strange old man with a pronounced British accent, waved them down.

"Girls!" she said. "Girls! I've got your basket here."

"Thank you, Iris," Audrey said with a smile, and reached to sweep up the basket, which was covered with a blue-and-white-checked napkin, and was faintly steaming.

But before she could, the old Brit caught hold of it.

"Wait a minute," he said. "What's in here?"

"Fresh bread," Iris said.

"And preserves," the old Brit added. "I assume these are homemade?"

Iris bridled at this, insulted. "What else do you think they'd be?" she asked.

But the old Brit was looking at Hannah and reaching for what was obviously the most tempting piece of bread in the basket. "You don't mind if I just . . ." he began, then swiped the piece of bread, slathered it with about half the contents of the jelly ramekin, and popped it in his mouth.

"Heavenly," he said.

At his appreciation for the quality of the victuals, Iris seemed to forgive him, her indignation relaxing into an indulgent smile.

While the old gentleman was lost in his ecstasy, Audrey took the opportunity to snatch the basket out of his reach.

But when Audrey got Hannah and the basket settled in a nook of the otherwise deserted dining area, Hannah got a taste of what he meant. The bread, the butter, the fresh blueberry preserves: it was better than any bread she'd ever had before—and probably any dessert. And in virtually no time at all, between Hannah and Audrey, half the loaf was gone.

Audrey sat back, satisfaction evident on her face.

But as Hannah brushed at the crumbs at her place, they both caught sight of motion beyond the window.

"Are the roads open already?" Audrey said with a sudden urgency that made Hannah realize that no matter what she was going through, Audrey was carrying her own weight—the disappointment of not getting to see Jared, even though he was stateside.

But before Hannah could answer, the two of them both got a good look at what had just pulled up beyond the windows of the cozy inn: a real-live old-time sleigh, straight off a Christmas card.

"Oh my gosh," Audrey said. "It's like we woke up in *A Christmas Carol*."

Hannah took a deep breath in response, to avoid saying what she really thought, which was that the world she had woken up in felt about as far as you could get from a holiday fairy tale.

"Look!" Audrey exclaimed, peering through the window. "It's Luke! And those two little girls! Could they be any cuter?"

Hannah leaned forward to get a better look just as, to her horror, Audrey started tapping on the window to get the attention of the inhabitants of the sleigh.

Luke looked up, yelled something that sounded faintly like "Bobcat!" and waved vigorously, as if Hannah and Audrey were a giant ship, slowly pulling away from port. Then he hopped down from the driver's seat of the sleigh, helped both girls down, and headed for the house, one under each arm.

A moment later, they heard a burst of squeals and a scamper of feet as the girls hurtled into the house. Then Luke appeared in the entrance to the dining area, grinning.

"Merry Christmas Eve, ladies," Luke said, with a booming voice.

Audrey giggled.

"Well, Bobcat," he said. "I owe you an apology."

"Hey, Luke!" Audrey said brightly.

Hannah looked up at him, not sure whether he was teasing again, or serious. "For what?" she said cautiously.

"The sleigh rides," Luke said. "I've been giving them all morning, but I'm afraid you're the only one who hasn't gotten one."

"Well," Audrey said, ignoring the fact that she obviously hadn't had a sleigh ride yet, either, "that's easy enough to fix."

Luke clapped his hands. "Well, Bobcat?" he asked. "What do you say?"

"Um," Hannah began, "I'm not sure I—"

"I forgot to mention," Luke said, "the sleigh rides here at Evergreen Inn aren't optional. They're actually a requirement for all the guests."

Hannah found herself trying to hide a smile. "Required sleigh rides?" she said.

Luke nodded. "Yes," he said, keeping his voice and expression both dead serious.

"And what are the consequences," Hannah asked, "if a guest doesn't go on the required sleigh ride?"

Luke grimaced. "We don't really like to get into that if we can help it," he said. "Much easier for all of us if you just come with me now."

Hannah couldn't suppress her smile

She looked across the table at Audrey, who grinned back.

"I guess I don't have any choice, then," Hannah said, rising.

"I guess not," Audrey said, looking as pleased as a cat. She watched Hannah follow Luke toward the door.

For her part, Hannah was simply grateful not to be lying in bed in the middle of the day anymore, or trying to figure out what else to do instead.

She couldn't have guessed, until she got up onto the front seat of the sleigh and felt the delicious slide of the runners as the old horse pulled forward, how much she would love the feel of it: the bracing wind on her face, the crunch and scrape of the snow, but most of all, what it was like to glide through a winter wonderland without being insulated from it behind glass, being blasted by the dry air of a car's heater.

It was chilly, but the chill woke her up and made her feel alive. And it was so beautiful outside that she barely noticed the cold.

"So you can drive a sleigh, too," she commented, as Luke steered the old horse through the woods, on a path he'd obviously cut before, with the girls. "So many hidden talents."

"Wait till you hear me yodel," Luke said.

"Oh, I've heard you yodel before," Hannah said, even though it was clear that he'd been joking.

Luke glanced at her, bemused. "Oh, really?" he said. "When was that?"

"Remember the time you bet me five dollars you could beat me across the lake at the old quarry?"

"I remember the time you jumped into the lake at the old quarry before anyone even told me we were racing," Luke said.

"I thought I heard you yodel then," Hannah said, with a mischievous smile.

"Oh, no," Luke said. "That wasn't yodeling. That was righteous indignation."

Hannah was surprised to discover that the smile on her face now was genuine. And surprised by how easy it was to joke with Luke. She'd tried joking with Trevor, in the first days they'd dated. But after a while, she'd given up. It wasn't that he didn't think she was funny. It was that all he ever did was smile and move on. He never picked up a joke and ran with it, like Luke did. She hadn't realized how much she'd missed it.

"Well," she said. "If you've known how to drive a sleigh all this time, I'm just surprised you never took me out in it when we were kids."

"It never worked when we were kids," Luke said. "It was stuck in the back of the barn. Half the time there was hay piled in it. I think Tim only got it fixed up in time for the—"

He caught himself before he said "wedding," but it was still totally clear to both of them where he had been going.

"I'm really sorry," he said. "Hannah, I didn't mean to bring that up."

Hannah took a deep breath, watching the glistening branches of the trees slide by.

"It's okay," she said.

Luke glanced away from the path to see her face. "How are you doing?" he asked.

Hannah looked down at her hands, lost in the thick fingers of a pair of gray-and-blue ski gloves.

"I just don't understand how I got here," she said in a small voice.

Luke piped up immediately, his voice hot with emotion. "That guy is an idiot," he said. "Any man in the world would be lucky to have you."

"Thank you for saying that," Hannah said.

"I'm not just saying that," Luke insisted. "I don't just say things."

She watched the snow disappearing under the sleigh for a moment, realizing that for as long as she'd known him, this had always been true about Luke. And that it hadn't ever been true about Trevor. He was brilliant at saying the right thing at the right moment. But no matter how long they were together, she never really felt like she knew if he meant it or not.

"It's not that," she said. "It's— You know what I keep wondering?" she asked.

Luke shook his head, deftly steering the horse around a gentle curve.

"I don't know how I ever wound up with someone like Trevor in the first place," she said. "When I was a kid, I always thought I'd wind up with someone more like—"

She stopped herself, realizing she'd almost said *you*.

"Like what?" Luke asked.

"I just think I got carried away with Trevor," Hannah back-tracked, trying to collect her thoughts. "He was just such a force of nature. He needed me so much. And he knew so much about the world. It seemed like he knew everybody. Sometimes it seemed like he knew every*thing*."

"Yep," Luke said, in a tone of voice that made it clear he recollected that quality in Trevor, too—but hadn't exactly found it an attractive trait.

"He knew where he wanted to go in life, and what he wanted to do, and I guess I just—didn't," Hannah said. "At least not when we first got together. And then I just started going along with him, what he wanted."

"What did you think you wanted?" Luke asked. "When you were younger?"

"Someone who loves his family," Hannah said. "Someone who likes the simple things. Just, simple pleasures. Nothing so fancy or complicated. Someone who knows how to do stuff."

She felt her face burning a bit as she said it, not just from the chill, but from the recognition that she was describing Luke, and the embarrassment of whether he'd realize it as well.

But instead of making the moment awkward, he just looked at her with the same teasing expression she'd known ever since they were kids. "Huh," he said, feigning ignorance. "Do you know anyone like that?"

Hannah smiled.

"Tell you what," Luke said, smiling back. "If I think of anyone, I'll let you know."

TWENTY-FIVE

"THOSE LOOK PERFECT," JEANNE said, glancing down at the chestnuts that Iris had been chopping into fine chunks.

"You think so?" Godwin said with a slightly incredulous tone.

Jeanne looked at him, trying to mask her exasperation. When she'd asked Iris to help her in the kitchen a few hours ago, Godwin, who had been chatting with Iris at the front desk, had followed the two of them into the kitchen as if he'd been invited, too. And since then, he'd kept up a steady stream of editorializing.

"She's the chef," Iris said tartly. "Not you."

Earlier in the hour, Jeanne had braced herself when Iris talked back to their cranky guest, expecting a blast of ill temper from him in response.

But by now she had learned that Iris seemed to know exactly how to handle him. Instead of snapping, he just settled back into his stool by the counter as Iris swept the last chopped chestnuts into a small silver mixing bowl.

"Where do you want them?" Iris asked.

Jeanne pointed toward the pot of broth, butter, and herbs she was preparing, to make the chestnut stuffing.

"In there," she said. "Let's give them a chance to soak up some of the flavoring."

Iris wiped her hands on the pale blue gingham half apron she had tied on when she'd come into the kitchen about an hour ago, at Jeanne's request, to help.

Jeanne didn't usually press Iris into service in the kitchen, but dinner tonight was a scheduled seating, on Christmas Eve: everyone at the inn, sitting down together at the same time, for a multicourse meal. That was quite a different prospect from sending out a handful of waffles at a time as people trickled down for breakfast, or sending out stacks of pressed sandwiches and ladling out potato leek soup for lunch.

"Anything else?" Iris asked, glancing around the kitchen like a curious bird, ready to help in any way she could.

Jeanne scanned the place along with her. Hiram's beef was roasting in the oven, giving off tempting aromas of garlic, rosemary, and butter. She had potatoes and onions cut and covered with water, ready to become mashed potatoes. Iris had already washed and dried an epic amount of greens for salads. And although the pies weren't done yet, Jeanne always liked to do those on her own. For some reason, when she baked, a kind of primal instinct took over, and if she had to explain to anyone else what she was doing, she was liable to make mistakes.

Not only that, but if she let Iris go, she was pretty sure Godwin would exit with her.

"I think we're good," Jeanne said, giving Iris a hug. "Thank you so much. I know it was above and beyond."

"I'll say," Godwin said. "You're doing more than double duty, running this hotel and serving in the kitchen."

Iris just shook her head at him, then turned back to Jeanne. "Oh, honey," Iris said. "I was cooking in this kitchen before you were born. It's a pleasure to spend some more time in it. I think I only ate about half the filling for those cinnamon rolls."

"Worth it!" Jeanne said. "You've been such a help."

"Okay," Iris said, waving as she went out the door. "See you at dinner."

To Jeanne's immense relief, Godwin followed Iris out.

Cassie, who had been lounging by the fire, leapt up as they went, and bounded after them.

When the door closed, leaving Jeanne alone in the kitchen, she sighed, feeling the irritation she'd been battling all afternoon rising up in her again.

To fend it off, she picked up one of the apples from the coral-colored ceramic bowl beside the sink, one of her favorite local thrift-store finds, and began to peel.

Her irritation wasn't at Iris, who had been a dream in the kitchen, or even at Godwin, whose barbs were too broad to take very seriously. It was at Tim. When she'd realized that she was swamped, sometime shortly after lunch, her first thought had been simply to press him into service. They'd started the inn, in part, because they loved doing culinary experiments themselves at home so much. He was her favorite sous chef, and the only one she could trust to do things just the way she wanted them done.

She didn't typically ask him to help out in the kitchen at the inn, because she usually had paid help for bigger events, and because there was so much to do around the place.

But today, she'd found herself almost nostalgic to work with him—and she seriously needed help from somebody.

It would have been the perfect cap to their wild ride the night before, to collect the ingredients for the day's meals, to prepare the last one with him. And since things seemed to have thawed a bit between them, part of her felt something she hadn't felt about him in quite some time: she missed just having him around.

So at first, she'd tried to get as far on the meal as she could herself, thinking that she'd ask him to join and help the next time he came into the kitchen—which couldn't be long, because what in the world could possibly need doing in the yard, with everything buried under at least two feet of snow?

But as the afternoon ground on, hour after hour, he didn't show. She called his cell phone to find that it was cradled in the charging dock on the far counter. As her anxiety mounted, she'd actually done a quick search of the inn and their own quarters for him. And by the time she discovered he wasn't anywhere inside, but must be out somewhere, roaming around, yet again, she was so out of patience that she no longer felt like working with him.

On her way back into the kitchen, she'd corralled Iris as her helper, thinking that once she got through the pre-dinner crush, maybe she'd feel a bit more generous toward Tim, wherever he was.

But she didn't. She felt even more irritated than before, because now he'd been gone, without any explanation, for even longer. And because it felt just like it had so many other times when she'd needed him for something, and he'd been out on his own, doing whatever he felt like doing, without consulting her.

She even felt an ache in her heart when she thought back on their sleigh ride the night before. It had felt like they were drawing closer then, but had it all been just an illusion? Had she been fooled by the situation into thinking things might actually change between them, when in fact, here she was, waiting and wondering again, just the same as it had always been?

By the time Tim finally did come in, she had put the finishing touches on half a dozen apple pies, topped with intricate layers of individually cut leaves made from the flaky crust, all arranged in a slightly different pattern, and just popped the first batch into their big oven.

"Hey, what smells good?" Tim said, grinning as he came through the back door, tromping snow everywhere and carrying some giant, unwieldy piece of plywood covered by one of his flannel shirts.

"All of it," Jeanne shot back, but without any welcome in her voice. By this time, she was less than thrilled to see him. "Dinner's ready," she said, in a tone of voice that added, *with no help from you*.

But, as so often happened, Tim didn't seem to pick up on her dissatisfaction.

He laid the dirty plywood in the middle of the counter she'd just cleaned and kissed her cheek, giving her a chill from his cold skin.

"You're amazing, honey," he said. "I don't know how you do it."

Then he caught sight of the pies beyond the oven glass. "How many pies did you make?" he said with a grin. "One for everyone?"

Jeanne's face darkened. As usual, he was picking on how generous she was with the food for the guests. "We've got almost twenty people here for dinner," she began. "Six is—"

Tim shook his head, raising his hands in surrender. "All right, all right," he said. Then he grinned. "Just as long as one of them's for me."

Jeanne's brow furrowed, as she was baffled by his unflappable mood. Had he just decided to pretend everything was fine between them now? Because everything was not fine with her.

"Honey," he said, glancing over at her. "Do you have a minute?"

Despite herself, Jeanne felt a jolt of nervousness. Why did

Tim, who never seemed to want to talk, suddenly want to talk? She didn't want to fight, not on Christmas Eve, not before the big dinner. But she couldn't think of any topic right now that wouldn't wind up as a fight, if they really tried to talk about it.

But she also couldn't think of a good excuse to give him. "Okay," she said warily.

"Okay," Tim said, steering her over toward the grimy plywood. "I have to tell you something."

"What?" Jeanne demanded, but Tim, as usual, would not be rushed.

When he got her where he apparently wanted her to stand, dead in front of whatever he'd just dragged in from the barn, he stopped and looked into her eyes.

"I know I don't always give you what you need," he said.

Jeanne watched him, waiting for the "but . . ." she was sure was coming, but he just dropped his eyes to the floor.

"I've never been good with words," he said. "And I know I get too focused on whatever's in front of me."

Jeanne agreed heartily with both those statements. But something in the humble, gentle way he said them took the will to fight out of her.

"I probably shouldn't have done this," Tim said, looking down.

Jeanne's throat tightened as he said this. What had he done? Taken out some crazy loan to try to save the place? Gotten a new apartment, so he could move out on his own?

Then she realized that he was looking down at the flannel that covered the lumpy plywood.

"I get the impression you would have liked to have me around instead of out there in the barn, working on this," Tim said. "But by the time I realized that, I was almost done making it."

He pulled back the flannel.

Underneath was a delicate model of a handful of small buildings perched on the top of a hill, surrounded by carefully placed model pines.

It took Jeanne a minute to recognize it all: the circle drive, the barn, the sloping drive to the road, the inn itself, all arranged in absolutely perfect detail, down to the wreath of blue blossoms on the front door, the very first thing she had made herself when they first came to the inn so many years ago.

A breath she didn't know she'd been holding escaped from her lips.

"It's our place," she said, threading her arm around his waist and leaning her head against his chest in wonder. "Did you make all this?"

"I'm afraid so," Tim said. "I'm sorry I left you alone so much. But I wanted . . ."

When he clammed up, Jeanne looked at him and saw that his eyes were bright with tears.

He shook his head, trying to smile them away. "I wanted you to have something of this place," he said, drawing a breath to collect himself, "that they couldn't take away. It's all made out of scrap wood from around here, our own pine needles and twigs, and leftover paint I found . . ."

Jeanne put both arms around him now, and squeezed. "It's beautiful," she said, her eyes soaking in every detail of the gorgeous model—and all the work it must have taken him. "Thank you."

Gratefully, Tim wrapped his arms around her.

"No matter what happens next," he said, bowing his head over hers, "we'll always have this to remember it by."

Twenty-Six

MOLLY HADN'T BEEN THRILLED to climb the steps back up to her room.

But when she and Marcus had tramped in the front door together, and she'd finally managed to peel off the damp snow pants and extra layers of wool socks, he'd suddenly turned distant again.

"Well," he said, standing in the front hall in a pair of thick pink wool socks that Molly was almost certain one of the girls had picked out for him, "I've probably kept you from your writing for too long."

"Oh," Iris said from behind her desk. "A little fresh air never hurt anyone." She smiled at Molly. "Clears the cobwebs, doesn't it?" she said. "The Vermont air's especially good for that."

Molly did her best to meet Iris's bright smile with one of her own, but in reality, Molly felt like begging Marcus to keep her from her writing for at least twice as long—not only because she'd enjoyed their walk so much, but because no part of her wanted to go back to that room, and the blank paper waiting for her there.

But when she got back to her room, something had changed.

At first, she couldn't tell what it was. She glanced around, trying to figure it out. She wondered if someone had just been in to clean. She had a sudden, quick hope that perhaps another goodie basket had been delivered in her absence.

Then she realized what it actually was: there was a story wait-ing for her. Maybe it had been there all along, and going for the walk had just knocked something loose in her, so that she could fi-nally recognize it. Or maybe it had arrived while she was gone.

But in any case, this time, she didn't hesitate.

She walked straight over to the desk, sat down, and immedi-ately began to scrawl a few lines on the blank piece of paper that had been waiting there for her for days. Then she filled the rest of the page with a bright sketch, set that page aside, picked up an-other piece of blank paper, and began to scrawl again.

When she looked up, hours later, the sun had dropped nearly to the horizon, and she didn't just have the few sheets of a re-spectable beginning, she had a serious stack of pages of a story that ran all the way from beginning to end.

Somewhere downstairs, a bell was ringing.

Had Iris said something about a dinner bell when she checked in?

In any case, she was more than ready to leave the room—and to have a bite to eat, especially now that she'd returned to notic-ing the signs of daily life around her, and could smell the incredi-ble scents drifting up from the kitchen, both savory and sweet.

But she wasn't ready to leave the manuscript behind. It had taken her so long to find the story, and it had come so fast, that she was half afraid that if she didn't take it with her, she'd come back upstairs later to discover the whole afternoon had just been some kind of daydream, and the proof of it had vanished.

So she scooped the pages up between the wings of a red leather manuscript portfolio, tucked it under her arm, and went downstairs.

When she reached the ground floor, it seemed that everyone else in the inn had already gotten the memo.

She tried to hide the portfolio as much as possible as she came downstairs, sure that Iris would catch sight of it with her eagle eye and begin to ask questions Molly wasn't sure she was ready to answer.

But to her surprise, Iris wasn't seated behind the desk.

And everyone was crowded together into the lobby and lounge areas, snacking on canapés and swigging what looked to be a spiced cranberry punch.

"Is it dinner? I heard a bell," she asked the first people she saw, a pair of older couples who had been swapping stories of Christmas in the 1960s, when one of the women had apparently gotten a Barbie for which she'd sewn a business suit, because she wanted her daughter to know she could be a businesswoman, not just a fashion model.

"In half an hour," one of the women told her. "It's just a warning bell."

"Not that we needed any encouragement," the other woman said, laying her hand on the arm of the man next to her. "Frank's been down here for an hour, lurking outside the kitchen like a puppy waiting for crumbs."

"I would *trade* a puppy for some of Jeanne's crumbs," Frank said.

Molly smiled and moved on, heading for a table stacked with appetizers, where she discovered Iris, explaining the hors d'oeuvres to Godwin, the grouchy old Brit.

"You'll want to try that," Iris told him, then looked over at Molly with a smile, to include her in the conversation. "It's cheddar, with a wonderful kick of horseradish."

"I've had cheddar horseradish spread before," Godwin said in a dismissive tone.

Iris just handed him one of Jeanne's handmade crackers,

topped with a healthy smear of the spread. "Not like this," she said.

When Godwin couldn't seem to find a way to contradict Iris after munching down the cracker, Molly decided to take her advice and try the cheddar spread, too, along with other tasty-looking foods from the buffet. The simple bites of sausage were so delicious that as soon as she tasted it, Molly immediately understood why it had been served plain.

But as she filled her plate, she felt a tug on the back of her pant leg.

"Molly!" Bailey said. "Molly! Come sit with us!"

Molly turned around to see Bailey and Addison, both standing at attention like a pair of sheepdogs ready to herd her home. Nearby sat Marcus, at the bench along the fireplace with two half-empty plates next to him.

She hesitated, not sure whether or not she was really welcome, but at Marcus's smile, she allowed the girls to lead her over, and sat down in the warmth cast by the dancing glow of the flames, balancing the folder on her knees.

"What's that?" Bailey asked immediately.

"Oh," Molly said, pulling it a little closer. "It's just a manuscript folder."

She could see interest light in Marcus's eyes, but before he could say anything, Bailey tugged on his sleeve and demanded, "What's a manuscript?"

"It's like a book," Addison said quickly, jumping in to make sure everyone knew she had the answer without having to be told.

But Bailey was no intellectual slouch herself. As soon as she had this bit of information, she had no trouble at all putting the pieces together.

"Is it *your* book?" she asked.

"Yes," Molly said.

As expected, Bailey began to bounce on her toes, and even Addison's eye grew wide.

"Is it *done*?" Addison asked.

"Honey," Marcus said. "Molly may not want to talk about . . ."

But Molly smiled at him to let him know it was all right.

"It is," she said. "I finished it this afternoon. Not all the drawings yet. That will take me some more time. But the story goes from beginning to end."

She'd never before had an actual kid around to celebrate with when she'd finished a book, even though all her books were for kids. And not one of the adults she'd ever shared the news of a finished manuscript with had ever had a reaction even remotely as satisfying as Addison's.

Addison threw her arms out in a kind of rapture, drawing in a huge breath. Then she clasped her arms around herself, shaking her head in wonder, as if Molly had suddenly been replaced by an angel sent from God himself.

"Can we read it?" Bailey demanded. "Will you read it to us?"

This seemed to snap Addison out of her trance. "Yes!" she said. "Read it to us!"

Molly glanced around, suddenly full of nerves. She still felt some of the fading exhilaration of discovering the story as she wrote it. But now she was moving into the phase after writing, when she just felt raw and vulnerable, and she had no idea whether what she had written was really any good or not.

"Pleeease," Addison said. "Please!"

The combination of the girls' rapture at hearing the story was done and the unapologetic begging was too much for Molly.

She glanced at the dining room, then opened the red folder.

"All right," she said, running her hand over the cover image she had sketched when she finished the manuscript: a silver fairy peeking out between the branches of a snowy pine. "Are you girls ready for a story?"

"Yes!" the girls chorused.

Molly felt so nervous when she flipped to the first page that at first she could barely read her own words. But when she was finally able to take them in, she grinned in delight. "'Jasmine was worried that their snowman might get cold,'" she began, "'so she made her little sister Ava give him her coat.'" It was a great opening, and the girls were immediately captivated to discover that the two main characters were a pair of sisters, one about five, and one about eight.

"Like us!" Bailey said, managing to bounce on Molly's lap with her eyes still glued to the page.

"Is it about us?" Addison asked.

"These girls might be something like you," Molly said. "I guess you'll have to wait and see."

The girls had been thrilled to hear about characters like themselves, but they were totally captivated when the story's young heroines discovered a Christmas fairy living in a pine tree in their backyard, caught her in a butterfly net, and began trying to use the ten wishes the fairy promised them in exchange for her freedom.

The problem was that none of the girls' wishes turned out just the way they had imagined. They wanted to get their father a new car, instead of the handmade cards they'd made for him in school. But there was no room for the big new car in their tiny garage.

So the girls wished for a bigger garage, but half of it appeared in the neighbor's yard, which made the neighbor furious.

So they wished for the neighbor to go away, but then the neighbor's daughter, one of their best friends, came over to announce that the family was moving, all the way out to California.

Eventually, the girls wound up living in a castle where their old house used to stand, complete with a moat and a hungry elephant bellowing in the backyard, and just one more wish.

"What would you wish?" Molly asked, before she turned to the last pages.

"She never wished that she could fly," Bailey said. "I wish that I could fly."

"I would wish for a hundred more wishes," Addison said. "And then when I used up ninety-nine, I would wish for a thousand more."

"Maybe I really should have you negotiate my next contract," Marcus joked.

"I'd wish for another plate of these cheese toasts," a man said.

When Molly looked up, surprised to see who had spoken, she realized that the guests of the inn had been drawn like a magnet to the story, and were all crowded around the fireplace now, waiting with bated breath to hear the ending.

The man who had spoken was a big, buff guy who Molly guessed was the father of the bride in the wedding that had been called off. He grinned for a minute at the laughter his joke produced, but then his face turned serious.

"Not really," he said. "If I had just one wish, I'd give it to my daughter. I'd give her anything she could wish for."

"Oh, Daddy," said a pretty brunette on the opposite side of the room, who was now standing close enough to Molly to be able to see the illustrations over Molly's shoulder. "I couldn't wish for a better dad than you."

"I'd wish for every Christmas to be as full of love as this one," said Eileen.

"And as full of apple pie," her husband added. "Could you folks smell that cooking, too?"

Standing beside the brunette behind Molly was a tall blonde, who Molly suspected must have been her bridesmaid. For some reason, tears had sprung to her eyes as everyone went around the room, saying their wishes.

As Molly watched, the brunette squeezed her around the waist and whispered, "I know what you'd wish for."

At this, the blonde shook her head and wiped away an errant tear.

"What would you wish for?" Iris asked Godwin, the grouchy old Brit, who was standing beside her near the back of the horseshoe-shaped crowd.

"They don't come true," he grouched. "Not if you tell them."

"Oh, come on," Iris said, giving him a friendly swat.

At first, Godwin's face turned even grouchier. But then he got a faraway look in his eyes. "I guess," he said, "I'd wish to come back here."

The gathered crowd let out a little sigh at the kind words, which were even more surprising coming from him.

"What would you wish?" he asked Iris.

"Oh," she said. "I always thought I was going to travel the world one day. Maybe I'd wish for that."

"But *what happens*?" Bailey finally bellowed, cutting through the chatter, as more and more people blurted out their wishes, and the people around answered with their own.

Suddenly, all eyes were on Molly again. But this time, she wasn't nervous. She couldn't wait to share the ending.

And when Molly turned the page, what the two sisters in the

story actually wished was that everything would go back to just the way it had been. In the end, the only thing that had changed was them. Suddenly, they realized how much they loved everything they already had.

"'The end,'" Molly said, reading from the last page, where the final words were surrounded by a sketch of a ball of glowing light at the end of the fairy's wand as she flew away into the night.

As she closed the red folder, the whole lounge erupted into applause.

Then, to her surprise, someone began to sing. Almost immediately, the whole group had burst into a noisy, laughter-filled, and not completely in-tune rendition of "Joy to the World."

And just as the last verse drew to a close, a bell began to ring.

Twenty-Seven

"DINNER," AUDREY SAID WITH a sigh, squeezing Hannah's waist. "Finally."

"No," Hannah said, pulling away from her. "It's not the same bell."

"Then what is it?" Audrey said as the bell rang again. She glanced out the window. "Did you see that?"

Hannah peered out into the night beyond the windows, and the ghostly blue drifts of snow that still covered everything she could see. "See what?" she asked.

"I thought I saw someone out there," Audrey said.

"Santa?" Hannah said. "Maybe he comes early in Vermont, because we're so far north."

Audrey didn't even laugh at her joke.

But although the gathered crowd had now launched into a version of "We Wish You a Merry Christmas," apparently Hannah and Audrey weren't the only ones who had heard the bell.

At the back of the crowd, Iris detached herself, and headed for the lobby.

"The door," Audrey said, clutching Hannah's hand. "The door!"

Then, before Hannah could ask her what she was talking about, Audrey pushed her way through the crowd and vanished into the lobby.

A moment later, all the singing was brought to an abrupt halt as a piercing scream cut through the song and silenced it.

As one, the gathered crowd turned toward the lobby. Molly stood up from the fireplace bench so that she could see, along with the father of the two children she had been reading to, who drew his daughters closer to him.

For a long moment, they stood there frozen, not even murmuring to each other.

Then Hannah's father began to stride forward, barreling toward the lobby as if he was willing to take on whatever had just come through the door, man or bear.

But before he even reached the boundary of the lounge, a couple appeared in the wide entryway.

Cassie, who had been hoovering up any scrap of food that anyone let fall to the ground, suddenly came to attention as the crowd turned to them. Her barrel chest thrust out, her ears came forward, and her tail waved tentatively, not sure whether to bark a warning at a stranger or pounce on an invited guest with canine glee.

It took Hannah a long moment to even recognize that the woman was Audrey, and another to understand who she was clinging to: Jared, who was barely recognizable in the snow gear he was wearing, and because of his red face and what seemed to be ice clinging to his eyebrows. But he still had the same unmistakable grin that would have given him away to anybody who knew him.

When Audrey turned back to the crowd and saw the somber, even frightened faces of the other guests, her smile faded for a minute. "Wait," she said. "What happened?"

Then she realized why all the faces were turned to her. "Oh my gosh," she said, her smile lighting up her face again. "I didn't mean to scare you! I was just so happy. This is my husband, Jared! He just made it all the way from Philly."

Instead of defending the gathering from Jared, Hannah's father was the first to embrace him in a bear hug, with Audrey hanging on for dear life, because she wasn't about to give up Jared's arm herself.

"I'm sorry it took me so long to get here, baby," Jared said, looking down at Audrey after Hannah's father had released them. "I went back to the airport at five a.m. and sweet-talked an airline clerk into giving me the first flight that landed me anywhere near Vermont. Turned out they had an early-morning flight to Philly. They took pity on me and let me ride in a jump seat with the crew since I was military. And I even managed to get a car when I got there, but when I got to Vermont, they'd closed the roads. So I tried the first drive I found, and I met this old farmer checking on his sheep with a snowmobile. We found a ewe of his who'd fallen in a ditch, so I helped him pull her out, and when I told him what I was doing there, he gave me a ride here. Longest snowmobile ride of my life."

"Cool," crooned the voice of a small child by the fireplace, with breathless wonder.

Everyone laughed, and Audrey reached out, lovingly brushing the chunks of ice out of Jared's hair.

"I can't believe you're here," she said, tears running freely down her face. "I can't believe you're here."

"And you were trying to act like you were all cool with me not coming for Christmas," Jared said, laying a formidable kiss on her cheek, then leaning back to look at her with a big grin. "I knew you didn't mean it."

"Well," Iris said, following the two young lovebirds into the room from the lobby. She'd apparently been the one to open the door for Jared. "I guess we've got one more guest tonight. I'm just not sure where we're going to find the room," she added with a wink.

"There's room!" Audrey called joyfully. "There's room for him!"

"I did notice," Iris said, raising one eyebrow archly, "that you two failed to observe the mistletoe tradition when this young man arrived at the house."

Jared looked from Iris to Audrey in confusion.

"You didn't kiss her!" Iris said. "Back in my day, that would have been the first order of business!"

"Well," Jared said, taking Audrey in his arms. "We're very sorry. Let's fix that right now."

As he kissed Audrey, another bell began to ring: this time the same one that had drawn the crowd together a little earlier that evening.

"That's the dinner bell," Audrey said, turning to Jared. "You're just in time."

And as Jeanne came out of the kitchen, carrying a gorgeous, gigantic roast scented with garlic and rosemary, Audrey and Jared followed her, leading the rest of the guests in.

As the lounge began to empty, Hannah felt as if her own heart were emptying out with it. She was overjoyed for Audrey. If she could have made any wish that night, it might have been that Jared would somehow be magically transported there in time for the holiday. Audrey didn't complain about much, but Hannah knew being separated from Jared hurt her—not to mention the disappointment of having gotten her hopes up in the first place, only to see them dashed by the storm.

But now that he was here, it just reminded her that this was supposed to be her rehearsal dinner. And tonight she was alone. She didn't blame Audrey for it, not in the least. In fact, it made her wonder how often she'd made Audrey feel the same way, when Hannah got lost in her own world with Trevor and forgot that, with Jared deployed, Audrey was often on her own, just as Hannah was now.

She especially didn't want her own failed wedding to cast any shadow on the joy of Audrey and Jared's reunion. There was no reason for them to spend even a second thinking of that, when they were just so happy right now to see each other.

But she couldn't help but wonder if this was what the rest of her life would be like: watching other people find a happiness that always eluded her.

She shook her head, but the thought clung there stubbornly until she felt an arm thread through the crook of her own elbow.

Before she even turned her head, a hint of rosewater lotion perfumed the air—her mother's familiar scent.

"Hey, honey," her mom said. "How are you doing?"

Hannah didn't answer. She didn't have an answer to give. But something in her mom's eyes let her know that she understood.

Instead, she just hugged her mom, laying her head on her shoulder just like she had when she was a little kid.

"We love you so much, honey," her mother said, stroking her hair.

"I love you, too," Hannah said.

Dinner, when they walked in, was already a riot of sounds and smells.

Jeanne and Tim had pulled all the small square tables in the dining area together to form one long one, right down the center of the room, and even before Jeanne laid the roast proudly in the center, the table was piled high with delectables.

Baskets of golden rolls with ramekins of butter and jam in glistening jewel tones: purple, red, deep orange. Bowls of green salad with slices of oranges, almonds, and mint leaves, beside silver boats full of some creamy vinaigrette, loaded with fresh chives. Dishes full of mashed potatoes, their brown skins still peeking through, as well as a sweet potato parsnip mash, and bowls of fluffy stuffing. Green beans and carrots both glistened with butter, and the carrots were also garnished with honeycomb.

Between all the tempting dishes were gorgeous arrangements of evergreen boughs, juniper, and bare branches tied together with thick wine-colored velvet that reached up toward the ceiling.

Chairs scudded as everyone found seats.

But before anyone could dive in, the booming voice of Hannah's father cut through the general din, along with the sound of silverware clanging on glass.

When the crowd turned to him, he was holding a water glass and a spoon, a serious expression on his face. "Just a minute, everybody," he said. "Just a minute."

Hannah's heart twisted with love as she realized what he was about to do.

"Well," her father said, glancing over the crowd as it grew quiet. "As I guess you all know now, this wasn't exactly the toast I was planning to give my daughter this weekend."

He glanced at Hannah, then glanced away before his voice could break.

"But I still want to make a toast to my daughter," he said. "She's the smartest and the kindest and the most beautiful young woman I know."

"Wait," Hannah's mother said beside him. "Are you saying I'm not young?"

As the crowd laughed, Bob put his arm around her and drew her closer to him.

"Hannah's been a constant source of amazement and joy to both her mother and me," Hannah's father went on. "But most of all, I've always been impressed by her strength. I still am, honey," he said, lifting the water glass toward her.

Hannah felt a deep pang of gratitude for her father, and she beamed up at him through tears. She felt completely and perfectly whole in this moment, surrounded by a room full of love and unexpected support. She forced herself to breathe and take it all in.

Then he looked around the room. "So I want to toast Hannah. And I want to toast Jeanne's hospitality. Jeanne's and Tim's."

"And Iris's," Godwin piped up. "This is her place, after all."

"That's right, that's right," Bob said with a smile. "The rest of us are just visiting. And I want to toast the rest of us," he said. "Because you've all made this such a special holiday. Not the one we imagined. But maybe," he said, "the one we needed."

At this, his wife squeezed him, and the crowd burst into cheers.

Hannah joined in with the cheers and hugged her father. Then everyone took their seats and dove into the meal, pausing between bites to exclaim how delicious it was.

"I think you must have a magic table out there in the kitchen, Jeanne," Hannah's father called down the table, as Jeanne brought out another round of one of the handmade sodas she'd produced for the meal: seltzer with a cranberry-and-pine syrup. "Like in the fairy tales, one that makes a new meal every time you wish. I pawed through your fridge the other day, looking for another grilled cheese sandwich, and I could swear there wasn't a darn thing there. I don't know how you did it."

"The only magic in that kitchen is Jeanne," Tim said, setting down a fresh basket of rolls and handing the empty one to Luke, who was already carrying a tray full of dirty dishes to the kitchen, pinch-hitting as a waiter for the evening.

As the other guests first took their places, Hannah had realized, to her surprise, that she had been keeping an eye out to see where Luke wound up. Iris was at the table, along with everyone else, and for a while there was a seat beside her, until Godwin, the grouchy Brit, took it.

When she finally did see Luke, though, he was marching in and out of the kitchen, refreshing bowls of mashed potatoes and refilling water glasses.

"Can I bring you anything at all, ma'am?" he asked at one point, stopping by her seat.

Hannah thought for a moment, trying to come up with the craziest request she could. "Pheasant under glass?" she finally said.

Luke had grinned at her. "Be careful what you wish for," he said. "Jeanne might actually have that out there somewhere."

But when the tables had been cleared of the remains of dinner and the serving dishes, Jeanne, Tim, and Luke all filed back out of the kitchen, each carrying two pies, one in each hand. And after serving slices all around, Jeanne and Tim pulled up their own chairs at the head of the table.

But Luke wandered down the table to where Hannah was sitting.

"How about some company for dessert?" he asked.

Hannah, who had been watching him out of the corner of her eye, started to scoot her own seat over as far as she could to make room for another chair. But Audrey, who had been sitting next to her, with Jared on the other side, began to poke at Jared's shoulder.

"Scoot back," she said.

Baffled but game, Jared scooted his chair back from the table, and Audrey plopped herself happily down in his lap.

"There's an empty seat," she said, nodding at the chair she'd just vacated. "What are you waiting for?"

Hannah shook her head, trying to suppress a smile as Luke sat down and set his own piece of pie on the table. Thankfully, Hannah's mother was deeply embroiled in a conversation with Frank and Eileen, apparently plotting a Caribbean vacation they all planned to take next winter, so she didn't seem to notice as Luke settled in.

At the first bite of pie, Luke closed his eyes in apparent ecstasy, took a deep breath, and opened them again before taking another forkful. "This is out of this world," he said. "I swear, I used to sit in that kitchen watching her work for hours, and I still don't know how she does it."

"I'm glad they let you sit down for dessert," Hannah said.

"What do you mean, dessert?" Luke said. "This is the first time I've eaten all night. It's dinner. When I have my third piece, that'll be dessert," he said. "The second one will just be seconds."

Hannah laughed.

Beside her, her mother turned, startled. She took a long look at Luke and then slowly, deliberately, turned back to her own conversation, as if trying not to do anything to disturb the situation.

"How'd you like dinner?" Luke asked.

"It was wonderful," Hannah said. And she realized, as she said it, that she meant it, even though it had been very different from the rehearsal dinner she'd expected to have.

"Yeah?" Luke said, almost surprised.

She nodded.

"I'm glad to hear it," he said. "I thought it might not be an easy night."

"It's better than I thought," Hannah said. As she said it, she realized that could mean two things: better than the awful night she thought she might have after the breakup, or better than the rehearsal dinner she thought she'd have had if she and Trevor were still together. She would never have guessed that anything could be better than the perfect dinner she had planned, especially not if Trevor wasn't there. But somehow this night still felt good.

"Hannah," Luke said. "I feel like I need to tell you something."

She felt a little flash of fear at the serious way he'd said it, and the look on his face when her eyes met his. What could he possibly have to tell her? Did he have a girlfriend he hadn't mentioned yet? And why, she thought, with faint annoyance, would that be the first thing that popped into her mind to worry about?

But instead of asking any of this, she just said simply, "What?"

"I've never met anyone else like you," Luke said quickly, like he wasn't sure he could get the words out. "My whole life. You're a really special girl. I hope you know that."

"Thank you," Hannah said, because she couldn't think of anything else to say.

"And you deserve someone special. Someone really special," he added, "who knows what he's got in you."

Hannah felt a twinge at this, thinking back on Trevor. How could she have been so stupid? How could she have given so much to a man who never really loved her back?

But Luke wasn't finished. "You should come see me some-time, out in the wilderness," he said. "I think you'd like it. It's a lot like this place is, actually."

"I always liked it here," Hannah said.

"I mean, I know now may not be a good time. For a couple of reasons," he said with a wry smile. "I try not to take people on wilderness adventures when there's three feet of snow on the ground, in general."

"I don't know," Hannah said. "You did pretty well with me yesterday."

"Still," Luke said. "Maybe not optimal. But just when you feel like it, sometime. You want to get away for the weekend, see something new." She met his eyes, which looked into hers, full of meaning. "Maybe in the summer. Or the spring," he added.

"That sounds . . ." Hannah began, but before she could finish, something down at the other end of the table caught her attention.

Jeanne and Tim were both rising and collecting the dishes of the guests around them. When Jeanne's eyes met Luke's, she gave him a meaningful nod.

"Duty calls," Luke said.

Hannah flashed him a little smile as he picked up his own plate, and hers.

As he walked away, Audrey leaned in.

"Did he just ask you out?" she said. "That sounded like he was asking you out."

"I don't know," Hannah said.

"Would you be happy if he did?" Audrey asked.

Hannah shrugged, and after a moment, Jared pulled Audrey back over to talk with him.

But as the party broke up around her, Hannah stayed still at the center of it. Would she be happy to go on a date with Luke? What would it even be like? And how could she even be thinking about Luke and not Trevor, on tonight of all nights? Hannah shoved the thought from her mind.

TWENTY-EIGHT

"NO, DADDY!" BAILEY SAID as Marcus reached down, trying to steady the giant plate of chocolate walnut brown sugar cookies that the girls had foraged from the kitchen before going up for the night. "I can do it!"

"Just because you can doesn't always mean you should, dear," Iris said, as they went by.

Bailey snatched the plate back and the cookies reeled crazily, but now well out of reach of Marcus, who was coming up the stairs behind Bailey with Molly trailing a step behind.

Addison, going up the stairs side by side with Bailey, glanced at the unsteady stack of cookies, and without turning a hair, planted her palm smack in the middle of the top one, stabilizing the whole tower of sweets, without eliciting a single peep of protest from Bailey.

When they got to Molly's room, the two girls carried the plate immediately over to the fireplace opposite the foot of Molly's bed, where Bailey set it down on the cold brick just beyond the grate itself.

"Not there," Addison said. "He might step on it."

In answer, Bailey dragged over a small antique table from its station beside a nearby chair, and plunked the cookies down on it.

"There," she said. "Now Santa will definitely come."

"Okay, girls," Marcus said. "Time to get ready for bed."

As the girls turned for Molly's office and their pair of day-beds, Marcus started to follow, but this time Addison looked back with a protest. "We can put our pajamas on ourselves," she said. "We'll tell you when we're ready."

"Okay," Marcus said, somewhat surprised as his girls disappeared into the other room and pulled the door shut behind themselves.

He looked ruefully down at the plate of cookies. "I've tried to get it through their heads that the snacks we leave out are a present we leave for Santa, because he brings us such nice gifts," he said. "But as far as I can tell, the girls seem to see the cookies more as bait."

"They might not be that far wrong on that," Molly said.

Marcus smiled.

"You do realize," Molly said, "that if you leave those cookies here in my room, they will definitely be gone by morning."

"You'd be doing me a favor," Marcus said. "If they wake up and there are still cookies on the plate, that's a dead giveaway. Especially when the cookies are this good," he added. "Not even Santa could pass them up, even if he's eaten hundreds of others."

"The girls still believe in Santa?" Molly said.

"Officially, they do," Marcus said. "Although I sometimes wonder if Addison has already wised up, and calculated she can ask for more outrageous things from Santa than she'd dare from her dad. What makes me suspicious is that she doesn't *seem* suspicious. It's Bailey who's been asking all the relevant questions this year."

He sighed.

"Probably I should have told them both by now," he said. "I just haven't had anyone to talk with about it. I hope I haven't already scarred them both for life."

Molly shook her head. "I highly doubt it," she said. "In fact, I suspect just the opposite."

"Well, you haven't known us very long," Marcus said with a smile.

"Long enough to at least know that," Molly said. "You tell them whenever you think is best. They're good girls. They'll handle it."

"Daddy!" Bailey cried, flinging open the door. "We're ready."

"Are those your pajamas?" Marcus asked, incredulity in his voice. Bailey was wearing a red flannel top, with a gigantic skirt made from seemingly infinite layers of tulle, complete with glittered stars.

"It's Christmas," Bailey said, in a tone that implied all normal rules of life were void as a result of the holiday.

"But don't you want to wear your skirt tomorrow?" Marcus asked.

Bailey nodded vigorously. "*And* tonight," she said.

Defeated by this logic, Marcus headed for the little office.

With a sigh, Molly sank down in the chair beside her unlit fireplace, watching him disappear into the office with a faint sense of wistfulness. There was something that felt right about the fact that his little family should all be together on Christmas Eve. But she already felt a tug of nostalgia for the night before, when she'd been the one the girls asked to read. And spending time with the girls in that warm little room, she realized, had been more pleasant than sitting alone in hers.

Suddenly, Addison appeared in the doorway, waving her hand frantically as if she were trying to flag down a passing ship.

"Hey, honey," Molly said. "Is everything okay?"

In answer, Addison just kept waving, this time with an increasingly vexed expression on her face. "You have to come, too," she said.

"Kiddo," Molly said, starting in to explain that the holidays were a time for family. "It's Christmas Eve—"

"Not without you!" Addison said.

Behind her, Marcus's big frame appeared in the doorway.

"They won't even let me read a book to them unless you're here," he said. "Do you mind?"

"Mind" was not at all the word for it, Molly thought, as she crossed her room toward the office. What she felt was grateful.

And when she entered the room and saw the delighted grins on the faces of both the girls, she felt a sudden rush of happy tears in her throat.

"*You* read to us!" Bailey said from her bed, waving a book around. "You're better than Daddy."

Molly looked at Marcus, to make sure it was all right, with a slight grimace at Bailey's criticism. But Marcus just laughed it off. "Kids," he said. "They're tough critics."

Then he sat down at the foot of Addison's bed, while Addison climbed in and snuggled under the covers.

"Here!" Bailey said, handing the book to Molly, who took a cue from Marcus and sat down beside her. As if it was the most natural thing in the world, Bailey ducked under Molly's arm and leaned against her, picking absently at the blanket, a little pouf of her tulle skirt poking out under the edge.

The story was an old Christmas classic, a beautifully illustrated version of " 'Twas the Night Before Christmas," and when Molly finished, Bailey seemed to have fallen completely asleep, her head on Molly's lap.

But Addison was alert, not willing to let any possibility pass her by.

"Now Daddy," she said, handing her father the book she had been reserving in her own hands.

Marcus gave Molly a look across the room, as if to ask, *Do you mind?*

Molly smiled in response. There was just about nothing, she was realizing, that she would mind less: him, and the kids, and the low, quiet rumble of his voice as he started to read. She knew the story he was reading as well, about a Christmas tree light that had always wanted to be free of its string, and wander the sky like a star. But it was hard to keep track of the story, because she kept getting lost in the sound of Marcus's voice, the soft light in the room, and a story she was starting to write on her own, almost without meaning to: that this might be the beginning of a much longer story, a story where their accidental meeting was just the beginning of a lifetime of days and nights like these, with the four of them together, almost like a family.

As Marcus read on, so did her story. The seasons changed, winter to spring, spring to summer. She saw the girls splashing happily in a summer lake, watched the leaves turn from green to gold and red, saw them getting bigger, and more confident. In no time at all, Bailey had learned how to read for herself. But no matter how the time and place shifted, they were all still together, and Marcus always had the same gentle, questioning glance and quick smile. She even imagined them returning to the inn in years to come, remembering this year as they settled in around new fires and new feasts.

When Marcus finally finished the book, Addison was still wakeful enough to offer a small protest. "Another one," she said sleepily. "It's Christmas!"

"That's why you want to get a lot of good sleep tonight,"

Marcus said patiently. "So you'll have lots of energy to open your presents and play with them tomorrow morning."

This rejoinder, along with her own sleepiness, seemed to set Addison happily off on the road to dreamland. But the end of the story, or Marcus and Addison's exchange, had woken Bailey out of her own slumber.

"Hey, sweetheart," Molly said, shifting Bailey so that her head rested on her pillow, instead of Molly's leg, and trying to tuck the tulle skirt down a bit so it wouldn't be a perfect nightmare of wrinkles in the morning.

"I have a wish," Bailey murmured.

"A wish, huh?" Molly said, glancing over at Marcus, who winked at her. "What's your wish?"

"I wish that you and Daddy get married," Bailey said. "So we can be together all the time."

Bailey's wish was so close to her own that when Molly heard it said aloud at first she froze, with the eerie feeling that somehow the little girl had been able to read her thoughts.

Then Marcus's voice broke in, still measured, but now filled with alarm. "That's not going to happen, girls," he said definitively. "Molly is just our friend."

Stung, Molly stood up quickly, then leaned over clumsily to give Bailey a kiss good night.

"Me too, me too!" Addison said.

Unable to look at Marcus, Molly engaged in an awkward dance with him, trying to reach Addison with her own good-night kiss.

Once she'd delivered it, she fled the office.

Back in the dim quiet of her own room, she stood for a minute, her heart pounding. All her instincts told her to flee this room as well. But it was her own room, after all. And where would she go? With the place still snowed in, there was no place in the house where she would be safe from running into Marcus.

Better to stand and face him now, she thought, and turned around just as he followed her out the door.

"Hey," he said. He winced as she finally met his eyes, then glanced away about as quickly as he could. "Wow. I'm so sorry about that. They have very . . . vivid imaginations."

Molly shook her head. "It's a compliment, really," she said. "It's sweet."

Marcus breathed a sigh of relief.

"Thanks for understanding," he said, already heading for the door. "Uh, good night."

Then he stepped into the hall and pulled the door shut behind himself, leaving her alone.

Twenty-Nine

"THE CHEF! THE CHEF!" someone called from the kitchen door as Jeanne stood at the counter, wrapping up a tray full of the remains of the parsnip-and-sweet-potato mash.

When she turned around, the older couple who had taken refuge with them the day before, Frank and Eileen, came through the door, followed closely by Bob and Stacy, Hannah's parents.

Frank was applauding loudly, joined by Bob. "Bravo!" Frank called. "Bravo!"

Tim, who had been scraping plates at the wash sink, looked over his shoulder curiously.

"I couldn't stop him," Eileen said, smiling. "I told him you were probably busy cleaning up."

"Heck, after that meal," Frank said, "I'm willing to help!"

Luke, who had followed shortly on the heels of the two couples, carrying a large tray of dirty glasses, deftly navigated around them and laid the glasses down on the counter with a slight clink.

"Be careful," he said. "She might not put you to work, but I will."

Frank grinned. "I don't usually barge my way into the kitchens of fine restaurants," he said, "but I had to see this one. Just to make sure you didn't really have a magic table hidden back here."

"That meal was fantastic," he said. "Out of this world."

Jeanne smiled at the praise, but some part of her still hummed with anxiety, making it hard for her to soak it up. She couldn't believe they'd managed to get the food they needed last night. Or put it all together into a meal for so many guests, with the skeleton crew they'd had to operate with.

Eileen rubbed Frank's back affectionately. "When we got here, we were just grateful to have a roof over our heads," she said. "We had no idea this was going to be one of the best experiences we've ever had as travelers."

"The best," Frank said. "I'll say it. I think it's been the best."

"And it's not just that incredible meal," Eileen said. "Everything about this place is so . . ." She paused a moment, searching for the word. "Thoughtful," she finally finished.

"Oh, Jeanne doesn't do anything around here without putting thought into it," Tim said over his shoulder, but he was smiling as he said it, and when he winked at Jeanne, she smiled back.

"Look, I like a nice wallpaper as much as the next guy," Frank said, "but what I really love about this place is the way you took us in and made us feel like we were part of something."

"They've always done that," Stacy said. She and Bob looked happy, but they were far less effusive than the newer guests, and Jeanne could guess why. "From the very beginning," Stacy added.

"We weren't sure how this Christmas was going to feel," Eileen said. "We booked this trip because it was our first holiday in over twenty years without the kids."

Stacy nodded sympathetically. "That's a big change," she said.

"Yep." Eileen nodded. "But you welcomed us in as if we were family. Even though you'd never met us before."

"That's what we always hoped to do here," Jeanne said. "Treat everyone so well they feel like family."

"Well, mission accomplished," Frank said. He slapped his hand on the counter and pointed at Jeanne. "And don't think you're rid of us after this time, either. Because we're coming back!"

"I've already talked with Iris about booking sometime in June or July," Eileen said. "I can't wait to see what this place looks like in the summer, all in bloom."

Tim came up behind Jeanne and gave her a squeeze, checking to make sure she was okay. But Jeanne managed to smile.

"We would love to see you here this summer," she said, which was absolutely true.

"Okay, well," Frank said. "We don't want to get in the way."

"Then pick up a towel and get to work!" Luke joked, heading out to the dining room to collect another tray of dishes.

"You want?" Frank said, picking up a stray towel from the counter.

Jeanne laughed and shook her head. "Maybe the next time you come," she said.

"All right, then," Frank said. "Thanks again."

Eileen gave Jeanne a warm hug, and the two of them trailed out the door, while Stacy and Bob lingered.

When the door shut behind them, Stacy just looked into Jeanne's eyes, trying to smile. But after a moment, her eyes filled with tears.

"Hey," Jeanne said, gathering Stacy up in a hug as well.

Stacy hugged her back warmly, from the heart. Then she pulled away, wiping the tears from her eyes. "I'm sorry," she said, shaking her head. "I know it's Christmas Eve. I shouldn't be crying."

"It's always okay to cry," Jeanne said. "You've got good reason."

"Ah," Bob growled, realizing the subject of the conversation. "Good riddance."

"I just wish—" Stacy said. "I wish—" Then she fell silent, leaving the sentence unfinished.

"I know," Jeanne said. "It wasn't what any of us expected."

"No, it wasn't," Stacy agreed, leaning into Jeanne as Jeanne slid her arm around Stacy's shoulder. Then she looked at Jeanne with a faint smile. "But if it had to happen," she said, "I'm glad it happened here. This was the only place in the world where Christmas could still feel even a little bit like Christmas to us under the circumstances. Thanks for that."

"Of course," Jeanne said, squeezing her arm. "To tell the truth, Christmas wouldn't feel like Christmas to us without *you*."

"Well," Stacy said. "Hopefully this won't be our last one. We'll have to see what the new year brings."

"That's right," Jeanne said.

As Stacy and Bob turned to go, Luke came through the swinging kitchen door again. Bob caught it and held it for him, and then Bob gave Jeanne a little salute as the two of them filed out.

"Okay," Luke said. "I think that's it from the dining room." He clapped his hands. "What do you need in here? Put me to work."

Jeanne shook her head. "Oh, no," she said. "You're done for the night."

Luke looked around at the kitchen, still half-full of platters of food and dirty dishes.

"You sure?" he asked.

"Absolutely," Jeanne said. "You get out there and have some fun."

Luke glanced at the kitchen door. "Fun, huh?" he said.

"See what Hannah's up to," Jeanne said, trying her best to sound nonchalant.

But Luke stared at her until she couldn't help but grin.

"I smell what you're cooking," Luke said. "And I'm not saying I object. But . . ."

"But what?" Jeanne said.

"Doesn't it feel like a little soon?" Luke asked. "I mean, she was supposed to be getting *married* this weekend."

"If you ask me," Jeanne said, tossing a spoonful of stuffing into an aluminum storage tray with unusual vigor, "we didn't get rid of Trevor soon enough. And as far as anything else goes?"

When she looked up, Luke was hanging on her every word. He was more interested in Hannah, Jeanne realized, than she had even guessed.

"Yeah?" Luke prompted.

"I don't think it's too soon to spend some time with her," Jeanne said. "Especially not tonight."

Luke took a deep breath, then let it out. "Okay," he said. "Wish me luck."

Instead, Jeanne gave him a quick kiss on the cheek. "Thanks for everything," she said. "Merry Christmas."

"Merry Christmas," Luke said and walked out, the door thunking behind him.

"Okay," Jeanne said, almost to herself. She surveyed the kitchen and all the work that still remained, then picked up the nearest storage container and started filling it with leftovers.

But as she did, her eyes filled with tears. She tried to press on, hoping that they'd pass if she kept on working. But her crying only got worse.

Just as she finally reached a hand up to wipe her tears away, she felt Tim's arms circle her waist.

"Hey," he said. "You okay?"

Jeanne nodded.

"Really?" Tim said, gently joking. "Because I don't usually cry when I'm okay."

"Did you hear them?" Jeanne said. "Making reservations to come back next year?"

"I heard," Tim said quietly, and gave her another squeeze.

"It's not just them," she said. "I just realized . . . I'm going to have to cancel all our reservations. Everything that's on the books now."

"We'll split it up," Tim said. "I'll help."

Jeanne leaned back against him, letting herself rest for perhaps the first time since the storm began. "Thank you," she said.

For a moment she just enjoyed the feel of his arms around her. But then she asked the question that had been echoing in her own mind. "What are we going to do?" she asked.

"I think now might be a good time to thank God," Tim said. "For everything we still have."

At another time, a stubborn resistance might have built up in Jeanne, wondering what they had to be thankful for, when everything they'd built seemed to be falling apart. But tonight, somehow, she knew what he meant.

"All the years we got to be here," she said.

"That's right," Tim agreed. "And that we still have each other."

Jeanne squeezed his hands, linked together over her belly. "That's right," she echoed quietly.

"And then," Tim said, giving her one last embrace, and stepping back, "we finish these dishes."

But before he went back to the wash sink, he stopped to give her a lingering kiss.

"I just wish I knew what was going to happen next," Jeanne said.

"Me too," he answered.

Thirty

NO MATTER HOW MOLLY tossed and turned, she couldn't seem to find a place where the starlight streaming in through the windows didn't keep her awake.

Finally, she sat up in bed.

She'd covered the clock at some point earlier, because she couldn't stand how fast it sometimes seemed to go, and also how slow, so she had no idea what time it actually was.

In the faint blue light reflected off the fields of white snow that glimmered beyond the antique glass in the windows, she surveyed the room.

Usually, when she couldn't sleep, her policy was just to get up and do something quiet until she felt sleepy again. But beyond the door, the girls were sleeping just feet from her writing desk, which was where she'd naturally gravitate in a mood like this. And the attic, while beautiful and rustic, was hardly light- or soundproof. Anything Molly did in the main room was liable to be seen or heard in the office, slipping through the gaps around the door, which had warped so much in the years since it was first installed that it now had uneven, gaping spaces on all sides.

If she moved around too much, or even turned on a light that was too bright, she was worried about waking one or both of the girls.

Which was pretty much the last thing she needed right now.

It was thoughts of the girls, in fact, that had been keeping her up. She'd spent a lot of her life with kids, and she loved them. Some part of her, in fact, was probably still a kid—at least that was one of the things she always liked to say at readings, when people asked how she'd decided to write books for children, instead of doing something else.

She'd met lots of great kids before, and she was close to the children of some of her friends and family as well. She relished the role of buddy and aunt, getting to be the silly grown-up who didn't have to enforce the rules.

But something was different about these girls. Or maybe, Molly thought, something was different about the family.

It wasn't just that she had a crush on Marcus. "Crush," she realized when she finally let the word surface in her mind, wasn't really even the word for it. It wasn't butterflies and blushing, although she couldn't deny that his strong frame and blue eyes did something to her knees when she looked at him for too long. Even deeper than that, though, was a strong connection, a meeting of the minds. It felt like it had been there since before they met, a way of seeing the world, and talking about it, that they shared in common, and that was far harder to find than butterflies in your stomach.

She had thought that Marcus must feel it, too—not necessarily a romantic interest, but at least that sense of connection. And it had certainly felt like the girls were attached to her, even if it had only been a short while.

So she had been surprised by how much it had stung to hear Marcus so quickly, and so sternly, dismiss Bailey's wish that they might be a family.

Of course, once Marcus hurried out of the room, leaving

Molly alone with her thoughts, she realized how crazy it had been to think that he could have done anything else. They had only known each other for a few days. A person would have to be crazy to be thinking about sharing their whole lives in such a short time. And the hopes and hearts of little girls like Bailey and Addison were not to be played with, especially after they'd already gone through so much in losing their mom. If they were entertaining hopes that were never going to come true, the right thing to do was to let them know as quickly and gently as possible.

Which was exactly what Marcus had done.

But although Molly could organize her thoughts along these lines, she couldn't seem to make her heart stop ringing as if it were a big bell that had just been struck a heavy blow.

Because the fact was that the time with Marcus and Bailey and Addison had made her think about her whole life.

For who knows how long, she had been lying in bed, tossing and turning, trying to tell herself that she was just crazy to be dreaming about joining her life with these three strangers who she barely knew, that she needed to get over it, and soon. Or preferably, *now*.

But as soon as she gave up on the attempt to fall asleep and sat up in the dark, she realized something.

It wasn't just that she had fallen madly in love with Marcus, or was certain that she wanted to be part of his little family.

Instead, she realized, the time with them had woken her heart up to what it could be like to be part of a family. When she spent time with other kids, it was always in a classroom, or with their mom nearby, ready to jump in. And when she dated, it was always just her and whoever she was dating.

But this weekend had given her a taste of something she'd

never experienced before: what it was like to take the place of a mother and wife in a sweet young family.

She'd been able to tell herself that might not be for her, and to believe that was the case. And for a long time she'd also felt like there wasn't much she could do about it either way: for whatever reason, the world hadn't presented her with the right man, or the right chance to have children.

But now that she'd had a taste of it, with Marcus and the girls, she suddenly knew that was something she wanted, and wanted deeply.

And as she'd tried to erase these thoughts with sleep, Marcus's words had echoed again and again in her head: *That's not going to happen.*

It hadn't just felt like a way to calm down the girls' inflated expectations, Molly realized. It bounced around her thoughts, a rejection of the possibility that she could ever have anything like this for herself. For reasons she could never really understand, it just wasn't going to happen.

Molly took a deep breath and shook her head.

Now she knew more than ever that she needed to get out of bed, to break the hold of these thoughts and calm her mind so she could get at least a few hours of rest before Christmas morning.

But the last thing she wanted was to wake the girls so that they lost sleep the night before the big day or, God forbid, decided that they wanted Marcus to come back upstairs to help put them back to bed again.

She pulled the scarf she'd thrown over the clock away from the glowing digital face so that she could check the time.

Two o'clock.

Had she really been caught in these thoughts for so many hours?

In any case, she thought, everyone in the house would be asleep. Since a change of scene always helped clear her head, at least now she could creep downstairs and grab an evening snack from the kitchen without running into Marcus, or anyone else.

A moment later, she had thrown on her favorite baby-blue satin robe over her white cotton nightgown and padded out the door, so silently that she would have been surprised if the girls could hear even a single footstep.

The old stairs, to her relief, proved to be incredibly quiet— probably due to more precise and thoughtful renovations by Jeanne and Tim, who must have realized that the normal creaks of an old house would keep all the guests awake, carrying sound to all the floors along the wide stairwell.

In what seemed like no time at all, without meeting another soul, she stepped gratefully into the kitchen, where she caught the swinging door before it could even begin to make any noise whispering back and forth before it came to a stop.

Then she turned around and saw Marcus sitting at the kitchen island, caught midgesture, a forkful of apple pie frozen halfway to his mouth.

For a brief moment, Molly calculated wildly, trying to believe there was even the smallest chance that he hadn't seen her yet, and she could just slip right back through the door and flee to the safety of her room upstairs without having to say anything.

"Molly," he said, not quite as if he was greeting her, but with a bit more wonder in his tone, as if some strange creature had just materialized in front of him and he was naming it as a way to get his bearings.

Then he let his fork drop to the plate and stood up.

"Hey," he said. "I was just getting a midnight snack. You want something?"

"Um," Molly said, drawing her robe around her. Somehow, even in sweatpants and a T-shirt, Marcus looked fresh and put-together enough to run a business meeting.

She lifted her hand to her hair in a nervous gesture, and realized that she hadn't even looked in a mirror before she'd come downstairs. God only knew what she looked like.

"Here," Marcus said, cutting a piece from the pie pan in front of him, then grabbing a small plate from a clean stack nearby.

He set the plate down next to him and pulled back the counter stool beside him.

"Please," he said. "Don't let me midnight snack alone."

Molly managed a smile, and took the seat next to him, but huddled down as if she might possibly be able to make herself small enough that he would forget she was there.

The first bite of the pie, however, did act like a tonic on her, sending a surge of irresistible joy through her as she tasted the tart apples and the buttery crust and the hints of vanilla and cinnamon.

"Look," Marcus said. "I still feel terrible about what happened earlier. With the girls."

"Oh," Molly said, waving her hand like a policeman directing traffic to a halt. Maybe she could just stop the conversation before it even began.

But Marcus was apparently unfamiliar with the basic signals of the road. "I mean it," he said earnestly. "I don't know what got into them. Why they'd ever say something like that."

At the look of horror on Molly's face, it finally seemed to sink in through Marcus's skull that he might have said something wrong. "I mean," he said, "not that the right guy wouldn't be lucky to have you. I mean, anyone would. But you know that already," he said, dropping his eyes to the remains of his pie.

At this, Molly's own eyes grew wide. She most certainly did not know that, she thought.

"It's just," Marcus rambled on, desperate now to find a way to stop talking, "they should never have presumed to say that. I mean, I would never presume . . ." He looked up, his eyes practically begging for her to throw him some kind of lifeline.

His obvious distress finally jogged Molly out of her own crippling embarrassment. She shook her head in a way that she hoped looked nonchalant and carefree.

"Please," she said, "don't worry about it. I mean, I can understand where they were coming from. It was very sweet to get to spend time with—"

She hesitated for a moment, trying to choose between "them" and "you."

"You," she said, settling on the word she really meant. "It even made me think about what it would be like to be a little family, too."

She shook her head, looking down at her own pie now. "I know that's crazy," she said. "All of us only just met. I think it was just that—"

"You were thinking that, too?" Marcus blurted out.

Molly looked up and met his pale blue eyes, feeling even more abashed to have just admitted that her own dreams as a grown woman were just as childish as the little girls' had been.

But when she met Marcus's eyes, something in them made

her realize that he wasn't surprised because she had been thinking the same thing as his girls. He was surprised that she had
been thinking the same thing as him.

And before she could think of anything else to say, he pushed
her plate aside and kissed her.

Thirty-One

IRIS CARRIED HER CUP of hot mint tea with honey out of the kitchen and sat down at her usual spot, a rocking chair by the window in what now served as the inn's dining room. She looked out the darkened front window at the first small traces of the light of dawn and sighed.

Ever since she was a girl, she'd loved waking up before sunrise. It wasn't just that a sunrise was a whole different ball game than a sunset: the beautiful reawakening of hope as light flared up in the darkness, rather than the gorgeous final celebration of a day before it slipped into night. And it wasn't just that so many fewer people ever saw a sunrise than a sunset.

Instead, it was those few quiet moments that the early morning hours gave her to herself. When she was a child, she had thought she needed them because otherwise the house was crowded with other kids, her brothers and sisters, her parents—even the occasional farm animal who had wandered or been smuggled in, across the strict division her mother was always trying to hold between the house and the barn.

But as she'd grown into a woman, she'd realized that she wasn't just making an escape from company. She was looking to connect with something—sometimes herself, sometimes the Lord—to focus, even for a few minutes, on what really mattered, before the press of the day got into full swing.

And now that she was an older woman, without as many re-sponsibilities and emergencies as she had once had in her life, she treasured it even more than she had as a child. It was one of the most selfish reasons she'd sold the property to Jeanne and Tim in the first place. She couldn't seem to give the tradition up—sitting at this very window, watching and reflecting. Jeanne and Tim didn't seem to mind her traipsing over here at all hours to enjoy the view.

In fact, one of the things she loved best about her stolen early-morning moments was the way they took her back to her childhood and collapsed the years between her life as a girl and the one she lived now. She stared out the same window she'd looked through her entire life, out onto the same fields and hills, and the same mountains beyond, the trees a bit bigger now than maybe they were once, but generally in the same places.

She loved the feeling it gave her, to be both young and wise at the same time, carrying the exuberance of her youth with her into her current life, and looking back on her younger days with a perspective that made them richer, because she still stood in the same place now, doing the same thing: sending up a little prayer as the morning began.

But as she settled into her chair this morning, ready to watch her regular morning show of sunlight beginning to creep into the world, she heard a footstep on the stairs.

She got up quickly and peered into the hall.

She was interrupted so rarely in her morning ritual, and she did it so much earlier than most people rose from bed, that her first thought was that something must be wrong with one of the guests.

But when she saw who had just stepped from the staircase into the lobby, she smiled. "Geoffrey," she said, whispering so that she wouldn't wake up Luke and the other young gentleman, who she'd found slumbering peacefully in the lounge when she came in from her cottage.

Geoffrey froze in his tracks.

But almost instantly, he turned his head, recognized Iris, and broke out into a grin that transformed his entire craggy face.

"Iris!" he whispered back. "I don't think I could have said this sincerely if you'd been any other inhabitant of this establishment. But this is a pleasant surprise."

"You're up early," Iris observed, coolly taking a sip of her tea.

Geoffrey sighed and leaned against her desk, parking his rolling suitcase quietly at his side.

"It's an old habit I picked up from the time I was a boy," he said. "I always liked to beat the sun out of bed. It gives you a little bit of time for yourself, no matter what else happens that day."

Iris smiled. "I find that's true myself," she said.

"I suspect you do," Geoffrey said, looking at her with the same close look she'd noticed several other times during his visit, the one that made her feel as if he was taking in her characteristics in order to be able to describe her later as some kind of a specimen.

She looked out the window, where the very first gold and pink of dawn were just beginning to spill over the horizon. "And look," she said. "There it is."

"Yes," Geoffrey said, his voice almost gentle. "There it is."

For a long moment, both of them simply stared out the window, side by side, watching the light of day break into the world.

Then Geoffrey shifted, still watching the dawn. "You know what else I've always loved about it?" he said, without even looking over to see Iris shake her head. "It's always the same, any-where you are in the world. But always different, too."

"It's always different even if you watch it from the same place every day," Iris said.

This time, Geoffrey did glance away from the sunset so that he could meet her eyes. "That's what you've done, isn't it?" he asked.

Iris nodded. "You can learn a lot in just one place, too," she said.

"Well, I'm not sure everyone does," Geoffrey said. Then he smiled. "But I'm willing to believe you have."

Iris smiled back as Geoffrey reached down to pull something from his bag.

"Am I all set with the room?" he asked. "Do you need any-thing else from me?"

Iris flipped open the house version of the guest register, double-checked the column by Geoffrey's name, and nodded.

"All set," she said. "Thank you for staying with us."

"It's been a pleasure," Geoffrey said. "A wonderful surprise."

Iris beamed. "Are you sure you wouldn't like to stay for breakfast?" she asked.

Geoffrey shook his head. "It's not a matter of what I'd like, at this point," he said. "It's a matter of where they expect me, and keeping my promises. The interstate opened this morning shortly after midnight. I need to get back on the road."

He bent over again, rummaging in one of his bags, and Iris expected him to straighten up again, hands free, to make his final exit.

But instead of taking his first strides out the door, he laid something on the richly varnished counter of the front desk.

"This is for you," he said with a twinkle in his eye.

Iris picked up the package, which looked like a book, wrapped in paper.

"What's this?" she asked, surprised.

The book wasn't wrapped in decorative paper, but in what looked to be a page of an English newspaper, printed on pink paper, rather than the standard American gray.

"It's a little gift for you," Geoffrey said.

"For me?" Iris said, her voice rising in surprise so that she shot a worried look at the lounge, worried that she'd been loud enough to wake the sleeping men.

Geoffrey nodded, clearly pleased at her reaction. "I just thought it was a little something you might enjoy. It's a book on travel. In case you ever decide you'd like to see the sun rise on some distant shore. I thought it might give you some ideas."

"Well, thank you," Iris said, falling back on her manners in the midst of her pleasant confusion. "I'm afraid I don't have anything for you."

"Oh, no," Geoffrey said. "This place has already been a gift. And so have you," he said.

As he smiled at her, Iris looked down at the wrapped book in her hands, surprised by how shy she felt.

As she did, he took the opportunity to head for the door. But before he went out, he turned back.

"Merry Christmas!" he said.

"Merry Christmas," Iris whispered back as he went out into the early morning light.

As soon as she saw his car nose down the drive, away from the inn, Iris tore that paper off.

Inside was a beautifully illustrated travel guide, describing picturesque but out-of-the-way destinations on every continent.

How in the world had he managed to have such a perfect gift

for her on hand? There was no way he'd been able to go out shopping in the midst of the blizzard. Iris flipped through the first pages until she came to a scrawl of handwriting.

Iris, it read, in handwriting that was almost as confident, and crabby, as Geoffrey himself. *If you ever decide to travel to any of these places, or anywhere else, please consider letting me know. I'd be very glad to meet you again, anywhere in the world. Geoffrey.*

It wasn't until she read his signature, still feeling a little thrill at the words they'd been signed to, that she realized his name was mirrored somewhere else on the page: just below the title.

With a sudden shock of recognition, she slammed the book shut to get a better look at the cover.

There was Geoffrey's name again, in one-inch letters, standing at the foot of the mountain that decorated the cover. But Geoffrey Peterson, the book's author, had a different last name than the one Geoffrey had used to check in.

That's when she saw the type that ran across the top of the book, just above its title: "*New York Times* Bestselling Author."

THIRTY-TWO

JARED'S EYES WIDENED AS he took his first bite of breakfast, glancing around the table at Audrey, Hannah, and Hannah's parents, who were all seated in a little alcove by the window in the dining area.

"What is this?" he asked when that bite was finished, looking down at his plate of pancakes as if they might have suddenly been transformed into something completely different.

"Nothing fancy," Audrey told him, rubbing his shoulder. "Chocolate chip pancakes."

"A traditional Christmas-morning meal," Hannah's father joked. "Dating back to the time of the English kings."

Jared shook his head. "I don't know if it's fancy or not," he said. "But they taste like someone just snuck into heaven and stole them."

"You like them, huh?" Audrey said, glancing over her own plate with an appraising eye.

"We have two options," Jared said. "Either we can stay here forever, or we can kidnap the chef before we go. I don't care which. You choose, honey."

Audrey shook her head and kissed him.

"How about option three?" she said. "I'll see about getting the recipe."

As Hannah took another bite of her own pancakes, she felt a touch on her shoulder.

"Dear?" Iris said, leaning close and speaking low. "Would you come with me?"

Gratefully, Hannah put her fork down and stood.

The quick, worried glances of everybody at the table only reminded her why she was glad to have any excuse to escape for a moment. Her mother and father, Audrey and Jared—they might all be having the time of their life right now, in a snug inn, feasting on Christmas breakfast, if it weren't for her. But none of them could forget the reason that had brought them all there originally, or the fact that today was supposed to have been Hannah's wedding day.

At the same time, nobody could bring themselves to bring it up, at least not at the breakfast table, in front of everyone. And watching them tiptoe around it, each taking surreptitious glances at her, someone checking her face after almost every comment or joke, was driving her crazy.

They all just wanted her to be all right, but none of them seemed to have any idea what that meant, and neither did Hannah. She didn't know if she ought to be enjoying herself as much as she could, because the place was beautiful and the food was good, and because Trevor shouldn't have the power to ruin a good day. On the other hand, maybe she should be way more upset than she actually felt at the moment, getting all her emotions out, because there certainly must be a lot of them in there somewhere when you're left at the altar by your fiancé.

Trying to figure out how she should act in front of everyone just made it harder for her to figure out how she actually felt. Which this morning, actually, was tired, deeply tired, as if she'd run a years'-long race and was only just now able to sit down for the first time. She was also surprised that she didn't feel more of the other things she'd been afraid she might feel—fear of the future, shame over the breakup.

And she didn't miss Trevor. That was the thing that surprised her most. In the moments after she talked with him, it had felt like her whole world was breaking apart, since she had believed she was building it with him at the center. If someone had asked her then, she would have said that the worst part of the breakup would be the loneliness and the loss of not having him around.

But now, days later, she didn't miss him. She'd been angry at him, and exasperated with him, and even felt sorry for him. But she hadn't missed him.

And she didn't know how to feel about that, either.

So Iris's whispered request came as a relief.

"Everything okay, honey?" her mom asked as Hannah turned to follow Iris.

"Sure," Hannah said, giving her mother a smile that she hoped would ease her worries. "I'll be right back."

It wasn't until she was following Iris through the dining area that her relief began to turn to curiosity as she started to wonder why Iris had plucked her away from her breakfast.

But before her curiosity had formed into a question, she followed Iris around the corner to the lobby by the front desk and found the answer: Trevor.

He was standing just inside the door of the inn, surrounded by foul-weather gear and snowshoes, grinning.

At first Hannah felt the same rush of familiarity and pleasure she always did when she saw Trevor. But this time, right behind it was a wall of anger. It roared up to the surface of her mind and was stopped only by her profound confusion of what he was doing there at all.

But when Trevor saw her, he didn't hesitate. "Baby," he said, rushing forward and crumpling her against his chilly foul-weather jacket. "I'm so glad you're here. I was afraid I lost my chance."

"Your chance?" Hannah repeated.

But Trevor wasn't looking at her anymore. Instead, he was scanning his surroundings.

"It's nicer than I remembered," he said. "I have to say, I wasn't crazy about getting married here. Where is everybody? Your dad still here? Your mom?"

Hannah nodded.

Trevor kissed her. "Well, we need to tell them."

Hannah clung to him for a minute, comforted by the familiarity of his arms and his kiss. But then she struggled free and stepped back.

"Tell them what?" she asked.

"Tell them to get ready," he said. "I'm going to marry you today." He grinned at her as if he'd just delivered the most amazing Christmas present in the world.

Hannah felt something huge shift inside her, as if all the pieces of her life that she'd spent the last few days letting go of were straining to stand back up and fit together again. She felt a sudden rush of wild hope that everything could go back to the way she'd always dreamed it would be.

As she stared at Trevor, she heard a footstep behind her.

She turned, hoping someone had followed her out of the dining area—Audrey, her mother, even her dad, to help her figure out what in the world she should say next.

But it was Luke, coming out of the lounge, carrying a big backpack over his shoulders and keys in his hand.

"Hannah," he said, his face lighting up in a big smile. "I wanted to catch you before I went."

Then he recognized Trevor. When he did, his entire expression changed. Hannah saw a flash of deep dislike before Luke smoothed his features flat. "Trevor," he said.

Trevor looked at Luke in confusion. "I'm sorry, man," he said. "Have we met?"

Luke gave a brusque nod. "Few summers ago," he said. "You might not remember."

"Oh, sure!" Trevor said, sticking his hand out with a smile Hannah knew meant he was covering up the fact that he still had no recollection of Luke whatsoever. "Good to see you again."

Luke looked at Trevor's hand for so long that Hannah was afraid he might actually refuse to shake it. Finally, though, he clasped Trevor's hand back.

"What are you doing here?" Luke asked as they shook.

Trevor grinned and put his arm around Hannah, squeezing her to his side as she looked down, unable to meet Luke's eyes.

"I'm here to marry my girl," he said. "I'm a little late, but I made it."

For good measure, he kissed Hannah's cheek. When she glanced at him, still in shock, he was looking from her to Luke with a smile that seemed to be trying to apologize for being so charming, while at the same time saying that he couldn't quite help it.

Luke watched Hannah for a long moment, then resettled his bag on his shoulder. "Well," he said. "Good luck."

"Thanks, man," Trevor said.

Hannah ducked her head again.

"I'm gonna go," Luke said.

"Good to see you, man," Trevor said. "Drive safe. It's crazy out there."

Hannah watched as if frozen while Luke walked out the door without another backward glance.

But when the door thumped shut behind him, something snapped in her.

She pulled away from Trevor and crossed her arms over her chest.

"Who was that?" Trevor asked, glancing back over his shoulder.

"What makes you think we can still get married today?" Hannah asked.

This, finally, drove the grin from Trevor's face.

"Babe," he said. "I know. I messed up."

"Is that what you did?" Hannah said.

Trevor shook his head and pushed his hair back, his standard move in moments when he was distressed. "I spent all day thinking about it yesterday. It's just such a big step, you know? I just didn't know if I was strong enough to take it. You've always been the strong one," he said, stepping forward to take her hands. "But that's what made me realize," he went on, the grin creeping back onto his face.

"Realize what?" Hannah said.

Trevor stepped forward to gather her in his arms again. "I can't live without you, babe," he said. "It was the biggest mistake of my life, thinking I could. But as soon as I started thinking about life without you, I just knew—I can't do it. I've told you that a million times, but now I know it's true. So as soon as I heard the roads opened up, I got in my car and started driving, and—"

By this point, Hannah had begun to squirm so insistently that he finally released her, but without breaking his earnest eye contact, or the cadence of his speech. "—and here you are," he said. "And here I am. Everything's still here. Nothing's really changed. I say, let's do it. Let's get married, babe."

"Everything's not here," Hannah said. "The caterer couldn't get through the storm. The minister didn't come."

"Well, we'll get another one," Trevor said. "They've got to have some minister out here who's crazy enough to marry us."

Hannah stared at him.

"You've got your dress, right?" Trevor said.

Hannah nodded.

"That's all I want," Trevor said, as if it was the simplest thing in the world. "Just you in your dress, and that's everything I'll ever need."

He grabbed her hand, kissed her cheek, and drew her to him tenderly.

Out of the corner of her eye, Hannah saw a flash of Luke's jacket as he headed for his truck.

"Come on, baby," he said tenderly. "What do you say? Let's go tell everyone. It'll be a Christmas present they'll never forget."

At the thought of Trevor appearing in the dining area, grinning that same grin at her parents, the words Hannah had been searching for finally sprang into her mind.

"It's not all *I* need," she said.

Trevor looked at her, surprised. "What do you mean?" he asked.

"You're not the only one getting married, Trevor," Hannah said. "You're not the only one who gets to say whether it happens or doesn't."

"But you wanted to marry me," Trevor said. "I'm the one who wasn't sure."

"That was true two days ago," Hannah said.

Trevor looked around, like he was trying to figure out if someone was pranking him.

"What happened in the last two days?" Trevor said. "Did something change?" He took her hand again. "Because I didn't," he said.

Hannah didn't know whether to laugh or scream. But in a flash it came to her that Trevor wasn't lying. Even though he'd been the one to break off the engagement and then show up saying the wedding was back on, he was no different than he'd ever been, always up and down, never sure what he wanted.

Gently, she pulled her hand free from his.

"You know what?" she said. "Maybe nothing changed. Or maybe I'm the one who did. But in any case, we're not getting married. Not today, and not ever."

"Babe," Trevor began, but she was already pushing past him, out the front door to the porch, where she stood in the glittery snow that had dusted back onto the blue-painted slats after someone cleared it, scanning the yard for Luke's truck.

But by the time she got there, the yard was already empty.

Luke had gone without leaving a trace, not even the faintest rumble of his truck engine vanishing into the distance.

Thirty-Three

"SHHH!" ADDISON SAID, IN a voice loud enough to wake anyone still sleeping in the top two floors of the inn. "She's *sleeping*!"

"No, she isn't," Bailey said triumphantly, as Molly's eyes fluttered open.

Instantly, Molly shut them again.

She wasn't typically an early riser, or a fast one, and she hadn't exactly gotten a full, peaceful night's sleep.

Experimentally, she tried turning her head away from the girls, toward the opposite side of the bed, and pretending to fall back into a deep slumber. She hoped that if they padded quietly away, she actually might.

For a moment, both girls fell silent.

Then she could hear shuffling, and finally the patter of feet from the side of the bed where they'd originally woken her, around the bottom, to the other side, where they came to a stop, presumably the better to observe the progress of this last bout of sleep.

By now, Molly was wide awake, but still kept her eyes closed as she struggled not to burst into laughter, which would be a dead giveaway to the girls that she had been faking.

"She wants her present," Bailey stage-whispered.

"Maybe she wants to sleep," Addison said. Her tone conveyed the clear message that older sisters always knew things that younger sisters hadn't thought of yet.

"Would you want to sleep, or to have a present?" Bailey asked.

In the silence that followed, while Addison apparently debated the merits of this question, Molly managed to turn her head away from the girls again in a way that she hoped was convincingly sleepy.

For an instant, both girls fell silent, and Molly could almost feel the way both pairs of eyes must have fastened on her, watching like tiny, very cute hawks, for any sign of wakefulness on her part.

"Well?" Bailey whispered, while apparently poking Addison, which evoked an indignant "Hey!" and a brief scuffle.

"I'd rather have a present," Addison said. "But Daddy would rather sleep."

"Daddy *always* wants to sleep," Bailey complained.

This time, Molly couldn't resist the smile that came to her lips at the idea of the girls stalking Marcus this same way, morning after morning.

With a big, theatrical groan, she stretched, rolled over, and opened her eyes on the girls.

"Well, girls," she said. "Good morning."

For a moment, both girls looked at her wide-eyed. Then Bailey began her familiar dance, bouncing on her toes in celebration of the fact that Molly had decided at last to greet the day. "You're awake!" she sang, then turned to her sister with the next verse: "She's awake!"

But Addison, with her superior wisdom and knowledge, wasn't about to be taken over by rejoicing so quickly. "It's Christmas," she announced to Molly, in a slightly disapproving tone, as if she couldn't quite believe that any functioning adult would have let this crucial detail slip their mind, even in the first seconds after waking.

"Is it Christmas?" Molly asked in a slightly teasing tone. "Then there's going to be a lot of excitement this morning. Maybe we should all go back to sleep for a few hours, to make sure we get enough rest to enjoy it."

She closed her eyes again, but when she opened them, seconds later, Addison was grinning at Molly's joke, and Bailey was clambering onto the bed itself.

As Molly sat up and the mattress rocked slightly, Bailey lost her balance and tumbled, giggling, into Molly's arms.

"Well," Molly said. "Merry Christmas to you!"

"Merry Christmas!" Addison crowed, tossing a sheaf of paper on the bed.

"We made you a present," Bailey confided, curling up in Molly's lap.

"A present?" Molly said. "You girls didn't have to do that!"

"We used your pencils," Addison said, pushing the paper out of her way, toward Molly, and climbing up on the bed to join them.

From Molly's lap, Bailey stuck out her foot and dragged the stack of pages toward her with her toes. "Toes are like hands," she said. "They're just as good."

But before she managed to get it within reach of her actual fingers, Addison pounced, collected the pages into a rough approximation of a manuscript, and handed them to Molly with a high degree of ceremony.

"We wrote it ourselves," she said. "This morning."

Molly looked down at the cover, a charming rendition of what was clearly recognizable as the inn, complete with its green shutters and white siding, perched on the top of a snow-covered hill.

"Oh my goodness," she said. "This is beautiful."

"Read it!" Addison commanded, snuggling in under Molly's arm.

"You wrote all this?" Molly said, flipping through the pages, and realizing the girls had used up almost twenty of her drafting sheets. That wasn't any kind of a problem—she just couldn't believe how much work they had done.

"I wrote it," Addison said. "Bailey helped with the drawings."

"I'm going to be an artist," Bailey said with an impish grin. "Like you."

She tapped with her toe at the page in front of her. "I drew this one," she said.

"You know what?" Molly asked.

"What?" Bailey asked, squirming in her lap so that she could look up into Molly's eyes.

"I think you already are an artist," Molly said.

Bailey regarded her seriously for a moment, as if to make sure this wasn't a joke. Then a shy smile began to steal over her face. Before it could overtake her completely, she squirmed back around into a position where she could see the manuscript Molly was holding again.

"Read it!" she crowed.

As Molly read the first few pages, a familiar story emerged. A dad and his young daughters, both dressed in princess gowns in the most vibrant possible shades of turquoise and magenta that Molly's pencil box would allow, were caught by surprise in the midst of a terrible snowstorm.

But just as a large and quite convincing abominable snowman was opening his jaws to swallow their little red car, a snow witch appeared and chased it off.

When Molly got her first look at the drawing of the snow witch, she got a sensation the girls themselves must have felt when they first saw the drawings in her manuscript the night before, pictures that were obviously inspired by them. It was both thrilling and a little vertigo-inducing to see herself being drawn as a character, even in a book that had actually been written by children, because it offered such a clear mirror of what they thought of her, juxtaposed against what she hoped others might see when they looked at her.

But from the very first page where the snow witch appeared, the girls' vision of her was full of wonder. She was almost twice the size of their car, with bright red lips and long, flowing hair, all accented by a sky-blue-and-silver dress. Somehow, the two girls had drawn Molly as both more powerful and more beautiful than she would ever have drawn herself.

When the snow witch first joined the story, though, the little family wasn't sure if she was going to swallow them, just the way the abominable snowman had threatened to. As the snow witch waved her wand at them, the girls in the story had a nervous conversation about whether she was going to turn them into pillars of ice, or maybe tiny winter birds.

But when the snow witch waved her wand, she transported them to her magic castle, which was warm and cozy, and full of tables piled high with delicious food: stacks of buttery pancakes, gooey grilled cheese, and laundry-sized baskets of brownies.

She introduced them to her magical companions, who bore a suspiciously striking resemblance to a number of the characters from Molly's own books. And finally, with their dad's smiling permission, she taught both of the girls to be snow witches themselves, and they all flew off together in search of other lost travelers to rescue from the winter roads and take back to their vast but cozy castle.

At the end of the story, Molly had a feeling that she rarely had with books anymore, since writing and reading them had become her profession. Just as she'd often felt when she was around Addison's and Bailey's ages, she didn't want the story to end.

"Should we read it again?" she said, looking from girl to girl.

Bailey, thinking that Molly was making a joke, teasing her for always demanding to hear any story once more, burst into laughter.

So Molly just shuffled the papers together, lining them up with each other so that none of the pages would be out of order or have their corners bent.

She looked down again at the "cover" drawing of the inn, which she now knew was just the top bit of the good witch's castle, peeking up above the mountain it was hidden in, and where she could now see the face of the snow witch smiling from the corner of one of the windows.

"This is such a beautiful present," Molly said. "Thank you, girls."

But as she said this, she realized something: she didn't have a present for them.

Neither girl seemed to mind this, at least not yet. Both of them were still looking at her happily, gleeful with the pleasure of giving. And there was no reason to believe that either of them would expect a present from her. After all, when would she have had the chance to get them one, since they'd all been trapped together at the inn since the day they met?

Still, something in Molly yearned to give them something in

return for this story they'd worked so hard on. Almost selfishly, she wanted to have the pleasure of watching their faces light up the same way they had moved her heart this morning.

Gently, she lifted Bailey from her lap and pushed the covers back, as Bailey began to protest. "Hey, no!"

"Where are you going?" Addison called, as Molly went over to the table by the door, where the manuscript she'd written yesterday was sitting.

When she picked it up, she held it for a minute in her hand. She'd already taken photos of each page, backed them up, and emailed them to herself. She wasn't about to take a chance on losing a draft once it was finished.

But she'd always kept her first drafts, her very first drafts, before. In fact, she had a whole section of a shelf of them at home: her own private library of books that only she would ever see. The idea of not taking this one home to sit among its brothers and sisters gave her a moment of pause.

"Molly?" Bailey asked, in the same tone of disappointment she might use to inquire if a beloved game was finally over.

The sound of Bailey's voice drove away the last of Molly's hesitation. She turned around, slipping the manuscript behind her as she did.

"I'm not going anywhere," she said. "I just had to get the present I have to give you girls."

"A present?" Addison said, calculating quickly. "Where did you get us a present?"

Her voice got wobbly by the end from the sonic interference of her sister, doing her best to bounce on her heels while standing up on Molly's bed.

Half worried that Bailey would bounce herself right onto the floor before she got there, Molly almost dove for the bed, scooping Bailey up as she sat down and the girls crowded around, both craning their necks to get a look at whatever she was holding in her hands.

When Molly removed the manuscript from the folds of her gown, Addison piped up with consternation.

"That's your book," she said, as if it should be obvious to everyone that Molly couldn't give them her *book* as a present.

"That's right," Molly said. "And I want you to have it."

Bailey, for her part, didn't have any hesitation. She seized the pages and clutched them to her chest.

"Your book!" she said.

"Be careful!" Addison said, retrieving the pages from her as if Molly's hand-drawn sketches were actually the *Mona Lisa*. "This is the only one!"

"The only one?" Bailey said, looking up at Molly. "And you're giving it to us?"

Molly nodded. "Well, it won't be the only one forever," she said. "Eventually, I hope there will be quite a lot of copies. But no one will have this one. It's the first one, and there won't ever be anything else in the world quite like it. And that's just right, because there's nobody else in the world quite like you two."

At this, Bailey buried her head against Molly's chest. "Our own book," she said in rapture.

As she sighed, a knock came on the door.

"Daddy!" both girls chorused, piling off the bed as Molly grabbed for her robe.

But when the door opened, it wasn't Marcus, but Santa Claus, and not a Santa Claus with quite the same tall, fit build as Marcus, but one who looked quite a bit more like one of their refugee travelers, Frank.

"Ho, ho, ho!" he boomed. "I don't usually have to wake little girls up on Christmas morning, but I thought this time I'd make an exception. I'm so close to the North Pole up here in Vermont that sometimes I like to stick around to see children open their presents. And let me tell you, there are some very nice presents waiting downstairs for you to open."

As the girls squealed with delight, Santa stepped aside to let them barrel past, and Molly finally got a glimpse of Marcus, standing a bit down the stairs. It was the first time she'd seen him since he'd kissed her in the kitchen the night before, and she got a deep thrill at the sight of him, along with an undertow of uncertainty. She wasn't sure what the kiss had meant to her yet. And she had no idea what it had meant to him—if it had meant anything at all.

When the girls got to him, they stopped, creating a perfect traffic jam on the stairs. Between their "Merry Christmases" and hugs, Addison also managed to press the pages of Molly's manuscript into his hands and order, "Be very careful with this, Daddy! It's important."

As Molly watched, Marcus smiled indulgently, then stepped aside to let the girls and Santa slip by him, heading for the presents waiting on the main floor. But when he glanced down at the pages in his hands, he froze, then looked up toward Molly's room, where his eyes locked with hers.

"Is this your book?" he asked.

Molly nodded.

"Did they misunderstand?" he said. "Were you reading it to them again?"

Molly shook her head. "It's for them," she said.

Marcus took a step up the stairs toward her, but then the girls' voices floated up from the main floor. "Daddy! Daddy! Santa says we can't open our presents until you come down."

"Um," Marcus said. It was clear he had something to say, but totally unclear what. Did he want to let her know it had all been a terrible mistake? Did he want to kiss her again?

"Go!" Molly said, waving him down the stairs. "It's Christmas morning! They're going to expire from anticipation if you don't get down there soon! I'll be down in just a minute," she said in answer to his questioning glance.

"Daddy!" the girls chorused from below.

"I'm coming!" Marcus called. "We'll talk after?" he asked Molly.

And before she had even finished nodding, he dashed down the stairs.

THIRTY-FOUR

LUKE WANDERED AIMLESSLY DOWN the candy-and-chips aisle of the gas station convenience store, spent a good long time perusing the energy drinks in the coolers, and then came back up the aisle full of jumper cables and weird little dolls, before stopping at the cooler at the front of the store, which was stocked with frozen treats on Popsicle sticks, and frozen candy bars.

"It's Christmas. You're buying breakfast in a gas station," the woman behind the counter said. "I say, get whatever you want."

From the looks of the small pile in front of her, she had taken her own advice. She was sipping from both a large coffee and a blue slushie, and picking at a cinnamon roll from the warmer beside the counter.

"Um . . ." Luke said, trying to come to some kind of a decision.

He felt like something was missing, and he'd thought at first he must be hungry, but his brief tour of the convenience store had convinced him that he wasn't—or at least he wasn't hungry for anything in the convenience store.

Still, he didn't want to go on the long trip to Burlington on an empty stomach—especially because, with the storm and the holiday, there was no telling when he'd be able to find something decent to eat next.

He had pulled a banana and an orange from the fruit basket beside the lottery tickets, and was trying to decide if anything else nearby looked remotely healthy, when the bell over the front door dinged as the door swung open.

Luke recognized Trevor as soon as he walked in. But Trevor, who was wearing a bright blue parka coat with a ridiculous and mismatched brown wool deerstalker hat, didn't seem to notice there was anyone else in the place but him. He didn't even nod back to the woman behind the counter just inside the door when she nodded her greeting to him.

Instead, he stalked down the first aisle he found, as Luke made a quick turn away from him, pretending to take a deep interest in the various kinds of bottled water in the nearby cooler, because the last thing he wanted to do was have any kind of further interaction with Trevor.

So he was startled when Trevor blurted out, "What are you talking about?" in a loud, impatient voice.

Both Luke and the woman behind the counter looked over at Trevor, thinking he must have been talking to one of them. But Trevor was oblivious to them, and after glancing at him for another moment, Luke saw the mobile earpiece hooked over Trevor's ear, when Trevor leaned down to pick up a crinkly bag of cheese crackers.

He was on the phone with someone, Luke guessed. He hoped it wasn't some local minister Trevor was trying to talk into coming out for the wedding, who now had to deal with that kind of attitude on a Christmas morning. But in Luke's brief experience with him, Trevor had never worried much about anyone else when he wanted something.

Trevor threw the bag of crackers back down on the shelf as Luke turned away to make sure he still wasn't recognized.

"I don't see why that should matter," Trevor said. "Not when we've been together for six years."

It was all Luke could do not to shake his head in disgust. Who was Trevor browbeating now? Some poor local Vermont city clerk who he'd rousted out of bed and was now harassing about some local permit for the wedding? And did Trevor really think that whoever it was cared even the tiniest bit about how long Trevor and Hannah had been together?

But at the thought of Hannah, Luke felt a twist in his stomach. The idea of her winding up with anyone else but him was bad enough. But the idea of her winding up with this guy was unbearable.

He had several brief fantasies, all in a row, all of which involved running Trevor out of town somehow before he could get in his car and go back to Hannah. In one of them, he threw a bottle of water at Trevor's head. In another, he forced Trevor's pretentious little sports car, which was completely unsuited for the Vermont winter, back to the highway with his truck, then made sure that Trevor stayed in it, headed anywhere but back to Hannah.

But when those crazy ideas played out to their end, Trevor was still there, braying into his cell phone.

The only difference was that, having reached the back of the store, he'd now turned up the next aisle, and was coming up it.

"I don't know," Trevor said. "I have no idea what she was thinking."

Luke could relate to that, he thought wryly. He didn't blame Hannah for the decision she'd made. She'd been in a tough place, and he knew what it was like to be loyal to someone you'd cared about for years. But he did wonder what she was thinking, how she explained it to herself. And just the tiniest part of him also wondered something else—if she had thought about him at all before she made the decision to get back with Trevor.

By now, Trevor was standing directly behind Luke, pawing at the display of beef jerky on one of the convenience store's end-caps.

The hairs on the back of Luke's neck prickled, but he managed to hold steady, and hold his ground without shooting his mouth off, until Trevor let loose with his next volley.

"She just said no, Mom," Trevor said. "I tried to get her to change her mind." He listened for a minute, then let out an exasperated sigh. "I tried telling her that," he said. "She didn't care."

Suddenly, a different kind of thrill went through Luke. Was it possible that Trevor was talking about Hannah?

"You know what?" Trevor said. "I'm not sure Hannah ever really knew what she wanted."

This, coming from Trevor, who had called his wedding off and then showed up for it after all, all within the space of forty-eight hours, almost made Luke laugh out loud.

But instead, he just turned on his heel.

For the first time, Trevor realized he wasn't alone in the convenience store. Startled, he lurched back a little bit as he recognized Luke, almost as if he was afraid Luke might throw a punch at him.

Instead, Luke just grinned and started to stride out of the store.

As he passed the woman at the counter, she called after him. "Hey," she said, nodding at the fruit he'd left on the counter. "You want this stuff?"

"No thanks," Luke said. "I've gotta go."

And he walked out the door, straight back to his truck.

Thirty-Five

"LOOK, AS LONG AS you're at it," Jeanne said, looking down at Tim, who was busily patching the beautiful cobalt-blue tile below the mantel over the kitchen stove, "I think maybe it'd be best if you just tore out the whole stove and built me a fireplace this morning. I've been thinking it might be fun to cook over an open fire. Not many fine chefs in Vermont could claim to do that."

But instead of annoyance in her voice over Tim's constant repairs, this morning there was amusement.

"Hey," Tim said, plunking one last tile into place, and wiping away any stray mortar. "At least if I'm wasting my time repairing stuff, I'm doing it in the kitchen, not the barn, right?"

He stood up, wiped his hands on his work pants, and kissed her. "Togetherness," he said.

"Mmm," Jeanne answered, linking her arms together at his back as she leaned against him.

"Hey," Tim said. "You okay?"

Jeanne leaned back and surveyed the kitchen. "I think so," she said. "I'm going to keep it simple this morning. I just cut a bunch of grapefruits to caramelize brown sugar on under the broiler. And then I've got the famous Evergreen Inn Christmas-morning cinnamon rolls in already."

"Couldn't miss the smell of those," Tim said.

"Even when I had nothing in my pantry," Jeanne said, "I still had Indonesian cinnamon. And, of course," she said, "the remains of Hiram's sausage and bacon."

She laid her head back on his chest. "So I think we're good," she said.

Tim gave her a squeeze. "That's good," he said. "But actually I was asking about your feelings."

"My feelings?" Jeanne said, looking up at him with a mock-skeptical glance.

Tim laughed. "I know, it doesn't happen often," he said. But his eyes stayed locked with hers. "But seriously," he said. "How are you doing?"

Jeanne sighed. "Okay," she said. "A little sad."

"Me too," Tim said.

"It used to be when you did a fix-it project," she said, "at least we were building something together. Now . . ." She looked up at him. "It feels so strange to think of leaving it all behind."

Tim nodded. "Well," he said, "I can't help it. As long as I see something I can fix, I'm still going to do my best. Including us," he said, bending down to kiss her.

Jeanne smiled at him. "I could get on board with us both spending some time on that," she said.

But just as Tim leaned in to kiss her again, Iris came through the kitchen door.

"Jeanne," she said, somewhat breathlessly. "Jeanne, there's something wrong with the computer. I think I broke it."

"The computer," Tim said, letting Jeanne go with a squeeze. "The one thing I *can't* fix."

"How is it broken?" Jeanne asked, not at all alarmed. Iris's previous incidents of a "broken computer" had involved both accidentally changing the font in a word-processing document and inadvertently dragging their finance documents into Jeanne's recipes folder, both of which were relatively easily identified and remedied.

But she'd never seen Iris look quite this worried before.

"It's our guest calendar," Iris said.

Jeanne gave an internal sigh of relief. Iris had always been fiercely resistant to the online scheduling system, because she highly preferred the handwritten ledger system she'd developed on her own. It had always been a little source of friction between her and Jeanne, but never a big one, because they simply didn't get very many online reservations—or many reservations at all, these days. But the likelihood was that Iris had just forgotten how to use the system, because she'd never really wanted to learn it in the first place.

"We got a reservation?" Tim asked. "On Christmas?"

"It was Frank and Eileen," Iris said. "Eileen wanted to make a reservation for them to come back this summer, on Frank's birthday. So she asked me to put their name in secretly, so it would be a surprise for him, while he was helping the girls with their presents."

"And what's wrong with the calendar?" Jeanne asked patiently, trying to bring Iris back to the problem at hand.

"Well, it's full," Iris said.

"Were you looking at last year, maybe?" Jeanne said. "I do that sometimes. It's a little too easy to click the year-to-year view."

"No," Iris said. "I'm quite careful about that. It's next year. We were both looking at it, she and I. We could both see the date, for next year. And June of next year, when she wanted to book, is all full."

Jeanne's mind began to race. She knew exactly how many reservations they had in the new year, because there were only a handful of them. She had gone over and over them, hoping against hope that if she left them alone, they might multiply, maybe even enough to keep the place open. And in the process, she had gotten to know them, which was why she had been dreading canceling every single one.

"Maybe you accidentally blocked a whole month out," Tim suggested, then glanced at Jeanne. "You can do that, right? Mark a week as not available in the calendar? Maybe Iris accidentally marked a whole month."

Iris shook her head decisively.

"Or maybe you did," Tim said to Jeanne, to mollify Iris.

But Iris was not the least bit confused on this point. "It's not just June," she said. "They're almost all full. And the ones that aren't, while you sit there and look at them, suddenly the empty dates will fill up, without you even touching anything. It's like the calendar's haunted."

"I'll come take a look," Jeanne said, heading for the front desk, the two of them trailing behind her.

When she sat down in Iris's seat, Iris and Tim both looking over her shoulder, she clicked open the guest calendar.

Sure enough, when she flipped to January, the following month, almost all the rooms were marked full.

Frowning in confusion, Jeanne clicked on January, then February, then straight on through to the end of the year. It was just as Iris had described: some months, especially in the summer, were totally sold out, while others flickered with activity in any unclaimed space, which was liable to be reserved without warning, as Jeanne looked at it.

"How are they breaking into our calendar?" Tim asked, alarmed. "Did someone hack the inn?"

Jeanne suppressed a smile at his utter lack of tech savvy, then clicked for the first time on one of the reservations.

"This came in over our website," she said. "It's always been enabled to take reservations online. But we've never had more than a handful get made that way. Usually, we're booking repeat customers, and they're liable to call instead."

She clicked on another reservation. "I don't recognize any of these names," she said. "I don't think they've been here before."

"They're real reservations?" Tim asked, realization dawning in his eyes. "It's not some kind of glitch?"

"Seems like it," Jeanne said, opening another. "But why now? What are people doing, booking us on Christmas?"

"Is that a note on that one?" Tim asked. "What does it say?"

Jeanne clicked on the personal request that had been attached to the reservation Tim had pointed out, then peered down at the lines of text.

"It's a man booking a surprise weekend for his wife, for their anniversary," Jeanne said. "He says he wants to make sure that she's able to try our orange-lemon French toast, that they read about it in Geoffrey Peterson's article on this year's best country inns."

"Geoffrey Peterson?" Tim repeated.

Jeanne turned to meet his eyes. Geoffrey Peterson was the country's leading travel writer, by turns irascible and effusive, and the two of them had been devotees of his work for years. It was through his writing that they'd first learned of some of the jewels of the hospitality industry all over the world, and all the different ways individual innkeepers had invented to welcome and pamper their guests. He'd been a major inspiration for their work at Evergreen Inn. It was after reading about quilts made from scraps of saris at an establishment in India that Jeanne had gone on a hunt for the velvet crazy quilts that now graced all of their guest beds, for instance.

But it had never occurred to either of them that their inn would ever rise to the level of his attention.

"Did you say Geoffrey Peterson?" Iris asked.

Jeanne nodded. "He's the best travel writer living," she said by way of explanation. "And probably the most powerful. I just don't know how in the world he would have heard of us. And he would never write about a place without visiting it himself. So how did he write about us?"

"Well, he was just here," Iris said.

Now both Tim and Jeanne turned to her.

"Geoffrey," she said. "Our British gentleman."

"Geoffrey Godwin," Jeanne said automatically, with her perfect memory for the names of every guest that had ever passed under her roof.

Iris nodded and pulled a book out from under a sheaf of papers on the front desk. "When he left," she said, "he gave me this."

"*Travels Incognito*," Jeanne said. "This is the book that made his name." She flipped it over to look at the picture on the back, which showed a clean-shaven man about thirty years younger than the bearded Geoffrey who had just spent the past few days with them.

"No wonder we didn't recognize him," Tim commented.

"There's an article?" Iris said. "Did he write an article about us?"

Jeanne set the book aside, brought up an Internet browser, and typed in "Evergreen Inn" alongside "Geoffrey Peterson."

"I never thought I'd see those two names side by side," Tim said, squeezing Jeanne's shoulder.

But when Jeanne hit enter to get the results, they saw those two names side by side in hit after hit, all the way down the search page.

"It looks like . . ." Jeanne said, sifting through them. "It looks like he just posted his year-end list last night."

"And people are already making reservations?" Tim said.

Jeanne glanced back at him. "When he puts a place on a year-end list, it can sell out for years in advance," she said. "Do you remember how we wanted to book that tree house inn we saw in upstate New York?"

"But getting a reservation was going to take two years?" Tim said, disbelief in his voice. "Is that what's happening to us?"

Jeanne switched back to the calendar mode, just in time to see the last empty room in January turn red for reserved.

"These are all genuine reservations," she said, flipping from one to the next. "Credit cards, deposits, everything."

"Jeanne," Tim said quietly as she raised her hand to touch his hand on her shoulder. "This means . . ."

"What does it say?" Iris broke in. "What does he say in the article?"

Jeanne had to pause for a minute before she could bring herself to click on one of the links that led to the actual article.

When she did, all three of them gasped.

There, under the headline "World's Best Inns of the Year," was a photograph of Evergreen Inn, beside a prominent "#1." And although the headline promised a further list, Jeanne had to scroll for what seemed like pages before she came to entries two and three. And each of those only involved a paragraph-long blurb and small picture, nothing as long as the full article that Peterson had devoted to Evergreen Inn.

"The Inn at Sand Beach," Jeanne read in wonder. It was her favorite boutique inn anywhere in the country, so exclusive, and expensive that she and Tim had only been there once. But that trip had given her years of inspiration, and she still measured everything she did at Evergreen Inn against the standards of creative hospitality she had experienced at Sand Beach. "He rated the Inn at Sand Beach number three. And us number one."

"Scroll up," Tim said. "Read the article."

So Jeanne scrolled up and did, reading aloud, even though by now both Tim and Iris were huddled close, looking over her shoulder, because she could barely believe it was true if she didn't hear the words coming out of her own mouth.

It was all there: from the first bite of the brownies that had been laid out on the hall table when he came in, to descriptions of Jeanne's holiday decorations and the appointments of his room, to a lush litany describing Jeanne's Christmas Eve spread, and the nighttime sleigh ride the owners of the business had gone on to provision the guests, expected and unexpected, with homegrown, inventive fare, even in the middle of a major blizzard.

As Jeanne read, she felt her eyes filling with tears. It wasn't just that the flood of reservations the article had prompted had changed the whole prospects for their beloved home and business overnight. Even more than that, she was touched by the fact that, at last, her inn had been visited by the perfect guest, the guest she'd been preparing for since she dreamed up her first meal and envisioned the unique, welcoming elements of their first guest room.

Peterson wasn't the perfect guest because of his big name, or his wide audience. And definitely not because he was a model of agreeable manners himself. He was the perfect guest because he noticed everything, absolutely everything, every tiny detail that she had spent her time and thought on but secretly believed no one else might ever even see: the dried flowers mixed into the juniper swag, the playful burst of red paint she'd added to the underbelly of the blue shelves in Peterson's room, the three cheeses she blended together before she grilled her grilled cheese sand-wiches, every single one of which Peterson had been able to rec-ognize and identify.

Other guests loved Evergreen Inn, and Jeanne loved having them there, whether they had a sophisticated eye, and a sophis-ticated palate, or not. And she never did anything she did to show off.

But reading Peterson's article, there was something incredibly wonderful about feeling so thoroughly seen and understood. And the fact that Peterson wasn't just any guest, but someone who had seen so much of everything else the world had to offer, someone she had looked up to herself, made it hard to even take in.

"Well, he certainly seemed to enjoy your company, Iris," Tim commented. "I don't think I've ever seen him spend so many words on the check-in process."

Iris gave a coy smile. "Yes," she said. "We were actually think-ing of doing a bit of traveling together."

At this, Jeanne's and Tim's eyes met, both trying not to laugh out loud with the glee of it.

Then Jeanne stood up and threw her arms around Tim, who hugged her so hard that he pulled her feet up off the ground.

"This changes everything," she said. "Everything."

From the lounge, where the girls were opening presents, they could hear a squeal of joy, followed by a low roar of laughter from the gathered guests.

"Except for the way I feel about you," Tim said, and kissed her. "Merry Christmas, baby."

"Merry Christmas," Jeanne said, and kissed him back.

Thirty-Six

"HE DID WHAT?" AUDREY said.

"Is he still here?" Jared said, glancing out the windows at the blue-and-white world beyond.

Hannah, seated on the bench in the front hall where she'd taken a seat after Trevor left, shook her head. "He's gone," she said, but as she did, her mind flashed not on Trevor's petulant stomp out of the house, but on what Luke's back had looked like as he strode out the door.

Audrey sank down on the seat beside her and put her arm around Hannah.

"Honey," she said. "I can't believe it. How are you doing?"

To her own surprise, when Hannah looked at Audrey, she broke out in a grin.

"I feel . . . great," she said.

"Yeah?" Jared said, obviously confused.

Hannah couldn't blame him. She was having some trouble keeping up herself. "I don't even understand it. I mean, I knew Trevor couldn't be the one for me after he dumped me the day before the wedding. But this time—it was my choice. It's not just something that happened *to* me anymore. That feels different." As she said it, she could feel her grin widening. "A lot different," she said.

"I still wish I'd seen that guy," Jared said in a dark tone.

As they were talking, Santa Claus had come into the lobby from the lounge, where they could still hear the voices of the girls as they played with the toys and books and other presents they'd opened earlier that morning. He was followed by his wife, Eileen, who did have the neat white bob of a Mrs. Santa Claus, but wore an outfit that was significantly toned down to his red velvet and white fur: jeans and a soft red sweater.

"Ho, ho, ho!" Santa said, glancing around the lobby. "How are you kids doing this morning?"

"Merry Christmas," Audrey said with a smile.

"I can't believe you've spent all morning in that monkey suit," Jared said, shaking his head. "That's above and beyond the call of duty."

"Are you kidding?" Eileen said. "The problem I'm going to have is getting him to take it off."

"I think I should drive home in it," Frank said, pulling off his fake beard. "It's nice and warm. And if we get stopped by the police, they'll have to let me off with just a warning. After all, I'm Santa Claus."

"Is that how it works?" Eileen said with a smile.

"Now," Audrey said with a perplexed look, "do you always travel with a Santa suit?"

"That's a good idea," Frank said, turning to his wife. "Now, honey, why haven't we thought of that?"

"No," Eileen said firmly. "No, he does not. He managed to root this one out of the wardrobe in our room. Unfortunately, it fit like a glove."

"But the kids love it," Frank said.

"That I can't argue with," Eileen said. "The kids do."

"My kids don't get that excited about Santa anymore," Frank said with a wistful look.

"It was nice to see that," Eileen agreed. "We were thinking this year that Christmas wouldn't be Christmas without the kids."

"But then we figured out we could borrow someone else's!" Frank said with a grin. Then he tugged at the furry collar of his suit. "Much as I hate to, I'm going to go upstairs and get some regular clothes. This thing does get old after a while, even for me."

"I'll see you up there," Eileen said as he climbed the stairs. "You kids getting ready to head out?"

"Soon," Jared said. "I've got another few days with this beautiful woman, and I'm going to take her down to Boston to show her the lights of the big city."

"That sounds lovely," Eileen said. Then she looked at Hannah. "It was so nice to meet you and your family," she said. "We were very grateful to find room here, I can tell you. And very grateful to meet you. Even though the circumstances weren't ideal."

In reply, Hannah grinned at her. "I'm not sure I'd say that," she said. "It wasn't what I expected. But it might have been all right."

As she said it, she thought of Luke again, but pushed the thought out of her head. Enough had happened for one weekend. For a lot more than one weekend, actually.

"I'm glad to hear you say that," Eileen said. "Of course, I hoped you'd feel that way eventually. But it's nice to see you smiling today. It is Christmas, after all."

"That's right!" Audrey said, giving Eileen a hug. "Merry Christmas!"

"Merry Christmas," Eileen said. "And the happiest of new years to all of you," she said before she headed up the stairs.

"Well, babe," Jared said to Audrey when the three of them were left alone in the lobby. "What do you say? You want to run away with me?"

"Always," Audrey said. "But can I grab my bag first?"

"Nope," Jared said, slipping past her as she started up the stairs after Eileen. "I'm going to get it for you."

Left alone in the lobby, Hannah leaned her head back on the wall behind the bench and looked around.

In the months leading up to this day, she'd imagined it dozens of times, filled with ribbons and white flowers to give a wedding accent to the juniper swags, Trevor's family, her family, the minister, the carefully chosen drinks and canapés.

But looking around now, she realized she loved it the most just as it had always been, not dressed up, but with the simple beauty that had drawn her and her family back there, year after year.

Instead of Trevor and his family, she'd met Frank and Eileen, and Marcus and the girls still playing happily in the lounge where she had planned to have her wedding ceremony.

And from where she sat right now, that seemed like a pretty good trade.

"Hey, Hannah," said Jeanne, coming out of the kitchen with a basket of steaming cinnamon rolls, dripping with thick white frosting. "You want to taste-test these for me?"

She held out a blue-and-white cloth napkin with a roll nestled in the folds.

"Oh, yes," Hannah said. "These definitely seem like they need taste-testing. You wouldn't want to put out anything that's not absolutely top quality."

When she took a bite, she closed her eyes, to get the fullest possible experience of the buttery, doughy, spicy, sweet, warm confection.

"You know what," she said. "I'm not sure if these are any good or not. I may need to try another one."

Jeanne laughed, but as she did, a blast of cold air blew into the lobby from the front door.

When Hannah opened her eyes, Luke was standing there, clapping his bare hands to get some warmth back into them.

"Luke!" Jeanne said. "What are you doing back? Is everything okay?"

But Luke didn't break eye contact with Hannah, who he'd locked eyes with the instant he came through the door. "Um, yeah," he said, still looking at Hannah. "Everything's fine. I just—forgot something."

It didn't take long for Jeanne to take in the situation. Out of the corner of Hannah's eye, she saw Jeanne suppress a smile. Then she skirted around behind Hannah, carrying the basket of cinnamon rolls into the lounge, where they were met by peals of childish rejoicing.

"Hey," Hannah said. "I'm glad you came back."

"I just . . ." Luke said, then broke off. "I didn't want to leave that way," he finally finished.

Hannah smiled. "I didn't want you to leave that way, either," she said. "I went out after you, but you were already gone."

"You did?" Luke said, the urgency and worry on his face replaced by the dawn of a smile.

As he said it, he stepped closer. "What would you have said if you caught me?"

Now Hannah felt bashful, looking down at the coils of the cinnamon roll in her hand. "I don't know," she said. "I hadn't gotten that far. I just didn't want you to leave."

"Well," Luke said, taking another step closer, so that they stood almost perfectly face-to-face, "I'm here now."

Hannah stood there frozen. Part of her wanted to wrap her arms around him. Part of her couldn't believe she could feel that way so soon after the end of things with Trevor. And part of her wished that Luke would make the first move, so that she wouldn't have to.

But when she didn't answer, Luke stepped back, deflated.

"Look," he said. "I know this is crazy. It's way too soon to be thinking of anything like this. But I can't stop thinking about us, about what it could be like . . ."

At this, Hannah looked up, and Luke broke off, looking into her eyes.

"It's too soon," he said. "Isn't it? Of course it's too soon. I should have waited. I should—"

But before he could finish, Hannah took his hand.

"I waited a long time for Trevor to decide how he felt about me," she said. "A long time. And in the end it turned out he never really knew for sure."

"Maybe he never really knew you," Luke said.

"Could be," Hannah said. "But Trevor isn't what I'm interested in right now."

"What are you interested in?" Luke said softly.

"I'm interested in how you feel about me," Hannah said.

"I'm crazy about you," Luke said. "I think I always have been."

"What caught your attention first?" Hannah asked. "My terrible haircut or my braces?"

"You," Luke said. "I've always known how I felt about you."

"Well, we've known each other for years," Hannah said. "How could it be too soon?"

In answer, Luke kissed her.

Then he pulled back for a moment, laughing, to look at her.

And kissed her again.

Thirty-Seven

"UM," MOLLY SAID, LOOKING down at the perfect mess Bailey was attempting to stuff into her small blue suitcase covered with its silver stars. "Would you like to . . . ?"

Bailey looked up at her with a beatific smile, as if nothing in the world could make her happier than to do whatever Molly was about to suggest.

But when Molly surveyed the jumble of books, crayons, socks, wrapping paper, and tulle, along with what seemed to be an entire menagerie of stuffed creatures, including a giraffe and a brightly colored fish, she couldn't think of a way to finish the sentence.

"You know what?" she said, bending down to try to create some order amidst the chaos herself. "Why don't I just . . . ?"

And she began to tuck the corners of the tulle in so the skirt of the dress Bailey had worn to bed the day before wouldn't get torn up in the teeth of the zipper, stack the books, and try to settle the stuffed animals together in their own corner.

As Molly did, Bailey clung to her arm with a blissfully self-satisfied expression on her face, as if immobilizing Molly's arm was the most helpful thing Bailey could think of to do, after exploring all of her other options.

Nonetheless, Molly managed to tuck the most egregious outliers into the suitcase, tamp them down, and get the zipper closed.

When she turned back, Addison was already standing by the door of the office, her own suitcase neatly zipped, her boots already on.

"Okay, ladies," Molly said, scooping up both suitcases.

The girls trailed her out of the room and through Molly's own suite, until they got to the door where, to Molly's surprise, Addison balked.

"Hey, kiddo," Molly said, turning back on the stairs. "What's up?"

"Where's your suitcase?" Addison asked.

"Oh," Molly said. "It's up there. I haven't packed it up quite yet."

"You should pack," Addison said. "We're about to go."

Molly, who was painfully aware of this herself, tried to smile.

"Well," she said, to distract Addison from the question she was clearly interested in, which was getting Molly to come with them, "let's get these bags downstairs first."

Downstairs, the lobby was a bustle of activity.

Jeanne was pressing a package of brownies wrapped in wax paper into the hands of Stacy, Hannah's mother.

"Those are brownies," Addison identified with an eagle eye. For emphasis, she pulled insistently on the hem of Molly's shirt.

Stacy stashed the sweet treats carefully in her purse, then gave Jeanne a long, warm hug.

"I know this wasn't exactly the weekend we planned," Jeanne said when Stacy released her.

"But no matter what happened, it's always good to be here," Stacy said. "I'll see you in July?"

"You were one of the first reservations we had this year," Jeanne told her. "I can't wait to see you all then."

Molly skirted the two of them to set the girls' bags neatly beside the door. But as she did, she lost track of Bailey.

Finding her, however, didn't prove to be much of a problem, because of the volume at which she asked, "Where are *our* brownies?"

As Molly rejoined them, Jeanne laughed. "I think I must have left them in the kitchen," she said. "Don't worry. I'll be *right* back."

In the midst of it all, Iris was on the phone behind the desk. "I'm sorry, June this coming year is all booked up," she said. "Would you like to think about next December? Or perhaps the *following* June?"

At the sound of a step behind her, Molly turned, thinking it must be Marcus. She felt a little thrill of nervousness as she did. She'd spent a good part of the morning in the lounge with him and the girls and the two older couples, enjoying the girls' delight as they opened their gifts. But now that the day was almost over, they still hadn't talked about their kiss the night before.

She'd thought, when he'd knocked on her door a little while ago, that that might be what he was coming to talk about. But he'd simply said he thought it was getting to be time to pack up, which had sent the girls into a frenzy of activity, which they insisted he not help with, because they could do it themselves. Which of course had led to Molly doing half the packing and lugging the bags downstairs.

Not that she minded. She was glad to get any time she could with the girls, especially because she wasn't sure how much time she'd ever get to spend with them again.

But when Molly turned around, it wasn't Marcus behind her, but Luke, and Hannah's father, Bob, each weighed down with a hodgepodge load of rolling suitcases, garment bags, backpacks, and shopping bags.

"The simple life," Bob joked as they passed through the lobby, heading for the cars outside. "Just a few things we brought along for our weekend in the woods."

Hannah, who had trailed them down, stopped in the lobby to give her mom a hug. "I'm sorry about how this weekend turned out."

Her mom wrapped her in a ferocious hug. "Well, I'm not, honey," she said. "Not one bit."

"Thanks for everything," Hannah said.

"Oh, honey," her mother said, tears welling up in her eyes. "We'd do anything for you. Always. You know that."

As the two of them released each other, Marcus appeared at Molly's side. He had been so quiet, coming in from the lounge, that she hadn't heard him at all. And when he reached her, he touched her arm, which sent a jolt of electricity through her.

"Hey," she said, looking into his eyes searchingly.

"Hey," he said, glancing up the stairs. "I guess I'd better go up and get the girls' things."

Molly shook her head. "I brought them down," she said. "They're right over there."

When Marcus caught sight of the bags by the door, he nodded. "Thanks," he said.

Jeanne pressed through the crowd, carrying a small stack of her packets of brownies in waxed paper. "As requested," she said.

Marcus looked rueful. "Let me guess who requested those," he said. "I'm suspecting it was a female, under eight years old."

"That's amazing!" Jeanne said, pressing three of the packets into his hands. "How did you ever guess?"

She turned and handed the last packet to Molly, who noticed it was still faintly warm.

"We've loved having you here," Jeanne said. "Please come back and see us soon."

Molly glanced over at Iris. "It sounds like you're booked up now for years," she said.

"Well," Jeanne said, "for the right guest, we can always make room." With a wink, she slipped back into the crowd.

Molly turned to Marcus, and their eyes locked. Her heart fluttered with the thought that he was finally about to say something.

But he just ducked his head and looked out the door. "I've got the car warming up so it won't be freezing when I get the girls in," he said. "I'd better get our stuff out there."

"Oh," Molly said with a little pang. "Okay."

As he headed out the door, swinging the girls' bags up in one hand as if they weighed nothing, Molly knelt to see the two girls.

As if they'd choreographed it in advance, both Addison and Bailey leaned into her, giving her hugs from either side of her neck.

"It was so nice to meet you both," Molly said.

"Molly," Bailey said. "I love you."

It might not have been the declaration Molly was hoping for, or from the person Molly was hoping to hear it from, but there was no way she could resist it. "I love you, too, Bailey," she said, and gave both the girls a tight squeeze.

When she straightened up, she could see Marcus just outside, heading back in. He'd be inside in just an instant, so the girls wouldn't be left alone for long. And Molly didn't want to hang around, begging for a conversation that was never going to come, since he was clearly eager to get his family back on the road again.

So she gave the girls one last squeeze, then headed up the stairs to her room.

Inside, the pang she had felt when Marcus walked out the door turned into a deep ache. But she couldn't blame him for not wanting to start something more serious, and not knowing what to say to her about it.

It might not have meant everything she hoped, but her kiss with him had been a bright moment in a hard year. And she still couldn't think back on all the time with him and the girls with anything but pleasure and happiness.

And even if all they ever shared was this holiday, they'd shown her something about herself—what she really wanted, and what a fuller life could be like.

Idly, she began to collect the papers and pencils from her desk and stash them in the portfolio and art cases she'd brought with her. The ends of half her pencils were broken or blunt, but since this was just evidence of all the work the girls had done creating her Christmas present, they only made her smile.

She had the desk half cleared when she heard a knock on the door.

As she crossed the room to answer it, she scanned the place, looking for whatever the girls might have left: a stray shoe, a lonely stuffed animal.

But she didn't see anything obvious by the time she reached the door. And when she opened it, there was Marcus, without either of the girls.

"Hey," he said.

"Hi," she said.

"Listen," he began, looking nervous.

"You know what?" Molly said quickly. "It's all right. I under-stand."

Marcus looked at her in confusion. "You do?" he said.

Molly nodded vigorously. "It's fine," she said. "It's been great to meet you. And the girls," she added.

"Well," Marcus said slowly. "It's been great to meet you, too. And that's why I wanted to ask what you're doing for the next few days."

"Um," Molly said, confused now herself. "My reservation here ends today. I'm just about to pack up and head home."

"Well," Marcus said with a grin. "We were on our way to the Starlight Lodge down the road before we got stuck in the storm. I just checked with them, and they're honoring reservations that were interrupted by the weather, so it looks like we've got a few extra days of vacation. But they had to switch us to a different room to accommodate the different time. It's a suite, with a sep-arate bedroom off the main rooms where the girls and I will be. Got its own lock on the door and everything. I just thought, if you wanted to come along, maybe we could pay you back for your hospitality to us."

Molly hesitated, so surprised by the offer, and so confused by what it meant, that she couldn't answer.

"The girls would love it if you came along," Marcus said.

At this, Molly's face must have fallen, because he took a step toward her and linked his fingers through hers.

"And so would I," he said softly.

At this, Molly broke out in a wide grin.

"Um," she said. "I'm not all packed yet."

"Take your time," Marcus said. "We won't leave without you."

He leaned in to kiss her cheek, then turned and headed back down the stairs.

Molly stood there for a minute, feeling the faint impression of his kiss until it faded away.

Then she sprang into action, tossing together the last odds and ends that hadn't made it into her suitcase, pulling on a coat, and gathering the rest of her art supplies.

The last thing she packed was the stack of blank paper that had been both her inspiration, and her nemesis, for so many hours in the cozy room.

As she slipped it into her portfolio, she smiled at it like an old friend. She had completed the book she'd come here to write, but she was glad to see there were still plenty of blank pages left.

With the fresh, waiting pages tucked away, she slung her bag over her shoulder and started out to see what happened next in her story.